THE CURSED SWORD

RISE OF THE KING
BOOK THREE

TJ GREEN

The Cursed Sword
Published by Mountolive Publishing
©2020 TJ Green
Ist Edition 2018
All rights reserved
ISBN 978-1-99-004702-2

Cover Design by Fiona Jayde Media
Editing by Sue Copsey

Titles available in Rise of the King Series

Call of the King
The Silver Tower
The Cursed Sword

White Haven Witches

Buried Magic
Magic Unbound
Magic Unleashed
All Hallows' Magic
Undying Magic
Crossroads Magic
Crown of Magic

Invite from the Author

If you'd like to read more about Tom, you can get two free short stories by subscribing to my newsletter.

By staying on my mailing list you'll receive free excerpts of my new books, as well as short stories and news of giveaways. I'll also be sharing information about other books in this genre you might enjoy.

To get your FREE short story please visit my website - http://www.tjgreen.nz

I look forward to you joining my readers' group.

And so to bed; where yet in sleep I seem'd
To sail with Arthur under looming shores,
Point after point; till on to dawn when dreams
Begin to feel the truth and stir of day

— Alfred, Lord Tennyson (1809–92)

1 The White Wolves of Inglewood

Deep in the tangled centre of Inglewood, Tom eased his horse to a stop. In the silence that followed he listened for movement – the crack of a branch, the rustle of leaves, the skitter of footfall. Thick mist oozed around him, muffling sight and sound, and he admitted to himself he'd lost the hunt.

And now something was following him.

Tom heard the low throaty growl of the wolf moments before it leapt at him. He pulled Galatine free of its scabbard and lashed out, knowing he had only seconds before the wolf ripped his throat out. He felt its hot breath and thick matted fur, saw a flash of its wild yellow eyes, before feeling the sword cut deep into its side. It fell back into the trees, yelping.

Midnight bolted, and Tom grabbed the reins and held on, trying to calm her down. As they pounded through the wood, a branch whipped across his chest, knocking him to the ground. Midnight disappeared into the mist. Winded, Tom lay on the damp forest floor, wincing as he felt his ribs aching. He hoped Midnight hadn't gone far. Enisled was a long walk away.

He rolled to his feet and immediately froze as he again heard the low cunning rumble of the wolf, followed by a spine-tingling howl, repeated again and again as the pack arrived.

He was surrounded.

Pale yellow eyes glimmered through the mist. As the wolves crept closer, their white fur and sharp snouts inched into view, until Tom could see the whole length of their low crouching forms ready to spring at him. Now he hoped Midnight *was* a long way away. They would rip her to shreds, and him too if he didn't do something.

He couldn't possibly fight them all off. The nearest tree was only a few paces away. He inched backwards until he felt the rough bark pressing into his back, and then turned and scrambled upwards, grasping at small holes and irregularities in the trunk until he reached the first branch. He heard the wolves snapping and jumping for his feet, and swung himself up, higher and higher. By the time he reached a fork he could comfortably wedge himself into, his hands were scratched and bleeding, and sweat trickled down his neck.

Gripping a branch, Tom peered down. These wolves were lean, strong, and battle-scarred, and they gazed up at him with avid hunger, settling back on their haunches, preparing to wait him out. How long could he stay here? Already the chill mist was reaching into his bones.

If he could take out a couple, the rest might flee. From his precarious position, he pulled his bow round in front of him and aimed for the largest wolf in the centre of the pack. The arrow fell short. He knew he should have paid better attention to his lessons. He aimed again. This time the arrow streamed through the air, heading straight for the wolf … then it veered off, missing it completely.

A cloaked, deeply-hooded figure emerged from the mist and raised an arm towards Tom. Not knowing if the person was threatening him or protecting the wolves, Tom lifted his bow, preparing to fire. He felt a sharp tug at his waist and looked down to see Galatine moving, struggling out of its scabbard. His hand flew to the hilt and he gripped it tightly, securing it under his jacket and cloak. The figure continued to point and Galatine continued to wiggle, and Tom quickly took aim and fired at his unknown attacker who, with a quick flick of the hand, turned the arrow. It thudded into the nearest tree.

Tom was preparing to shoot again when he heard the sound of horses approaching, and voices shouting his name. The figure turned and ran, and the wolves fled too, disappearing into the trees.

Woodsmoke, Arthur, Merlin and Rek cantered into view. Tom smiled when he saw them, feeling relieved. They were all close friends now, particularly Woodsmoke and Arthur. Woodsmoke had been the first fey Tom had met, and was now a brother as much as a friend. And of course Arthur, who had been King Arthur, sitting astride his horse, looking fully in command. Tom's relationship with him changed constantly. Sometimes Arthur was a friend, sometimes a father figure, sometimes reckless, sometimes protective.

Orlas and Rek were in their stag form, the two shape-shifting fey standing as high as the horses. The pair had been a great help when it came to finding Merlin.

And of course there was Merlin himself, whom Tom could never categorise. Old, wise and powerful, he was completely changeable, his whims and fancies unpredictable. But a good friend regardless. Merlin had also shape-shifted into a stag, one of the wizard's favourite animals.

Tom shouted down, "I'm up here!"

As they halted and looked up, the stags changed into human form, Rek and Orlas's skin dappled in browns and creams, like deer markings.

"What you doing up there, Tom?" Rek called.

"Escaping from wolves," Tom shouted to the old grey-haired Cervini, as he climbed down to join them.

"I thought maybe you were trying to turn into a bird?" Merlin said, raising his eyebrows.

Tom landed with a thump. "Funny, Merlin."

"We've been following your trail," Woodsmoke said, sliding off his horse. He looked the same age as Tom, but was in fact several hundred years older. "We saw the wolves' footprints. Are you all right?"

"I'm fine, but Midnight has bolted. She headed that way," he said, pointing into the trees. "But someone is out there, with the wolves."

"What do you mean, someone?" Arthur asked, immediately on his guard. He scanned the surrounding area.

"I don't know who – I couldn't see their face, but they had magical powers, because they could deflect my arrows. And I think they were trying to steal my sword, sort of summon it with magic."

"Show us where," Arthur said.

Tom led them to the spot where the figure had stood. "Here. As soon as you arrived, they disappeared."

Woodsmoke examined the ground. "Strange. I can't see any tracks, not even the wolves'. I can't smell anything, either."

Orlas agreed. "Nor I. But here's your arrow." The Cervinis' leader was tall and muscular, with long dark hair. He plucked the arrow from the tree and handed it back to Tom.

"I wonder who wants to hide their tracks," Merlin said, deep in thought.

Arthur shook his head. "Well there's not much we can do about it now. At least you're not hurt, Tom."

Tom grinned. "No, I'm fine. Sorry I lost you," he said referring to the hunt. "I thought I was behind you, and then I hit a thick patch of mist and the next thing, you were gone. Did you find the boar?"

"We found *some* boars, and killed a few, but didn't find *the* boar," said Arthur. "For such a huge beast, the damn thing is able to disappear pretty quickly."

Arthur had organised the hunt for the Black Boar of Inglewood, as they had named it. The forest began a few miles beyond Enisled, in a deep valley on the edge of the moors. It was dark and damp, and prone to pooling mists that hung around for days. However, it was full of wild deer, pheasants, and boar (and wolves, unfortunately) and had become Arthur's favourite hunting ground. Since moving in to Ceridwen's old castle at Enisled, he'd established some of his old routines, one of which was hunting. Slaying the Black Boar was becoming an obsession. The animal had first appeared a few weeks ago, its size making it an obvious target. But it was quick. Tom half wondered if it was enchanted.

"Anyway," continued Arthur, "the rest of the group have taken back the spoils, and we came looking for you." He held his hand out to Tom and pulled him up to sit behind him on his horse, Cafal. "Come on. We'll help you find Midnight."

They found the horse's trail, and eventually spotted her grazing a few miles on from where Tom had fallen.

A few hours later they crested a low rise, and Enisled's castle appeared in the distance. It was early evening and lights shone from the towers, the rest of the building melting into the twilight.

The castle looked very different to when they had first seen it. Then it had been sealed up, access forbidden by Herne, due to the life-giving Ceridwen's Cauldron inside.

Tom and the others had been allowed to enter because Herne wanted Merlin to be resurrected.

Now that the cauldron had been destroyed by the sylphs, there was no further need for the castle to be sealed.

Up ahead, Orlas stopped to look at the view, changing to human form. "I still can't believe how different this looks, Arthur," he said, when the others drew level. "It was in a pitiful state when you bought it from me. And look at it now!"

Arthur laughed. "I have Merlin to thank for some of that. And of course the Cervini and my new employees."

"Are you really going to call it New Camelot?" Tom asked.

"Why not? I loved Camelot; it seems appropriate." Arthur seemed slightly put out that Tom should question his decision.

Merlin agreed. "It feels like home."

"But it's not very original!" Tom said.

"Isn't she beautiful?" Arthur said, gazing fondly at the castle and ignoring Tom's protests.

"Very," Woodsmoke said, rolling his eyes. He was used to Arthur extolling the virtues of his castle. "You stay and admire it, I'm heading back." He spurred Farlight on, racing across the moor, quickly followed by Rek and Orlas.

As if reminding him of the late hour, Tom's stomach rumbled. "Come on, Arthur, you're the host. No-one eats until you do. Get a move on!" And he raced away, leaving Arthur and Merlin to catch up.

As Tom strode through the door into his large second-floor bedroom, Beansprout flew from the seat in front of the fire and launched herself at him, hugging him fiercely. With the wind knocked out of him it took him a few seconds to speak.

"Beansprout!" he eventually spluttered. "Are you trying to kill me?"

"I'm just saying hello, Tom! It's been so long." She stepped back to look at him. "You've grown! And look at those shoulders! You've got all muscular, Tom."

"It's all the fighting practice Arthur and Woodsmoke make me do!" he said, feeling secretly flattered. "And it hasn't been that long – only a few months."

She smiled, and Tom couldn't help smiling back. Beansprout was his cousin, always happy and positive about everything, and she looked particularly relaxed at the moment. Her pale red hair was tied in a loose plait, and she wore a long vivid-green dress.

He gestured vaguely. "I think magic is suiting you, you look all smiley."

"It *does* suit me! Nimue says I'm a natural." Nimue was the priestess of Avalon who had now become the Dragon Sorcerer of Dragon's Hollow. She had replaced Raghnall, who'd been killed by Arthur and Woodsmoke after he tried to trap them in his weapons room. Without Nimue's protection spell, Dragon's Hollow would be a ruin inhabited only by dragons.

"Show us some magic, then," Tom said, curious to see what Beansprout could do.

"It's not a parlour trick, Tom," she said indignantly. And then she winked. "Maybe later."

"So Nimue was happy to let you leave?" Tom dropped his cloak on to the floor, before sinking into a chair and pulling off his boots.

"Not really. She said it's too soon, and I should have a full year of practice before leaving, just to learn the basics.

But I drove her mad asking, and in the end she said yes. I promised I wouldn't be long, but I *had* to come for the tournament." She grinned at her small victory, and sat in the chair opposite him.

Arthur had decided to hold a tournament in which his new friends and the local fey would compete in sword fighting, archery, knife throwing, wrestling, and horsemanship. So many wanted to take part or spectate that it had turned into a much bigger event than originally planned, and was now being held over three days. Arthur had asked friends to adjudicate, as well as compete. The competition would begin in two days' time in the castle grounds.

"By the way, Nimue says hello." Beansprout wrinkled her nose. "Tom, you stink."

"I've been hunting all day – I was nearly eaten by wolves! Of course I stink! How is Nimue?" Tom tried to sound offhand. Nimue was probably the prettiest, cleverest woman he'd ever met, and her green eyes haunted him.

"She's amazing, of course. She teaches me so much! One day maybe I'll know half of what she does." Beansprout leaned back with a sigh. And then she added, as offhand as Tom had been, "And how's Woodsmoke?"

"Woodsmoke's ... you know, like Woodsmoke. All Zen, except when Arthur goes a bit control-ish." He frowned. "Did you travel on your own?"

"No! Granddad and Fahey are here too. You've got a terrible memory, Tom."

"Oh, yeah," Tom said, as comprehension slowly dawned. "So they made it to Dragon's Hollow, then?"

"And loved it! They loved Nimue too." She smirked. "I think it's because she just let them get on with things. Unlike Fahey's sister ..."

Tom looked puzzled. "Fahey's sister? Who's that?"

"Driselda. Apparently she's been living with another sister for years, but they had an argument and she arrived just after you left with Woodsmoke, with her two daughters and three sons. I think. If I'm honest, I lost track," she said, looking sheepish. "In the space of one week she succeeded in turning their routine upside down." She giggled. "It sounds quite funny really."

Tom laughed. "I bet they didn't think so. So they've moved out?"

"Sort of. It coincided with their trip, but I think they're going to see how much they like living here."

Tom looked surprised. "Here? Jack and Fahey might move in?"

"Why, will they cramp your style, Tom?" Beansprout asked with silky sarcasm.

"No! Yes, maybe." At least the castle had lots of room. As much as he loved his grandfather, he wasn't sure he wanted to live with him all the time.

"Arthur wouldn't mind, surely. He has to put up with you," she said, grinning.

"Funny." And then he had a thought. "I presume you didn't encounter any dragons on the way?"

"No! Nimue has things well under control. You should come and visit – I'll be heading straight back after the tournament."

"Maybe, but I feel like I've only just got here." He was enjoying living in the Other and didn't want to go home, but every now and again he wondered what on earth he was doing, and now he just wanted to stay at Arthur's for a while.

"Anyway, Tom, I'm starving and you stink, remember? Get in that bath or no-one will speak to you all night."

2 New Camelot

Tom and Beansprout entered what Arthur referred to as his small dining room, on the first floor of the castle. Arthur was standing in front of the fire, resplendent in his black velvet tunic, holding a glass of his favourite beer. It was the Red Earth Ale from Holloways Meet – Arthur kept the cellars stocked with it.

Other guests stood around, chatting and catching up on news. Tonight there were just ten of them, including Jack, Fahey, Rek, Orlas and his wife Aislin, Woodsmoke and Merlin. Tomorrow the rest of the guests would arrive for the tournament, and Arthur had planned a banquet in the main hall of the castle.

Tom realised he and Beansprout were the last to arrive. He shuffled in quietly, looking sheepish, while Beansprout bounded in announcing, "Sorry we're late, Tom took forever to get clean."

"I was trying to have a relaxing soak in the bath, but someone kept yelling through the door at me!" he said, glaring at Beansprout. He headed to the long sideboard and poured himself a glass of beer.

"I don't blame you, Tom," Jack said, heading over to hug him. "We've had a long journey today. I could go to bed."

Tom grinned. "Hi, Granddad," he said, returning his hug, realising he should have greeted him properly. "You

14

look pretty good all things considered. I bet *you* weren't attacked by wolves." He caught Fahey's eye across the room and waved.

"No, I was not. Nor dragons, either. But it's a long way." He glanced round at Beansprout. "She's stronger than she looks. It was hard to keep up. And you've grown too."

"I know, Beansprout told me."

Arthur clinked his glass for attention. "Come everyone, let us sit, eat and make merry." He headed to the long candlelit table, the soft light showing Arthur at his most handsome and charismatic.

As they took their seats Arthur raised his glass. "To old friends—" he nodded towards Merlin sitting on his right, "and all my new ones, many of whom are very dear to me already."

They all clinked glasses with their neighbours, Orlas repeating, "To old friends and new!"

Tom sat next to Rek who smirked at him. "You're still getting used to all this, aren't you?" He gestured around him to the room, food and wine.

Tom nodded. "Is it that obvious?"

"Not really. I just pay more attention than most." He took a bite of bread. "Arthur's quite a force to be reckoned with, isn't he." It wasn't a question.

Tom nodded, a wry smile escaping. "When he has a plan, he sticks at it. First there was finding Merlin. I think you know how that went." He glanced over to where Merlin sat laughing with Aislin. "Being trapped in a spell and then almost being killed by dragons was ... interesting. And then this castle and the tournament have been plans number two and three."

"And are you number four?" Rek fixed his dark eyes on him intently.

"What do you mean?" Tom asked, startled, but knowing exactly what he meant.

"Sword training, archery, knife throwing, horse-riding. It's quite the education he's got lined up."

Tom swallowed a large chunk of chicken. "He says I need those skills to survive here. He's probably right."

"Well, it will help, but I think you were doing all right anyway." Rek looked across to where Woodsmoke sat talking with Beansprout. They hadn't seen each other in months, and had lots to catch up on. "What does Woodsmoke think?"

"He says it's a good idea. He's teaching me archery."

"You've got two good teachers," Rek said, reaching for a leg of chicken.

Tom laughed. "I have. I'm lucky. And you, of course – you've taught me lots." Ever since Rek had arrived he'd been assessing Tom's skills and sparring with him.

"It's good to practise with different people, my friend. I shall enjoy watching you in the tournament."

"Aren't you competing?" Tom asked, surprised.

"Only with the sword. My eyes aren't what they used to be."

Tom grinned at him. Rek may have been old and grey-haired, but he remained lean and fast, and he knew Orlas trusted his judgement completely. "I don't believe that for a second!"

Rek smiled back. "I figure I should give the young ones a chance." He nodded at Woodsmoke. "Besides, I think Woodsmoke's got the edge on archery. So who else is coming?"

Tom thought over the list of guests. "Arthur's invited Prince Finnlugh and some of his friends and family. It will be good to see him again."

"One of the royal tribes of the fey, I presume, with a name like that?"

"He lives in this huge Under-Palace not far from Woodsmoke," he said, remembering the labyrinth of rooms under the hill. "And Brenna arrives tomorrow, with some of the Aerikeen."

"Now that is good news," Rek said, raising his glass to celebrate. "Is she queen yet?"

"She'd better not be! I'm hoping for an invite. Any more Cervini coming?"

"Oh yes – Nerian, our shaman's arriving tomorrow. Remember him?"

"Of course! I'm not likely to forget the man who summoned Herne." Although, strictly speaking, all Tom could remember was a split-second image of the immense striding figure of Herne crossing the fire and breaking Nimue's spell, before Tom fell unconscious for days.

"Well he's coming with some of our best fighters. It will be quite the party, Tom," Rek said, winking.

At the end of the night Tom staggered to his room, full of food, and reflected on what a very interesting life he now led. There was no more school, housing estates, cars, traffic lights, computers, phones or TVs. Instead, here he was in the Other with King Arthur, his living-legend ancestor, in a castle on the soft green moors of Enisled. His best friends were a fey who was skilled in hunting, a shape-shifting bird who was heir to Aeriken, and his cousin, who lived with one of the most powerful witches in history (or legend, depending on your point of view), and who was now becoming one herself. His grandfather, a sort of bard in training, was best friends with Fahey, a skilled bard who conjured magic with words. Tom's newest friends were shape-shifting deer. And of course, there was Merlin, who now lived with them at New Camelot – the most famous sorcerer in the most famous castle of all.

Life was good.

Hours later he woke up, and couldn't work out why. He had heard something, but what?

He got out of bed and walked across to the window, pulling back the heavy brocade curtains. His room looked out across the grounds at the rear of the castle. The shadows were thick and velvety, and trees shimmered in the breeze. Far below, in the formal gardens, Tom saw a man-shaped shadow flit across an expanse of lawn. As if it knew it was being watched, the figure stopped and looked up at him, and then fled into the grounds. The howl of wolves started, piercing the silence of night. Tom shivered. It was unusual to hear wolves so close to the castle, and why was someone running in the grounds? It must have been a guard. Tom shrugged and went back to bed.

3 An Intruder

The next day the sun was high, the sky was a cloudless blue, and it was hot. Tom strode across the gardens with Arthur and Merlin, heading towards the area set aside for the tournament.

Servants were constructing two large pavilions on Arthur's fine green lawns. One was for food and drink, to keep the competitors fed and watered all day, and the other would store the weapons used for the events. Close to the pavilions were the areas marked out for the competitions. One area was for archery, and a fey dressed in dark green was pacing out the distance to the targets. The other area was for knife throwing, and had a similar set up to the weapons market in Dragon's Hollow. The targets were large wooden carvings of wolves, a wood sprite, boar, and trolls, plus some creatures Tom didn't recognise but which had a lot of claws and teeth. There was also an arena for sword fighting and wrestling, and a large enclosure filled with trees, bushes and obstacles, for displays of horsemanship.

Arthur's standards were very high. They stood before the food pavilion admiring the fine embroideries of dragons, woods and boars, the gold and silver thread glinting in the sun.

"I'm not sure these pavilions have enough gilding on them, Merlin," he said. "I really want them to catch the eye as the guests arrive."

It would be impossible to miss them, thought Tom. They were huge.

"Don't worry," Merlin reassured him. "I can burnish them if needed, I have just the spell for it."

"And Merlin, you *are* going to change into something a little more respectable, aren't you?"

Tom grinned as Merlin's face fell. Merlin maintained a look of constant distraction and disorder. His beard was unkempt, his hair long and messy, and he still wore the old threadbare grey cloak they had found him in, in Nimue's silver tower.

"I don't see why I should change," he muttered.

"Because you look scruffy," Arthur retorted. "It would be nice if you could make an effort."

Only Arthur could get away with saying that.

Before an argument could start, Tom decided this would be a good time to mention what he'd seen the night before. "I think I saw someone run across the lawns last night."

"What do you mean, Tom?" said Arthur. "When?"

"In the middle of the night. I saw someone run from over there." He pointed towards the edge of the lawns next to the gardens. "He, or she, seemed to look right at me, and then ran to the trees over there." He gestured to where the orchards began.

"Well I doubt it was an intruder, Tom. The walls are too high and strongly built for anyone to get in. And how could they possibly see you? You're three floors up."

"I know, but it seemed that way."

Merlin frowned. "I have put spells of protection across the walls. Only someone with magical abilities could get through."

That seemed to make Arthur's mind up. "Must have been a guard, Tom. Let's just finish the inspection."

"I'll leave you to it, Arthur," said Tom, unconvinced. "I'm going for a wander."

Arthur and Merlin waved after him distractedly as he headed to the orchards.

Within a short distance, the hum of noise from the activities dulled, and once he entered the orchard it disappeared completely. The trees around him were old and gnarled, their trunks a pale silver-grey. Branches twisted and knotted together, and the rub of their intertwined branches produced a slippery whispering noise that was disorientating. The orchard had clearly been here a long time, planted back in Ceridwen's day. Some of the trees had grown to huge proportions, particularly the walnut trees, but despite the long years of neglect they were still vigorous and covered with buds. Underfoot the grass was long, so evidence of an intruder should be easy to see.

It took a good while, but eventually Tom saw a patch of flattened grass, and followed a trail to the base of the wall. He examined the pitted stone blocks. It was possible to climb it; gaps in the stone provided small hand and footholds. But it would be tricky, and it was high. A fall could kill you. At his feet, something glinted in the sunlight, half buried in the soil. Pulling it free he brushed it off and held it to the light. It was a round silver disc, probably a brooch, with a pin and clasp on the back. In its centre was a wolf's head, carved in immaculate detail, and around the edge of the silver disk was a ring of paw prints.

Someone *had* been here. Tom wondered if it was the cloaked figure from the Inglewood. Whoever it was had possessed magical abilities, and they wanted Galatine.

Tom found Merlin in his tower. It rose from the centre of the castle, its windows looking out across the castle's grounds and walls to the moors beyond. The east window gave a view of the octagonal courtyard on the roof below, where Ceridwen's cauldron had been before the sylphs had blasted it to pieces. Merlin's was the only window that looked out on it. The other walls enclosing the octagonal space were windowless, making it completely private. Merlin said it reminded him of his own mortality – which Tom found odd, as the cauldron had been responsible for his rebirth.

The tower was square instead of round, but otherwise reminded Tom of the tower in the Realm of Air. Merlin had filled it with the things he had finally brought back from there. A long wooden bench ran down the centre of the room, the walls were lined with books, jars and pots, and the floor was made of solid stone slabs. Above him the thick wooden rafters were hung with dried herbs.

Merlin sat at the centre table reading a large, black, leather-bound spell book. His finger ran across the page and he muttered to himself softly. He jumped when Tom spoke.

"Merlin, I found something at the base of the walls by the orchard. I think our visitor left it."

Merlin's sharp blue eyes narrowed. "So you really think we have had a visitor?" He took the disc that Tom offered. "It looks a bit dirty, Tom. It could have lain there for years."

"But the ground was trampled, and there was a trail through the grasses," Tom insisted.

Merlin rummaged amongst the myriad objects on his table and finally pulled free a magnifying glass. "The detail is good," he said, examining the disc. "The eyes are obsidian."

"They're what?"

"Obsidian. It's volcanic rock from the Realm of Fire. And the pawprints have flecks of ruby in them. Tiny. Ingenious."

He handed the magnifying glass and disc to Tom, who was surprised to see Merlin was right. There was so much detail, it was incredible. He could see tiny blades of grass beneath the pawprints, and the fur on the wolf was so fine he could have sworn it moved.

"What does it mean, Merlin?"

He sighed. "I'm not sure it means anything." Taking it back he turned it over and examined the other side. "Probably an old brooch someone dropped."

"But who does it belong to?"

"I don't know, but leave it with me, Tom. I'll consult my books."

Leaving the tower, Tom found quite a commotion outside. Two-dozen riders on huge black stallions had filled the courtyard, their silver standards shining, dazzling everyone. Tom grinned, recognising them immediately. "Finnlugh! Over here."

A tall slim faery with shining white-blond hair turned and waved, then jumped from his horse and in seconds was at Tom's side, hugging him with surprising strength. "It's been too long, Tom! I *knew* you'd come back."

"Then you knew more than I did. I thought they'd abandoned me forever."

The last time he'd seen Finnlugh – Prince Finnlugh, Bringer of Starfall and Chaos, and Head of the House of Evernight – had been when Tom was returning to Earth and his granddad's cottage. Finnlugh hadn't changed; pale skinned, with sharp precise features and dark blue eyes, and the slight point to his ears that all royal fey had. His long hair was loose and he wore a midnight-blue tunic. Around his neck was a thick silver chain, the end tucked into his jacket. His clothes were immaculate, and of the finest cut and quality, and he emanated an aura of power and wealth. But for all that, he was friendly and genuinely pleased to see Tom. "You know they would never have done that," he said, shaking his head.

Tom shrugged. "I know, but I was starting to panic. I thought maybe they couldn't get back."

"Well, you're here now, and I hear you've been busy resurrecting Merlin and fighting dragons!"

Tom grinned. "It isn't something I'd have done back home."

"Home sounds like a very boring place – much better to have come back here. I presume you'll be in the tournament tomorrow?"

"Of course, but I'm not sure I'll be any good."

"There's nothing like competition to increase your skills, Tom."

"I know, but everyone else will be so much better."

"You don't know that. It's also meant to be fun."

They were interrupted by Arthur, who appeared from the hall behind them. "Good to see you, Finnlugh," he said, shaking his hand.

"Arthur – good to see you too. Impressive castle."

Arthur swelled with pride. "Come, I'll show you the grounds. You can pick your favourite spot. I presume you still want to stay in your tents?"

"Absolutely. We will appreciate being under the stars. Besides, there are rather a lot of us!" Finnlugh said, glancing behind him.

Finnlugh's companions had now dismounted and their horses were being led away by the grooms. They were a mixture of men and women, all tall, some with the same white-blond hair as Finnlugh, others with hair the colour of sunsets, forests, and blue skies. Tom had forgotten Finnlugh's royal family looked a little more otherworldly than other fey.

Finnlugh called to him. "I'll see you later, Tom. We have much to speak of." And with a theatrical wave he fell into step beside Arthur.

Tom watched them cross the main hall, wondering which events they would be competing in. His attention was quickly distracted by more noise, as a flock of birds wheeled overhead and then flew into the courtyard, swiftly changing form as they landed. Brenna and the Aerikeen had arrived.

Brenna was looking more like a bird, even in her human form. Her long black hair still fell to her waist, but the feathers along her hairline seemed thicker and they ran through her hair like down. The dark leather trousers and jacket she always wore also now seemed to be covered in tiny fine feathers, and her eyes were dark with almost no whites showing.

Her smile was so warm and friendly Tom felt a rush of affection. He had missed her, and wished she would come to live at New Camelot too. He gave her such a hug she protested. "Tom, you're crushing me!" She held him at arm's length. "You've grown. How dare things change when I haven't seen you!"

He smiled. "Well, you should visit more often then."

"Yes, I should," she agreed. "But unfortunately I've been kept pretty busy."

"But not busy enough to miss a tournament?" he teased.

"There's always time for one of those." She glanced behind her. "I'm being rude, let me introduce you."

A young Aerikeen with soft, brown, shoulder-length hair and feathers along her hairline and down her neck stepped forward. Her eyes were hazel brown, and like Brenna, there was almost no whites to her eyes. She was also very pretty.

"This is Adil, my cousin."

Adil nodded in greeting. "I've heard so much about you, Tom."

"You have?" he asked, puzzled.

"Of course, Tom. You helped save us." She blushed slightly, before stepping back.

Brenna introduced the others, and Tom knew he would never remember all their names. These Aerikeen were young, bright-eyed and eager to be involved in the tournament. "These are all survivors of Morgan," Brenna said, referring to Morgan Le Fay who had tried to kill them all at the Aerie in Aeriken. "They are helping to rebuild our way of life. I thought they should have some fun over the next few days."

Tom welcomed them, feeling it was his responsibility while Arthur was with Finnlugh.

"I take it Arthur has invited people to watch the tournament?" Adil asked. "There's a crowd of people on the moors outside the walls; a small tented city seems to have sprung up."

"He has, but I'm not sure how many," Tom said, slightly alarmed. "I think the competitors have brought their own supporters." He had a gnawing worry that Arthur wasn't in fact expecting this many at all. "I think everyone's excited apart from me – I'm just nervous."

Brenna laughed. "You'll be fine, Tom." She gave him another hug and big smile. "It's so good to see you." She lowered her voice and put her mouth to his ear. "I told you I'd miss our adventures."

He grinned. "Come on, I want to show you something." He led them into the main hall and heard Brenna's intake of breath.

"Arthur *has* been busy! Look at this place." She gazed at the tapestries, the rugs, the chandeliers, and the wooden table filled with trays of delicacies for the visitors.

"His small army of servants have been busy," Tom said wryly.

"I'm glad to see the profits from the dragonyx haven't gone to waste," she said laughing, and reached for a sweet cake on a gilded platter.

"Wait until you see the banquet he's prepared for later. Come on," he said, "I'll show you to your rooms. You're next to Beansprout."

4 The Incomplete Tale

After leaving Brenna, Tom headed back up to Merlin's workshop. Beansprout was there too, and they were examining the disc in front of the fire.

"Why have you got a fire going? It's really hot out."

"Some spells require fire, Tom," Beansprout said, distracted by the disc in her hands.

"Oh, so you're doing spells?" Tom was starting to sweat already. "Will I get in the way?"

"Not at all." Merlin beckoned him over. "We thought if we applied heat it might change the metal in some way, maybe revealing another image or message."

"Why? I thought it was just a brooch." Tom watched as Beansprout gripped the disc with forceps and held it in the flame.

"We're going to try it without a spell first, and see what happens," Merlin said.

The disc started to glow, and after a few minutes Beansprout took it out of the flame and placed it on a small table next to the fire.

After examining both sides carefully through his magnifying glass, Merlin let out a deep sigh. "Nothing. But that doesn't surprise me. Let's try a reveal spell. We'll start with the simple ones."

He held the disc in the flames, muttering softly under his breath. It seemed to Tom that the image of the wolf blinked, in response to whatever it was Merlin said. But Merlin sighed again and placed the disc back on the table. "No."

Tom felt a surge of disappointment and realised he'd been holding his breath. What had he expected to happen? All he'd found was some old brooch.

For the next hour he watched as Merlin tried spell after spell. Now and again he would stop to explain to Beansprout what he was doing, and to ask her questions. "Has Nimue explained the principals of fire to you?"

Beansprout nodded. "Yes, she covered all four elements."

"Good. In that case, show me how you would create fire in your hand."

Tom was alarmed, but Beansprout didn't look worried. She sat for moment in quiet concentration, holding her hand out in front of her. A small blue flame appeared, growing bigger as she concentrated. As Merlin nodded encouragement her confidence grew, and soon a small pulsing ball of flame hovered over her hand before she threw it in the fire. Tom was impressed, and started to see Beansprout as someone far more interesting than just his younger cousin.

Merlin clapped. "Well done, I see Nimue has done a very good job. But if I'm honest I expected nothing less. Now, back to this brooch."

He pulled the spell book towards him and flicked its pages absently. "Mmm, perhaps we should try a spell of awakening." He held the disc tightly in his hands and whispered over it, before blowing softly into his hands. When he opened them, nothing had happened. This was going to be a waste of time.

"Maybe it really is just a brooch and it does nothing?" said Tom.

"And maybe," Merlin said, raising his right eyebrow, the left staying firmly in place, "we haven't found the right spell yet."

"Spells can take time, Tom," Beansprout explained. "You have no patience."

"You're right. I'm going. I'll see you in the Great Hall."

They immediately turned their attention back to the brooch.

"Don't be late, you have two hours! And bring the brooch with you. I want to show it to Nerian."

The last two days had turned into a chore of fancy clothes and grooming. Tom returned to his room to find his clothes laid out for the evening. There was a fine linen tunic and trousers, and polished black leather boots. The bath was run, and a small tray of food had been left on a side table. While his room might not have had the opulence of the one he'd stayed in at Raghnall's, in the House of the Beloved, it was pretty close. He grinned. He wouldn't get this at home.

Two hours later he was standing at Arthur's side, greeting the guests as they came through the polished ebony doors that led into the Great Hall. This was not to be confused with the Main Hall, which was the main entrance hall of the castle. The Great Hall was on the first floor and overlooked the gardens at the back of the house. It had a high carved ceiling with a series of chandeliers down the centre. At the far end, tucked into a corner, was a dais for the musicians, and later for Fahey, who was going to enthral them with his stories. Long tables were set up down the centre of the hall and the room dazzled with silver and glassware, laid out on snowy linen cloths.

Out of the corner of his eye, Tom could see his grandfather and Fahey chatting quietly together. He felt a rush of guilt as he hadn't spent time with them today – but thinking about it, he hadn't seen them. They hadn't even been at breakfast. That was unheard of. They must have been preparing.

Finnlugh arrived and cornered Tom. "Tom, I absolutely insist that we speak later. It's been too long. And I have questions to ask about a certain sword I hear you have acquired from my recently deceased great-great uncle, second removed on my mother's side."

Tom was immediately baffled. "What are you talking about, Finnlugh?"

"Raghnall," he said, raising his head quizzically. "Remember him?"

Tom gasped, horrified. "He was your relative?"

"Don't worry, Tom. All of the royal tribes are related. It's down to years of intermarriage. I'm not grieving, it's all right." He smiled at Tom's discomfort, and Tom hoped Arthur couldn't hear. He was currently distracted with Finnlugh's cousin, Duke Ironroot.

"We didn't know! But …" Tom felt he should explain, "he did try to kill us."

Finnlugh patted his shoulder. "Later, Tom." And he moved off enigmatically into the mingling guests, a glass of Arthur's sparkling elderberry wine in hand.

The next person Tom wanted to talk to was Nerian, the Cervini shaman. He'd arrived that afternoon, with another dozen Cervini. Nerian hadn't changed either. His long hair was still matted into dreadlocks and plaited with beads and feathers. He wore a necklace of small interlinked animal bones, and tonight his ceremonial stag horns.

"Nerian, I haven't seen you for ages," Tom said, excited. "I've found something I want to show you."

Nerian narrowed his eyes. "It sounds intriguing. Something magical?" Then he paused. "Are you in trouble again?"

"I hope not! Can I show you later?"

He nodded. "Of course."

As he moved into the crowd, Tom wondered when he was going to have time to speak to everyone.

After another half hour of hand shaking, Tom was ready to sit down and eat. As enjoyable as it was to meet old friends and new, he was ready for food. Fortunately, so was Arthur. He stood next to Tom, taller and broader, his long dark hair falling to his shoulders. He wore a grey silk tunic and looked very regal, even without a crown.

Much like the previous night, Arthur had a speech of welcome prepared, but tonight it was about the tournament. "It will commence tomorrow morning at ten, and will run for three days. We begin with novice sword fighting, which will run at the same time as the knife throwing. On the second day there will be archery and advanced sword fighting, and on the last day, wrestling and horsemanship." He smiled magnanimously. "This will be a fine event that will prove our skills, and I hope to repeat it every year!" He raised his glass. "To new friends and new beginnings!" A cheer erupted and glasses chinked, and the banquet was underway.

It wasn't until much later in the evening that Tom was able to speak to Nerian again. On the far dais a small band was playing; the tables had been cleared and the dancing had started. Couples drifted around the room, cheek to cheek, or twirling around as the music demanded. Tom could see Woodsmoke dancing with Beansprout, and Brenna dancing with Fahey. Tom grinned as he saw his grandfather dancing with a stately Cervini elder. A few card tables had sprung up in an adjoining room, and he noticed Rek heading there, a look of serious intent on his face.

The fireplaces at either end of the room were filled with candles and flowers, and more candles burned in niches and sconces. Nerian sat with Tom in a quiet corner close to one of the fireplaces, his antlers shadow-fighting on the walls. Within seconds Finnlugh joined them, pulling up a free chair. "May I? I fear if I don't speak to you now, Tom, I might not get the chance tomorrow."

"Of course. Do you know Nerian?"

"We had the pleasure earlier." Nerian nodded to Finnlugh.

"I'm glad you're here, I wanted to show this to both of you." Tom pulled the brooch from his pocket. Beansprout had returned it to him, telling him that magic had revealed nothing.

Nerian looked at it thoughtfully, running his fingers over the design. "A wolf's head? I wonder …" He trailed off, gazing into the middle distance.

"What?" Tom prompted.

But Nerian was thinking and he fell silent, handing it over to Finnlugh's outstretched hand.

Finnlugh turned it over, examining the details. "I remember hearing about a Wolf Mage when I was young. I wonder if this has anything to do with him."

"Who's the Wolf Mage?" Tom asked.

"That's it," Nerian said, nodding. "The Wolf Mage. I was told his story as a young fawn. Where did you find it?" His pupils had rapidly dilated, and in that second Tom had a vision of him as Herne the Hunter, and almost forgot what they were talking about.

Shaking off his nervousness, Tom said, "I found it in the orchard, under the wall. I thought I'd seen an intruder so I went to check it out. The ground was trampled, and I found this in the dirt." He asked again, "Who's the Wolf Mage?"

Nerian stirred from his reverie. "If I remember correctly, he's the brother of the Forger of Light, who made Excalibur and Galatine, the sword I believe you now have?"

"How did you know I had Galatine?"

"Word gets around, Tom," Finnlugh said. "Did *you* know the Forger of Light had forged Galatine?"

"I suppose I did," Tom said, trying to remember what Arthur had told him. "I think Arthur called it the sister sword to Excalibur. It was made for Gawain, his nephew. Why, does that matter?"

"Galatine was indeed given to Gawain by Vivian, as a reward for his loyalty to Arthur," Finnlugh explained. "However, according to the myths of the fey – if I remember correctly – the sword was not made for him, and isn't really a sister sword. It predates Excalibur, and was made for the Forger of Light's brother, the Wolf Mage." He sighed, looking puzzled. "I am not entirely sure why it was given to Gawain. The roots, the details of the story are lost, at least to me. It was a very long time ago."

Tom was shocked. "It was made for someone else? I didn't know that. I don't think Arthur or Merlin do either."

"Why would you?" Nerian asked. "It's an old story, almost forgotten. But I believe this is his image, so someone knows of him."

"Are you saying the intruder is something to do with the Wolf Mage?" Tom asked, still confused. He looked around the room as if someone might suddenly reveal themselves.

"Maybe, or why is his brooch here?" Finnlugh said. "It's too much of a coincidence otherwise."

"The intruder must have been the same person I saw in the wood," Tom said, the events now starting to make sense. Finnlugh and Nerian looked confused, so he continued. "I was separated from the others in the Inglewood, and someone wearing a hooded cloak tried to summon my sword with magic."

"And was that cloak pinned by this brooch?" Nerian asked.

"They were too far away for me to see. Tell me more about the Wolf Mage." Tom's curiosity was now piqued.

"His name was Filtiarn," Nerian said. "He had the rare ability of being able to communicate with beasts, and was particularly fond of wolves. He ran with them, lived with them, almost was one. Years ago he was very powerful, as was the Forger of Light, but neither of them has been seen for many years. By now they must be dead. That's all I know."

"Are they part of the royal tribes – like you?" he asked Finnlugh.

He shook his head. "No. They were of different tribes, possessing different magic – such as skills in metal forging."

"But they were good?" Tom asked, trying to assess how far someone would go to get the sword back. "I mean, we should have nothing to fear from anyone who might know them? Surely the Forger of Light was good if he made such powerful weapons."

Finnlugh looked thoughtful. "It depends how you define good. Each weapon or object he made was for a purpose. Excalibur helps Arthur cheat death, and consolidate power. It is a weapon that bestows righteous kingship, or leadership. Where Arthur walks, others follow, yes?" Then he shrugged. "But nevertheless, such weapons can almost be curses."

Tom was shocked. "And Galatine? Is that cursed?"

Nerian corrected him. "The swords are not cursed, Tom, they are powerful, made by magic to give the bearer greater power. All magical weapons do so. I have no idea what powers Galatine may have. Unfortunately power can be a curse. It is much envied by the stupid and the greedy."

"You remember the weapons in Raghnall's weapons room?" Finnlugh asked. "They were all full of strange powers, but of course not all were forged by the Forger of Light. They were coveted by many and have passed through numerous owners, and will again. And if you recall," – his hand flew to his chest where he kept the Starlight Jewel – "I have had problems of my own regarding this." Tom caught a chink of blue in the candlelight.

"I couldn't possibly forget the weapons room or your jewel," Tom said. "Both nearly got us killed." He sighed, feeling suddenly out of his depth. "But Galatine doesn't seem to have great powers. I've had it for months and it's fine. I'm fine. I can't believe anyone would want it, especially after so long. Surely they must be dead?"

Nerian eyes dark eyes were unfathomable. "Well, if this brooch has only been recently left here – and it seems it has, considering the disturbance of the ground – then the two brothers would be the most immediate suspects."

"Or someone who wants to help them," Finnlugh pointed out. "Wait, why don't we call Fahey? He has a rich store of tales." He stood, looking around the room, and then darted away, returning in seconds with Fahey.

"Good evening, gentlemen," Fahey said, grinning and pulling up a stool. He was looking very dapper tonight. His long hair was pulled back into a tight ponytail, and he was wearing a well-tailored jacket, and trousers of the finest dark green linen. "I gather you want me?"

"Yes, we want to know if you've heard of the Wolf Mage," Tom said.

"The Wolf Mage! Why are you asking about him?" Fahey asked, intrigued.

"So you've heard of him?" Tom said, leaning forward in anticipation.

"Of course I've heard of him. It's my job to know," he said, preening slightly. "He was the original owner of your beautiful sword, Tom."

"Why didn't you tell me before?" Tom asked, thinking of the weeks he'd spent at Vanishing Hall.

Fahey shrugged. "I presumed you knew."

Tom rolled his eyes. "So what else do you know about him and the Forger of Light?"

"Well, the intriguing thing is," Fahey said, looking at them one by one, "that neither of them has a completed tale."

"All right, I'll bite," Nerian said, laughing. "What do you mean by that?"

"Well, they just disappeared. Filtiarn first, back around the time of the dragon wars, and then Giolladhe – the Forger of Light – not long after he made Excalibur. And nobody knows where they went or what happened to them."

"We found this," Finnlugh said, handing him the brooch.

Fahey held it up to the light. "The Wolf Mage! I have seen this image before. Where did you find it?"

"In the orchard," Tom said, "under the wall."

"How exciting," Fahey said, his eyes shining. "This means the tale is not yet over – and we will be part of it!" He leapt to his feet, handing the brooch back. "No time to talk. The dancing is over, and it's time for your tale Tom, and how you resurrected Merlin. We will speak later." And with a swirl of his coat tails, he headed to the dais.

5 When the Wolf Moon Rises

At one point it felt like the party would go all night, but eventually the competitors decided they wanted to be at their best for the next day and began to head off to bed. Finally only a few remained: Arthur, Woodsmoke, Beansprout, Brenna, Tom, Finnlugh, Nerian, Jack and Fahey. They sat in front of the fire, having a nightcap and winding down.

"I had such a great time," Beansprout said, leaning back in her chair and kicking her shoes off. "I haven't seen so many people for ages."

"You certainly know how to throw a good party," Jack agreed. "I think your story went well, Fahey."

Woodsmoke laughed. "Well, you can't go wrong with a tale about the return of Merlin, and all set in this castle!"

Fahey smiled and sipped his mead. "The trick is to know one's audience."

"You know that brooch I found, Merlin?" said Tom. "We think it belongs to the Wolf Mage."

"No," corrected Nerian, holding up a finger. "I said it symbolised him."

"What brooch?" Arthur asked, looking between them.

"Sorry, Arthur," Tom said. "I found this earlier." He pulled the brooch out of his pocket and gave it to Arthur. "It was at the bottom of the orchard wall. I showed it to Merlin, and then Nerian, Finnlugh and Fahey."

"Oh, leave me till last," Arthur complained.

"You were busy," Tom pointed out.

Merlin ignored them both. "Well I have never heard of the Wolf Mage. Who is he?"

Finnlugh explained the connection to the Forger of Light. "It's no wonder you haven't heard of him."

"But," Tom interrupted, "it seems Galatine was made for the Wolf Mage. We think someone wants it back."

Arthur now looked exasperated. "No, Galatine belonged to Gawain."

"But it wasn't made for him, Arthur," Nerian explained softly. "Vivian appropriated it."

Arthur shot to his feet and starting pacing up and down. "That woman always interferes!"

"Arthur," Merlin remonstrated, "she acts for the best."

He snorted. "Whose best, though?"

"Yours, usually," Merlin said, scratching his chin.

That seemed to deflate Arthur's anger, and he sat with a huff. "Do we need to worry? I mean, are they dangerous?"

"Maybe," said Finnlugh. "It depends who's after it, and how badly they want it. And ..." he paused thoughtfully, "what they want it for."

"Where is Galatine now?" Woodsmoke asked.

"In the armoury, of course," Tom said.

With unspoken agreement everyone got to their feet and set off, through dark corridors and down shadowy stairways to the basement, where the armoury was kept. They came to a halt in front of a large solid wooden door with two locks, and two iron bars across it. Standing to attention was a huge Cervini, who Tom recognised as Dargus, one of the Cervini who'd been eager to help Arthur on his return.

"Evening, Dargus," said Arthur. "Has anything unusual happened here tonight? Have you seen or heard *anything*?"

"No, Sir," he said. "Everything is quiet as usual. The last activity was about six hours ago when the Cervini locked their weapons away for the night, after final practice this afternoon."

"Good. Open the door so we can check a few things, please."

Dargus looked confused, but did as he was asked.

The weapons room was windowless, made of solid stone with a paved floor. There were racks and racks of weapons, most of them belonging to visitors who were here for the tournament. They were grouped together into swords, knives, shields, lances, and others. Adjoining the weapons room was a smithy for making repairs to the weapons.

After lighting the lamps, Tom led the way to the far side of the room where the swords were housed. Excalibur was mounted on a rack in pride of place, and next to it was Galatine. Despite knowing it was securely locked and guarded, Tom felt relief wash over him. "It's here."

"May I?" Finnlugh asked. He lifted the sword and held it under the nearest lamp.

Galatine's hilt had a simple design of curving interlocked symbols, and on both sides, embedded at the cross, was a yellow gemstone with swirl of black. Fine engravings ran down its blade. Tom had often puzzled at these – they looked like writing, but he couldn't read it, unlike Arthur's which clearly read, "Take me Up" and "Cast me away."

"Have you ever wondered what the gemstone is, Tom, and why it is yellow?" Finnlugh asked.

"Not really," Tom said, feeling a little embarrassed.

"It's a fire opal. And I believe the yellow represents a wolf's eyes. Or rather, Filtiarn's wolves' eyes; their eyes were only ever yellow."

Tom thought back to the wolves he'd been surrounded by the other day. They'd all had yellow eyes.

Finnlugh continued, "There's something written here in ancient fey script. I must admit, I can't read it. Nerian?"

Nerian examined it carefully. "That's because it's magical script, very old now, and not commonly used. There are two lines – one on each side."

"What does it say?" Tom said.

"When the Wolf Moon rises," he turned the blade over, "so shall the Wolf Mage."

"What does that mean?" Arthur asked, sounding annoyed. Arthur hated not knowing everything.

"That makes things a little more worrying," Nerian said. "The Wolf Moon rises next month."

"What's the Wolf Moon?" Beansprout asked. "It sounds romantic!"

"It occurs once every thousand years. Everyone will celebrate it," Nerian said.

Woodsmoke agreed. "Yes, there's nothing sinister about it, it just doesn't happen that often."

"Well there may not be anything sinister about it normally, but it says here the Wolf Mage rises on the Wolf Moon! Is he some kind of werewolf?" Jack said, casting a worried glance at Tom and Beansprout.

Fahey sighed. "No, he is not a Werewolf. What a vivid imagination you have, Jack."

"Can I suggest we continue this elsewhere?" Beansprout had started to shiver, and she shuffled on her feet, trying to keep warm.

Woodsmoke immediately threw his jacket around her, and Arthur came to a decision.

"This can stay with me overnight, and I'll double the guard on the armoury." He picked up Excalibur as well.

Woodsmoke grabbed his bow and arrow and hunting knife, and Brenna reached for her sword.

Arthur tried to reassure them all as they walked up to bed. "The castle is full of the finest warriors. I think whoever came here is just looking. He won't be fool enough to attack. You should all go and sleep. Tomorrow will be a long day."

6 The Tournament Begins

When Tom walked out to the pavilions the next morning, a large group of fey were already mingling and chatting to each other, clearly excited at the coming day. Breakfast was set out on long trestle tables, and most of the food had already been eaten. Small bets were being wagered, and Tom could see the steady passing of cash into the hands of two satyrs. A stream of people were going in and out of the weapons pavilion.

It was going to be another hot day. Benches had been set up for spectators, who were saving seats with hats and flags. Tom tingled with anticipation – once his event was over he could really enjoy the tournament. He'd only entered the sword fighting competition, as he wasn't confident about his archery skills – or his sword-fighting if he was honest. But at least he was in the beginners' category.

All of his friends were entering several events. Arthur was of course competing in the expert category in sword fighting, and Tom couldn't imagine anyone beating him. Arthur was also in horse showmanship, but Tom was pretty sure Finnlugh would win that.

The opening rounds were on at the same time, so the crowd would be moving around. As Tom strolled between the pavilions, he scanned the crowds for anyone who looked out of place or suspicious – but he knew trying to spot the intruder would be almost impossible. When Arthur had learned about the tented village that had sprung up outside, he'd opened up the castle grounds to the visitors and they had flooded in, many setting up small stores and cooking areas.

"You look miles away, Tom."

Tom looked around, at first not recognising the voice, and then he grinned. "Bloodmoon! I didn't know you were coming."

Woodsmoke's cousin was as blond as Woodsmoke was dark. Tom shook his hand, pleased to see him. "The last time I saw you, you beheaded the lamia and covered me in blood!"

Bloodmoon laughed. "But I saved your life! Don't worry, no lamias on my agenda today, just healthy competition."

"Does Woodsmoke know you're here?"

"Not yet, I've just arrived." He became serious. "So what were you looking for Tom? Or who?"

Tom filled him in on the intruder and the attack in Inglewood. Bloodmoon narrowed his eyes. "I saw many wolves coming through Inglewood, more than I'd normally expect. It made getting through there without losing blood a little more complicated than usual." He thought for a moment. "I'm not sure if they all had yellow eyes, though. On the day you were attacked, did you think the mist was unnatural?"

"I don't think so. You know Inglewood, it's always murky and misty. I just happened to have got separated from the others."

"Well it seems to me, Tom, that an attack in the woods and an intruder here is not a coincidence. I think you should be careful." Bloodmoon was clearly concerned and seemed oblivious to the party atmosphere around him. "Are you using Galatine today?"

"No, I'm using my old sword. We're not allowed to use magical weapons in the competition."

Woodsmoke appeared out of the crowd with Brenna and Beansprout, their faces breaking into smiles when they spotted Bloodmoon. Woodsmoke looked relieved to see Tom. "I've been looking for you everywhere. You shouldn't wander around on your own, you might be in danger."

Bloodmoon nodded. "I agree. Tom's filled me in on the news."

"I'll be fine! Stop worrying." Although Tom wasn't convinced. He couldn't shake off the feeling of being watched.

Woodsmoke just nodded. "The beginners' sword fighting is the first event – shouldn't you be getting ready?"

"I know, I know. I'll head there now."

Tom set off for the weapons tent, wishing he didn't feel so nervous and annoyed. He couldn't believe he was in danger – not here, not now. It was unlikely anything would happen, it was just a lot of worry over nothing.

The young fey and Cervini who had registered for the beginners', headed out behind the tent for some last-minute practice. They were joined by those competing in the knife-throwing event, which was on at the same time. At least the crowd would be divided between the two, Tom thought, relieved. He collected his sword and shield and started loosening up. He missed Galatine; it was so well balanced that although it was heavy, he found it easy to handle. Consequently, going back to his old sword was difficult and he felt at a disadvantage. And he still found using a shield difficult. It covered a good third of his body, and was of plain design, made of a metal the fey called Arterium, that was light but very strong. And of course it had been made in Dragon's Hollow, like most weapons.

Now it was nearly time, Tom started to feel nervous about all the people who would be watching him. His thoughts were interrupted by a loud bell reverberating through the grounds, summoning them to the draw that was to take place at the edge of the designated areas.

As they left the tent, the two groups separated. The raised benches were now full, and Orlas stood waiting, looking imposing. His tanned skin and deer markings glowed in the sun, and the gold torcs around the tops of his muscled arms reflected the light. Next to him was Duke Ironroot, a relative of Finnlugh and an expert swordsman, who'd been chosen to adjudicate. Ironroot was a huge dark-haired fey with thick eyebrows and eyes the colour of flint. His beard was flecked with purple and his expression was permanently grim. Few argued with him.

When the sixteen competitors were ready, Orlas dipped his hand into a silver helmet and randomly selected two names. There were to be eight fights, and those who lost would be eliminated, the fights progressing down to the final two.

The first two opponents stepped forward – a fey who had arrived with Finnlugh, and a Cervini. The other competitors watched, Tom wondering how good they would be. As the pair entered the ring, the crowd fell silent.

They started slowly, circling, weighing up each other's strengths and weaknesses. The aim was to either cause their opponent to lose their sword, or break through their defences with a move that would cause injury – but stopping short, of course.

The first match didn't last long. It started slowly, but within a couple of minutes both swordsmen lost their nervousness and forgot the watching crowd, advancing on each other, thrusting and parrying quickly. The crowd got behind them, and cheers and groans filled the air.

The fey was quick, but the Cervini was strong. Several times they rolled across the ground to avoid the other's advance, shields rising quickly as they regained their feet.

Tom started to worry. They were really good. He couldn't possibly hope to beat either of them.

And then it was over. The Cervini's strength had prevailed and he had brought his sword up under the fey's and, without Tom seeing how it happened, the fey was barehanded and the Cevini's sword was at his throat.

They stepped apart, breathing heavily as they bowed to each other. The fey grimaced, barely polite, but the Cervini beamed and bowed to the crowd as he accepted their cheers.

As they left the ring, Orlas drew two more names from the helmet. Again Tom had to wait. The next fight was between a Cervini and a satyr, well matched in size and strength. This bout was longer, and by the time the satyr had won, both competitors were sweating and panting heavily. The crowd were on their feet, cheering and yelling.

As Orlas stepped forward again they fell quiet, then resumed cheering as the next two names were called. Tom's was one of them. His opponent was Adil, Brenna's Aerikeen cousin, who grinned at him with what Tom thought an overly confident swagger, her shyness from the other day gone. If she fought anywhere near as well as Brenna, he was in trouble, and his stomach churned as he entered the ring. He heard a shout of encouragement from a voice he vaguely recognised as Beansprout's.

They started pacing around, testing each other's speed. As Tom challenged her, Adil responded quickly, blocking him then attacking his left side, forcing him to bring up his shield before he struck back. He forgot the crowd, concentrating only on her next moves, trying to stay one step ahead. The sun was now high overhead and he blinked, trying to get the sweat from his eyes. Adil seemed to be coping better with the heat than he was, and she was really quick. At one point she almost got beyond Tom's shield and he stepped and rolled, using his shield as a springboard. Surprised by his move she hesitated, giving him the upper hand, allowing him to get in close and finally flick her sword out her grasp.

Adil's eyes hardened, but she managed to control her anger, nodding to Tom as he realised he had won. After bowing to her, he turned to the crowd, grinning. Adrenalin surged through him, and he almost ran out of the ring. Now he couldn't wait to fight again. Buoyed by success, he started to relax.

Over the next half hour they watched three more fights, and Tom paid attention to the competitors' fighting styles, weighing up his chance of future success. Adil stood next to him, looking him up and down. "You fought well, Tom. Who taught you?"

"Arthur mainly, but also my friends Woodsmoke, Rek, and Brenna of course."

"She speaks highly of you and your friends, for what you did for us. And you saved Merlin. You're quite the hero," she said, with a cheeky grin.

He shook his head, embarrassed. "No I'm not. I just helped a little."

She smiled. "If you say so." She looked at their group of competitors, all watching the current fight. "Have you noticed the odd one out?"

"What?" Tom looked at her, wondering what she meant.

"The fey with the dark hair, over there, standing at the edge of the group. He watches you, very discreetly."

Tom's attention slid from the fight as he stared at the fey she had pointed out.

"Not so obvious, Tom, he'll know you're onto him."

"How long has he been watching me?"

"Ever since our fight, but he's careful not to be obvious."

"Maybe he's watching everyone. I have been too, you know, checking out the competition."

"No," she said. "He only watches you."

"Who is he?" Tom felt a stir of discomfort as he wondered if this was the intruder. But surely this fey was too young to be one of the brothers?

"I have no idea. He doesn't seem to mix with the other fey."

They looked away from him as they talked, Tom occasionally risking a glance whilst pretending to scan the crowd.

The fight finished and Orlas called the last two competitors. "Elan and Gelas."

The dark-haired fey glanced briefly at Tom as he passed.

He fought with a quiet intensity that was mesmerising to watch. His movements were precise and deft, and Tom had the feeling he was far more skilled than he was letting on. The fight was over in little more than a minute, the Cervini he fought startled by the speed of his defeat. The crowd seemed to feel cheated too, and gave a slow applause as the competitors left the field. Duke Ironroot turned to watch him pass, a slight frown on his face, as if he were trying to place him.

Orlas announced a short break before the second round, and the benches emptied rapidly as people left to find drinks.

"Well, that's me finished," Adil said. "I'm going to practise for the archery – let's hope I do better in that. I'll make some enquiries about Elan, but in the meantime, be careful."

Tom looked around for Elan, but he had disappeared. He headed for the food pavilion where, glad to be out of the sun, he grabbed a long cold drink and large slab of cake and went in search of his friends. He spotted Woodsmoke, who was carrying a tray of glasses filled with ale.

"Good work, Tom!" he said, slapping him across the shoulders with remarkable dexterity, the drinks not wobbling at all. "I knew you'd rise to the occasion. Excellent footwork, and a very impressive roll. Just remember to keep your sword raised at all times. Follow me, we're out here," he said, before Tom could get a word in.

Woodsmoke led him to Brenna, Bloodmoon, Beansprout and Arthur.

"Excellent start, Tom," said Arthur, beaming. "Just remember to keep your sword up." He raised his glass to Tom before taking a healthy gulp.

"I'm almost hoarse with shouting," Beansprout said, her shoulders shrugging up and down with excitement. "Brenna said you beat one of her best!"

"Yes, you did. But I'm secretly pleased you won, Tom." Brenna held her finger to her lips and Tom laughed. "I'm in the knife-throwing event next, so I won't see you fight – good luck!"

Tom had been about to tell them his suspicions of being watched, but in the light of all this excitement it seemed stupid, like he was imagining it. And he didn't want to worry the others while they were having so much fun. "So you're enjoying it, then?"

"Best idea I've had all year, Tom," Arthur said. "I've already decided I'm doing it again next year. Maybe make it five days rather than three."

He continued to describe his plan, but Tom switched off as he saw Elan out of the corner of his eye. It looked as if he was returning from the orchards. As he disappeared into the crowds, the bell sounded for the next round.

"Better go," Tom said, and he headed back to the fighting area, good luck wishes ringing in his ears.

7 The Enemy Within

Now there were only eight competitors assembled around the fighting circle. They stood nervously, trying to avoid each other's eyes while the crowds settled like a flock of birds onto the benches. Elan was standing close to Tom, and was at least a head taller.

Orlas announced the second round and pulled two more names from the helmet. The satyr was called to fight the Cervini from the first fight. The contest was close and hard fought, both of them muscular, tall and broad shouldered. The Cervini's skin with its dappled markings seemed to ripple in the sun, and the satyr's deer feet moved nimbly, his horns and yellow eyes making him look malevolent. But as Tom now knew, their appearance was deceptive – satyrs were in fact the most social and even-tempered creatures in the Realm of Earth. Tom watched them both, admiring their skill and strength, but once more he was distracted by Elan, which annoyed him. Again the satyr won and Tom thought he would probably win their section; he seemed too good.

He was jolted out of his reverie by Orlas, who called his name with Elan's. Inwardly his heart sank, but he headed into the ring, head held high, buoyed by his earlier success. They bowed to each other and Elan looked him in the eyes, showing only contempt. Tom had the feeling this wasn't going to be a normal fight.

Elan started quickly, testing Tom's reflexes with quick jabbing movements and sweeping attacks, and Tom had to keep defending, finding no gap in which to retaliate. But then Elan seemed to falter, almost stumbling, and Tom took his chance to attack before realising Elan's move was a feint, designed to lure him in and then throw him off balance. Elan struck and Tom retreated rapidly, only just able to defend himself and hold on to his sword. He heard the crowd's sharp intake of breath. His heart pounded and sweat streamed down his face, and he chided himself for his stupidity. He took a deep breath to calm himself, and heard Arthur's words of advice from the many sessions they had fought together: *Sometimes, Tom, you just need to let your opponent wear themselves out.*

Rather than attack, he just kept defending. The crowd's cheers turned to jeers, but Tom ignored them, pleased when Elan became frustrated, his attacks becoming more wayward as he grew angrier. It was time for Tom to seize the advantage. As Elan finished a flurry of attacks that saw Tom bringing up his shield and side-stepping furiously, Elan fell back, out of breath, and Tom ran forward, mercilessly attacking. Finally he swiped at Elan's legs, and he fell. Before he could roll away, Tom stood over him, holding his sword to his opponent's neck, exerting just enough pressure to make him uncomfortable.

Tom had won. He stared Elan down, as Elan scowled back at him, furious.

Tom withdrew his sword and stepped back, then bowed to the roaring crowd who had clearly enjoyed the fight. Then, suddenly, there was a collective intake of breath, and shouts of warning. Out of the corner of his eye he was aware of movement, and he ducked and rolled quickly, narrowly avoiding Elan's sword.

This was no longer a contest, it was a proper fight.

He barely registered Orlas and Duke Ironroot stepping forward before he ran full charge at Elan. He was furious – what was Elan thinking? The air rang with the clash of swords, and Tom felt a sting across his arm as Elan cut him. He retaliated and slashed Elan across the cheek, a line of blood immediately welling up. But before they could continue, Orlas and Ironroot intervened and Elan ran for a gap between the benches and the competitors' area. He was fast, and his run was so unexpected that he was gone before anyone could catch him.

Woodsmoke vaulted over half a dozen benches, closely followed by Bloodmoon, and the pair gave chase.

Arthur joined Tom, Orlas and Ironroot in the ring. "What in Herne's name is going on?" he said.

"I have no idea – he attacked me! Although I gather he's been watching me."

"How do you know that?" Orlas said, looking worried and examining Tom's arm. "I didn't see anything."

"Adil, the Aerikeen I fought, noticed him." He shook his arm free from Orlas. "Don't worry, it's just a flesh wound."

Ironroot hustled them all to the side of the ring as the crowd started to murmur. He pulled them aside, his arm muscles flexing impressively. "Let's get on with the last fight, Orlas," he said.

Orlas nodded his agreement and raised a hand to still the restless spectators. He announced the next fight while Ironroot stood impassive, carefully watching the crowd. He had a stark warning for the last two competitors. "No funny business, or you fight me." The pair glanced at each other nervously and then stepped into the circle.

While they fought, Arthur said, "Why didn't you tell me?"

"Because I thought it was nothing, or that maybe he had a grudge for some reason." He shrugged, not wanting to worry Arthur. He already had enough on his plate today.

"Tom," he sighed. "I know you're lying." His tone was hurt, but trying to be patient. That of a worried older brother rather than a father figure.

Tom rolled his eyes. "Arthur! I'm fine, so stop fussing. He's gone now, and I have another fight. Go!"

With Elan gone Tom felt able to relax a little, and even enjoy the final fights. All too soon they were down to the final four and he was called to fight Clia, a female Cervini. Orlas proudly introduced her, but gave Tom an encouraging grin too.

As Tom started the fight he realised he'd found a rhythm he hadn't had before, even when he'd been practising for hours. In the short time of the competition he'd actually learnt a lot. Arthur and Woodsmoke had been right, as usual. Although he was hot and sweaty, and his muscles ached, a thrill of adrenalin kept him alert and strong. Clia was a good opponent, but he found he could anticipate her moves. Before he knew it he had disarmed her and won. They bowed respectfully to each other and then to the crowd, and left the ring. Tom was in the final.

The crowd hushed in anticipation. Tom stood in the ring looking up at the satyr, Satini, thinking his luck might have run out. The sun was now falling towards the horizon, and shadows were stretching across the grass. The grounds, however, held the heat, and a trickle of perspiration fell between Tom's shoulder blades.

They bowed and the fight began.

The arena rang with the clash of steel and Satini's and Tom's grunts. Both advanced and fell back, testing the other's strengths and weaknesses. Every time Tom defended a blow he staggered back. Satini was strong. Tom blinked the sweat from his eyes and tried not be intimidated by Satini's size, or his Otherwordly appearance. He couldn't help noticing that Satini didn't seem to sweat or tire, and realised he was losing ground.

The crowd followed them step by step, blow by blow. With one final, enormous swing of his sword, Satini flicked Tom's from his grasp, and Tom sank to his knees. He had lost.

Satini bowed graciously to the crowd, then grinned and pulled Tom to his feet, engulfing his hand. "You fight well," he said in his gravelly voice. "You are a worthy adversary."

"You fight better," Tom said, breathing heavily. "But if I had to lose to anyone, it would be you." He shook Satini's hand and then both turned to Orlas and Ironroot. The crowd was bellowing and a few satyrs started singing something Tom didn't recognise. It seemed the party had begun.

8 First Blood

Tom was hot and sweaty, but he was also very happy. Arthur was waiting for him with an ice cold beer. "Congratulations, Tom!" he said, shaking his hand. "You've made me proud. Satini was an excellent opponent, you acquitted yourself well."

"Cheers, I was taught by the best." Tom took a long glug of his beer with relish. "And thanks for the beer, this is just what I needed. Shall we go and find the others?"

"I've got to head off Tom – I have host obligations, but I'll see you later." He gave Tom a final powerful squeeze of his shoulder before disappearing into the crowds.

Tom turned to find Adil behind him, appraising him with a slow smile. "Well done, Tom. I'm quite impressed."

He felt himself blushing. "Ch-cheers," he stammered. "You were watching, then?" He inwardly smacked himself. *Obviously* she was watching.

"Of course. Are you going to be around tonight?"

"Around?"

"You know, around the campfires, celebrating?"

"I guess so."

"Good, I'll see you later." And with a long last look at him, she headed into the crowds, leaving Tom wondering if his heart was beating faster because of the fight, or something else.

The awards would be held on the final day, so Tom waved to the crowd then headed to the food tent. He grabbed some kind of faery meat pasty and headed to the knife-throwing. A few people patted him on the back as he passed, which was embarrassing but nice, and he found Beansprout standing on the edge of the enclosure, a look of concentration on her face. Following her gaze, Tom realised she was watching Brenna.

"How's she doing?" he asked.

She turned to him, shocked. "Sorry, Tom, miles away. Very well. You?"

"Came second." He shrugged. "I was beaten by the best. Satini is amazing."

"Awesome! Really sorry I missed your final match, but I saw you in every other round. You're really good! I always tell you to trust yourself more."

He grinned, pleased Beansprout had watched many of his fights. "Cheers, I surprised myself if I'm honest."

"Well done." She leaned over and kissed him on the cheek. "Now shut up, I'm watching Brenna."

Before he could say anything else, Woodsmoke appeared. "I've been looking for you."

They stepped out of the crowd's hearing.

"Did you find Elan?" Tom asked, suddenly anxious.

"No. But we found his trail. We followed him over the wall and tracked him to Inglewood. Unfortunately his trail disappeared quite quickly."

"You went to Inglewood! But that's miles away."

"We travel quickly when we need to, Tom. Besides, he disappeared hours ago. You've just been sidetracked."

"Where's Bloodmoon?"

"Investigating, he's good at that. And congratulations on coming second."

"Thanks. I had fun." Tom rolled his shoulders and winced. "But I think I'm going to ache tomorrow."

"You'll live. So, who's Elan?" Woodsmoke wasn't going to let this drop.

"I don't know," Tom said, exasperated. "He just appeared in the event. Maybe the officials will know more? He must have registered with someone. Although no-one seemed to know him, and I didn't see him talking to anyone."

"Well he seemed to know you. I just can't work out what he was doing. I mean, was he trying to kill you, beat you, humiliate you? It's not like he could have done much with everyone watching," Woodsmoke said thoughtfully.

"He tried very hard to hurt me!"

"Come on," Woodsmoke said, pulling him along. "Let's ask Finnlugh or Ironroot."

They found both in the weapons pavilion, already talking about Elan.

"Ah, there you are Tom," Finnlugh said. "I've just been hearing about the attack from the mysterious Elan."

"So you don't know him either?"

"No," Ironroot said. "But I suspect he may be from the fey lands beyond Inglewood, close to the shore and the string of islands they call the Serpent's Tail. You probably noticed he had dark hair and suntanned skin."

"Is that in any way related to the Forger of Light and the Wolf Mage?" Woodsmoke asked.

"No idea, but I'll find out what I can," Finnlugh reassured them. "In the meantime, enjoy the tournament. There's nothing else we can do at the moment."

Tom left for his room – he really needed a bath – after which he'd come back for the evening's entertainment. He wandered through the crowds, glad to be alone with his thoughts. The day had been busy, hot and exhausting, and his head was buzzing with all sorts of things.

Closer to the castle the grounds became emptier, and he strolled down the garden paths wondering why he hadn't seen his granddad or Fahey during the day. He presumed they'd been lost in the crowds. He passed the guards at the big back entrance of the castle, and made his way down empty corridors, hearing the occasional muted shout from outside.

He trudged up the stairs and into his room, and at once all thoughts of exhaustion left him. His room had been ransacked, and Jack and Fahey were lying motionless on the floor, both with bleeding head wounds. Jack lay face down on the rug outside the bathroom, and Fahey was halfway to the door. His heart skipped a beat and he felt suddenly sick. He stuck his head into the corridor shouting, "Help, Help! Come quickly!" He then ran over to Fahey and Jack. "Granddad, Fahey!" He reached Fahey first and shook him, pleased to see his eyelids flutter. He then ran to his granddad who also stirred slightly as Tom shook his shoulder. "Granddad, can you hear me?" he said urgently. A pool of blood was soaking into the floor, and there was a thick matted clot on the back of his head.

Jack didn't respond.

Turning back to Fahey, he shook him again, then gently checked his head. There was a large gash on the side of his head too. Someone had struck them both and just left them here. And for what? Panic rose as he realised they could die if they didn't get help soon.

He looked up to yell again as Merlin appeared at the door, a twinkle in his blue eyes. "Did I hear...?" His voice trailed off as he took in the scene, then hastened over to Fahey and Jack.

"Any idea when this happened?" Merlin asked as he examined them.

"No. I just got back. But why are they in my room, Merlin?"

"At this stage, Tom, we have far more questions than answers. Before we do anything else we need to move them. It's a good job I told Arthur to set up an infirmary." He looked up from where he was crouched on the floor next to Jack, calm and resolute. "They'll be all right, Tom, but I need you to go and find Nerian. Bring him to the infirmary. Now!"

As Tom ran from his room he heard Merlin shout, "And send the servants to help!"

Fifteen or so frantic minutes later, Tom finally found Nerian in conversation with a grizzled satyr – they appeared to be discussing stages of the moon and old prophecies. With muttered apologies he dragged Nerian away, breathlessly trying to explain what had happened.

The infirmary was on the ground floor, next to the kitchen and stores and overlooking the walled herb and vegetable gardens. It had been chosen because of its big windows and the natural light that flooded in. Merlin had started cleaning Jack's and Fahey's wounds. A young female fey stood at his side, handing him strips of linen, and helping him staunch the bleeding.

Jack now looked ashen.

Nerian immediately assessed the situation. "Run to my room and bring me my large leather bag, Tom." He turned his attention to Jack's wound.

"And bring my large spell book, you know the one," Merlin added.

Dusk had fallen, and the candlelit sick room was filled with the pleasant smell of burning oils and the spicy rich aroma of incense. Tom sat by the open window, letting the warm evening breeze wash over him, breathing in the soothing scent of the lavender oil. He was exhausted, but his mind raced with the events of the day.

A servant had been sent to fetch Arthur, Woodsmoke, Brenna, and Beansprout, who had joined them now that the final knife throwing event had finished. The rest of the guests were celebrating in the pavilions outside. Three boars had been roasting all afternoon, and the party promised to be a long one.

Finnlugh had also stayed a while, using the Starlight Jewel to aid the healing process, before leaving at Arthur's request to help keep an eye on the crowds.

Arthur was standing by the fire, looking grave. "I think I should cancel the rest of the tournament. It's clear someone is using it as cover to attack us." His voice shook with anger.

"There's no point now, Arthur," Merlin said. He was sitting by Fahey's bed, watching the slow rise and fall of his chest. Fahey's head was wrapped in bandages, but his colour was good and his breathing steady. "Just double the guards on the castle and lock all the doors except for the ones at the rear and the main hall."

"How can you say that after what's happened?" Arthur said. "I feel guilty about all of this. And I presume it's to find Galatine."

"And *have* they found it?" Tom asked, having forgotten all about his sword.

"No. It's very well hidden and protected, exactly where I put it earlier."

Tom had another thought. "Have they attacked the armoury? Surely that's one of the first places they'd have looked?"

Leaving Nerian and Merlin in the sick bay, the others raced to the armoury, where Dargus had been on guard the previous night. As they ran down the long corridor they saw the door hanging open. There was no-one in sight.

Tom's heart was pounding. *Please*, he thought, *let the guard be OK.*

As they entered the room they heard a hammering on the door of the inner forge, and a voice shouting, "Help, I'm locked in!"

Arthur unlocked the door and flung it open. Dargus stood on the other side, covered in grime but otherwise well.

"Thank Herne you've found me," he exclaimed. "I thought I'd die in there."

Arthur looked angry but relieved. "You fared better than some," he said. "Can you remember what happened?"

Dargus frowned. "Not really. I remember letting a woman into the weapons room, but I didn't know why I was doing as she asked. And the more I thought about it the more my head hurt. Then she suggested I should be in the forge, so I walked in and the door slammed behind me. That's all I remember, until I woke up in here."

"A woman? Who?" Arthur asked.

"I don't know, I've never seen her before. And for the life of me, I can't remember what she looked like." He clutched his head. "Ow, the more I try the more my head hurts."

Arthur sighed. "You'd better head up to the infirmary too." He nodded to the floor above. "Go on, I'll arrange a new guard. And Dargus," he added, as he watched him go. "Keep this quiet."

Brenna placed a hand on Arthur's arm. "This isn't your fault. None of us could have had any idea this would happen."

"I still think I should cancel the tournament," Arthur said.

"No." Brenna shook her head. "Woodsmoke's right. You've spent months planning this and it would be harder to stop it."

"I agree, and we can watch the crowds, see if anything unusual happens," Beansprout added. She leant against the wall, looking pale and tired.

Arthur paced up and down and ran a hand across his face. "This reminds me of a time when my other castle, Caerleon, was attacked." He said it so casually, like everyone had other castles. "It was during a visit by the neighbouring princes of Ireland, who had come to discuss trade. Someone tried to sabotage the deal by attacking the delegation, so Lancelot, Gawain, Galahad and I set a trap, and it worked well."

"A trap?" Tom said, feeling alert for the first time in hours.

Arthur continued to pace up and down, his usual activity when he had a lot on his mind. "I need to think on it, but for now we say nothing, and I'll cover this place in guards. Whoever it was may return, because they haven't found what they were looking for."

"We presume they're looking for Galatine? They might not be," Woodsmoke said.

"No, maybe not," Arthur said thoughtfully. "But then, what else is going on?" He shook his head, frustrated by the events. "I'm returning to the party. I want everything to look normal, and we act as if nothing's happened. Come on everyone, let's go."

"Everyone?" Beansprout said, reluctance written all over her face.

Arthur winked. "Just a few hours, my lady," and he held out his hand. "We are to look carefree."

Beansprout grudgingly took his hand and he led her from the room, followed by the others. Locking the armoury door, they left to find a new guard and then headed to the party.

They strolled across the grounds, past stalls selling all manner of wares – jewellery, clothes, food, amulets, weapons, charms and more. Laughter and singing were everywhere. Tom had never experienced anything like it, and he found his energy returning with the excitement of it all.

A large fire was burning in front of the colourful tents belonging to the royal tribes of fey, and another half a dozen smaller fires were scattered around the grounds, where other visitors had set up camp for the night. The tents of the royal tribes were distinct from the others, partly because of their size – they were like mansions – and partly because of their unique design. Trees and bushes had sprung up where before there were none, weaving together tightly to make organic tents, with small lights sprinkled in the branches. The insides were lined with silks and velvets, and carpets were rolled out across the floors.

They found Bloodmoon, Orlas, Aislin, Rek and Finnlugh sitting around a small fire in front of Finnlugh's tent, deep in conversation. They stood to greet them as they arrived, but Arthur spoke first. "I don't want anyone to know of what happened," he said quietly. "We keep it between us."

"I've heard about the attack," Bloodmoon said. "Unfortunately I have been able to find out very little. Elan kept to himself. He wasn't witnessed talking to anyone. However, he was outside the grounds this afternoon, we know that. That means someone else attacked Jack and Fahey."

Arthur groaned. "You're right, Bloodmoon. Now we have two to worry about. Dargus was attacked by a woman, she must have attacked the other two as well."

"What are you planning Arthur?" Orlas asked.

"I'm not entirely sure yet, but someone here is intent on causing trouble and I intend to find out who."

"And how are Jack and Fahey?" Aislin asked, concerned, her large brown eyes looking molten in the firelight.

"Recovering slowly," Woodsmoke said. "I'm tempted to head back to Inglewood to search for Elan; that's where he disappeared to earlier."

"If you go, I'll come. I can't wait to get my hands on him," Rek said, looking grim.

Finnlugh shook his head. "That would be madness, although I understand your reasoning." He gestured to the stools set around the fire. "Come, there is nothing else we can do tonight. Sit, eat, drink." As everyone found a seat, he said, "You know, I have been thinking about this Wolf Mage, and I think it may well be worth me visiting my cousin's Under-Palace – it's not far from here. One of our ancestors, who lived there years before, wrote books about famous fey; I wonder if that's where I've seen the name."

Aislin protested. "But you'll miss the tournament!"

"No, I'll be there and back in a day," Finnlugh said, looking excited at the prospect of action. "I shall leave at dawn, and I'll be back for the horsemanship event, you can be sure!" He turned to Brenna and Tom. "And now there's nothing to do except celebrate your third position with the knives today, and Tom's second in the sword fighting!"

Brenna grinned as she accepted a drink. "I had stiff competition."

"Sorry! I forgot to ask," Tom exclaimed. He'd been so caught up in other events he'd completely forgotten about the competition.

"Don't worry, Tom, you had a busy afternoon." She held up her glass. "Here's to your success too."

By the time Tom got to bed that night it was very late, and the moon was high overhead. He realised with a feeling of guilt that he hadn't seen Adil at all. He promised himself he'd try to find her tomorrow. At least no-one would be creeping across the grounds tonight, he thought, as his head hit the pillow. He slept like the dead.

9 The Clash of Steel

Early the next day Tom headed to the infirmary. Nerian was there, his matted hair bound back, his necklace of bones and feathers more clearly visible as a result. Like the other Cervini, he wore a sleeveless animal-skin jacket and trousers, and was barefoot. He was bent over a small pot hanging from a chain over the fire, stirring a viscous dark green liquid, the heat already making the room warm. An unmade bed indicated where Nerian had slept, and he looked up as Tom entered.

"How are you, Tom?" He looked tired, his eyes heavy.

"Better than these two, I think."

Jack and Fahey were still unconscious, but both looked better, particularly his granddad, his colour looking brighter.

"And you? Long night?"

"Not so bad," he said, with a small smile. "I've slept a little. They are recovering well, I'm not sure how good their memory will be, though."

"At this point I'm just glad they survived." Tom stood looking at Jack and Fahey, feeling terrible he hadn't been around to stop this.

As if he'd read his thoughts, Nerian said, "Tom, this is not your fault."

"I still can't work out why they were in my room," he said, frustrated. He sat down next to Nerian, watching him absently.

"I'm wondering if they were under some sort of spell."

"A spell? Why do you think that?"

"Your granddad and Fahey wouldn't willingly have led someone to your room, unless of course they knew them, but that's unlikely. And they knew someone may be after Galatine, or something else. It just makes me think they didn't know what they were doing, and therefore won't remember anything about who it was or what they wanted. And if you recall, Dargus was also enchanted." He finished stirring the pot and took it off the heat, adding in one final herb. "I fear we are dealing with someone very dangerous."

"How *is* Dargus?" Tom looked around the room. "Where is he?"

"He left earlier – he was fine."

"This could happen again, but how can we stop them if we don't know anything!"

"Do you remember the satyr I was talking to last night?"

"Yes, he looked very old." Tom remembered he had a white beard, flecked with red, and his horns were gnarled and very long.

"He is an elder of their tribe, well versed in ancient lore and the ways of the land." Nerian again stirred the liquid and Tom did a double take. It was now a pale golden colour and smelt of a rich spicy pepper that made him want to sneeze.

"What did you do to that?"

"I added a herb called clarian. This brew helps heal the mind." He started to pour the thick liquid into two cups. "I asked him about Filtiarn and Giolladhe. He remembers a saying in their lore that says when the moon waxes yellow in the lupine sign, the wolf mage will rise and shed his skin until the moon falls for another thousand years, unless he can draw down the moon."

"Waxes yellow in the lupine sign? He'll shed his skin? That sounds disgusting. I don't understand that at all," Tom said, exasperated.

"It refers to the engravings on Galatine, Tom, remember? The moon waxing yellow in the lupine sign refers to the moon cycle of the wolf, or Wolf Moon, which starts in a few days."

Tom sighed. "I'm still confused about this moon cycle of the wolf stuff."

"All moon cycles here belong to different animals or spirits. Some recur frequently, others not so. The wolf cycle comes every thousand years, and usually brings a deep yellow moon. It is a time of great celebration – the fey wear masks and throw parties."

They were disturbed by Merlin who swept in, wearing his usual long grey robes, closely followed by Arthur.

"Morning, any news?" Arthur asked immediately. His hair was tied back and he had trimmed his beard, probably because today he was competing in the sword fighting.

Nerian filled him in on what he had been telling Tom.

"The wolf moon cycle?" said Merlin. "I must confess this is unfamiliar to me. I am far more familiar with the lores of Britain. What does 'shed his skin' mean?"

"Unfortunately, he doesn't know. It's an old saying, its origin lost in time," Nerian said.

"We need to know more about Giolladhe and Filtiarn," said Arthur. "Until then we can do nothing. The root of everything lies with them." He turned to look at Fahey and Jack, full of concern and frustration. "We *will* get our revenge. But in the meantime I'm going to go and win the sword fighting." He looked so determined, and his skills were so good, that Tom didn't doubt it for a second.

Tom stayed with Nerian and watched him and the female fey try to wake Jack and Fahey, until Nerian looked at him. "Go Tom," he said. "There's nothing else you can do. We'll send a message when they're awake."

Tom found Beansprout at breakfast, and after reassuring her about Jack and Fahey, they wandered out to the grounds. For the next few hours they meandered amongst the stalls, catching up with friends and watching the events. They visited Finnlugh's tent and found he'd left before dawn on his big black stallion. They hoped he would bring back news. The archery was on at the same time as the sword fighting, so they divided their time between watching Woodsmoke in the target area, and Arthur, Bloodmoon, Orlas, Rek, and Ironroot, who were competing in the sword fighting. There were new judges who Tom didn't know at all, and they were very strict.

The day flew by in a blur of sunshine, tension, food, and cheering. The competition in both events was intense, and Tom was enthralled with the sword fighting, which he watched avidly, trying to pick up skills. The competitors moved swiftly, almost a blur at times, rolling and jabbing and circling each other, until he was exhausted just spectating. The crowd was equal parts cheering, and silent with suspense.

The fey were quick, lithe, and strong, but of course this raised Arthur's competitive spirit even further. Tom often forgot that under Arthur's debonair attitude and easy-going manner lay a core of steel. Weapons of power had been banned as they offered an unfair advantage, but even so, Arthur's skills surpassed all, including those with a certain natural magic and enhanced skills at their disposal. Watching him again, Tom experienced a jolt of the unfamiliar as he remembered who he was watching and where he was.

In one of the earlier rounds he watched Arthur and Bloodmoon compete against each other. Bloodmoon never said much about where he'd been or what he'd been up to, but Tom got the impression it was always slightly shady. His fighting skills were good, and the crowd were on their feet watching them. Tom liked Bloodmoon, but he wanted Arthur to win, so he was relieved when Arthur finally flicked Bloodmoon's sword from his hand.

After many rounds, some fights lasting a long time, Arthur ended up in the final against Ironroot.

Meanwhile, Woodsmoke was battling a highly skilled female fey from north of Dragon Skin Mountain. The archery competition comprised three distances, as well as shooting several targets at the same time, and finally, moving targets.

The fey seemed to have taken a shine to him, and was a little flirty. Tom watched with amusement as Woodsmoke first tried to ignore it and then accepted her attentions with discomfort.

He turned to Beansprout. "Why aren't you competing? I thought you were getting pretty good with your archery?"

"I haven't really practised lately, I've been so busy with magic. Any sign of Elan today?"

"No." Tom sighed. "I've been checking the crowds, but I guess he won't dare return now."

"Woodsmoke is so skilled – they all are," Beansprout said, distracted. "I wouldn't stand a chance anyway." And then she leapt to her feet, cheering Woodsmoke's latest shot.

Tom headed back to watch Arthur and Ironroot. The crowd was silent as the pair walked into the centre and faced each other. They bowed, and then the clash of swords shattered the silence. The crowds cheered and they were off, fighting furiously, their concentration intense. Neither would give an inch, and they were well-matched, both quick and strong with extraordinary skills. Tom could barely keep track of their movements, and wondered if he would ever be as good. The match was prolonged, but the crowd's attention never wavered. Arthur finally won, after somehow managing to throw Ironroot to the ground and pin him there with his sword at his throat. Ironroot was clearly furious at himself, but stood and shook Arthur's hand. Arthur raised his sword, grinning at the crowd. Tom laughed; he had never seen Arthur look so happy.

Tom found Beansprout heading away from the archery. "How did Woodsmoke do?"

She grinned. "He won, of course. Beat *that woman* easily!"

"Great, so did Arthur. Let's grab some food." He shepherded her across to the pavilions.

As the light faded and long shadows spread across the ground, they celebrated around the campfires with the others for a while, finding Arthur, Woodsmoke, Bloodmoon and Brenna with the Aeriken.

Adil smiled as they approached. "Tom, what happened to you yesterday?"

"Oh, you know, stuff. Sorry." She looked very pretty, he thought, in the evening light, the flames throwing shadows everywhere.

She patted an empty seat next to her. "That's OK. Come and tell me what you've been up to."

Beansprout raised an eyebrow, but Tom ignored her with a lofty look, and sat down, smiling at Adil. However, it wasn't long before they received word that Jack and Fahey were awake, and so they headed back to the infirmary.

10 Hidden Histories

Jack and Fahey were sitting up, sipping soup and the golden restorative drink. Both smiled weakly as their visitors arrived.

"It's about time," Woodsmoke said, relief washing over his face.

"Fahey awoke first, a few hours ago, then Jack, but we thought we'd let them have a few hours of peace," Merlin said softly, his blue eyes solemn.

"I've got a pounding headache," Jack said, grimacing.

Beansprout sat next to him, kissing him gently on the cheek. "You had us worried. That was quite a thump you had."

"You don't have to tell me!" Jack said. "This drink's working wonders, though."

"I think I got off lightly," Fahey said.

"Your injury's still bad enough," Brenna said, settling in the chair next to him. "Can you remember anything?"

"Nothing at all. The last thing I remember is heading down the corridor with Jack to see the games."

"Same here," Jack said.

"I doubt you'll recall anything more," Nerian said, looking exhausted as he sat by the embers of fire, the shadows making his eyes enormous.

The windows were wide open and warm summer air drifted gently through the room. From outside they could hear muted shouts, laughter and music drifting across the grounds. A feeling of peace washed over the infirmary as relief at Jack's and Fahey's recovery sank in.

The kitchen staff brought platters of food and drink, and they sat and chatted about the events of the day. Despite their ordeal, Jack and Fahey were keen to know what they had missed.

About an hour later, Finnlugh swept into the room, his bright white hair shining in the candlelight. He looked none the worse for his long journey.

"You have news?" Arthur paused expectantly, a drink halfway to his mouth.

"I do indeed, very enlightening news! My cousin has an excellent library," Finnlugh said, as he sat on the edge of an empty bed.

From a pocket deep in his cloak, Finnlugh pulled out a small leather book. "I have found the diaries of the ancestor I mentioned, who we called the Gatherer – he was forever searching for scraps of knowledge about this and that. He wrote books, some good, some bad. There are a few very interesting entries I would like to read you. Unless …" He looked to Fahey. "Would you like to do the honours?"

"Great Herne, no," Fahey protested from the depths of his pillows. "You go ahead."

Finnlugh opened the book, pulled a candle close, coughed gently to clear his throat and began.

"The Waning Hawk Moon

"I arrived in Dragon's Hollow over a week ago, travelling the blackened land over Dragon Skin Mountain. Despite the protection cast by Raghnall, the dragon tamer, I found it a perilous journey, and hardly slept. I have been staying in Raghnall's

house, which he has called, quite precociously, the House of the Beloved. It is a small affair of black marble at the moment, but he assures me it will get bigger. If he wasn't a relative I would have nothing to do with him. I find him insufferable, even more so now he has ensorcelled the dragons. The Hollow is becoming quite the place to be, houses are springing up everywhere, and Raghnall has become a bit of a dandy.

"I am in Dragon's Hollow to meet Giolladhe and Filtiarn, the two brothers who have great powers — two more additions to my book. A couple of days ago Raghnall finally introduced me to Giolladhe, or the Forger of Light, as everyone calls him. He is a peculiar man. Very skilled, generous with his powers — although he charges exorbitant fees — and full of knowledge of things dark and light, and things that should remain hidden. Giolladhe's abilities have called him far and wide across the Realm of Earth, making objects of skill and power. He has made rings of beauty, lockets of wisdom, chains of servitude, shields of strength, lances of purity and swords of power. He supplies the djinns of the desert and fire, the sylphs in their airy palaces, the water sprites in their cities far beneath the rolling waves, and the fey who roam across meadows and forests.

"He arrived here during the Dragon Wars. The mountains are rich with dragon gold and seamed with thick deposits of metals and gems. The Hollow speaks of him reverently. But, like Raghnall, he is full of pomp. I told him I was documenting great

works for my book on skilled fey and he was only too pleased to show me his forge. I went there today.

"It is a large place – a cave, in fact – underneath the right shoulder of the mountain. There is a small winding passage cut into the rock that leads to it, sealed by a heavy copper door, covered in filigree and runes. The way it is constructed you would think it is meant to be a secret, but everyone knows its whereabouts, although anyone infirm would have trouble reaching it along the narrow path up the craggy mountain side. Fortunately I am relatively fit.

"The passageway winds to and fro, eventually reaching the main room, from which several doors lead off. The forge itself is huge. The fire glowing within makes the place stiflingly hot, but along the workbenches and wall are articles of great beauty. He showed me the objects he had been commissioned to make, as well as those he designed for general sale.

"He was at that stage working on a sword called Galatine, quite beautiful, with two fire opals set one on either side of the hilt. He said he was making adjustments for his brother, Filtiarn, the person I am planning to interview for my book, whose skills lie not with metals, but with the power to speak and understand any creature. He arrived in Dragon's Hollow just before Giolladhe. His skills have also brought him fame and wealth, as he is used by the many realms to help them communicate with creatures and resolve disputes. He had endeavoured to communicate with the dragons in their harsh guttural language, trying to broker peace,

which brought him great respect amongst the sylphs – who of course have battled with the dragons for years. However the language barrier proved too difficult, and common ground could not be established, the dragons unwilling to relinquish their gains. In truth, I believe Filtiarn's sympathies lay more with the dragons, they had been there first. But their destructive powers were such that he stood aside when Raghnall cast his spells.

"According to Giolladhe, Filtiarn has decided that in order to avoid future miscommunications he wants his sword enhanced to improve his power of communication – I believe he wishes to re-open negotiations with the dragons, so there is no need for Raghnall's spell. In addition, such is his affinity with wolves (the reason he is called the Wolf Mage), he also wants to run with them, especially the white wolves who howl his name and follow him across the forests of the realm. He has asked Giolladhe to give his sword the power to turn him into a wolf at will – I find that astonishing.

"All afternoon I have listened to Giolladhe boast that it will be one of his greatest achievements. He has drawn down the power of the moon, specifically the Wolf Moon, and I wondered why he chose the Wolf Moon when it only came every thousand years. He assured me, however, that it could be used on any full moon, although the Wolf Moon will be the most potent. He says there are limitations on the transformation. It will only last one month, and to reactivate the spell, the ceremony of transformation must be performed again. This of course makes sense, for a wolf can hardly carry a

79

sword! The enhancements are nearly finished, and the additional engravings are quite exceptional. He has also manufactured a receptacle for Galatine, a magnificent moonstone, into which the sword fits, and which will be embellished with some precious metals. He is to show his brother soon, and he says I may come too. It will be an excellent chance to meet him.

'The Waxing Wolf Moon

'This afternoon I again went to the forge. Filtiarn was already there. Unlike Giolladhe, who is blond and green eyed, Filtiarn is dark – his hair almost black – and he has dark blue eyes. He was accompanied by a young wolf, which followed him around the room. It was quite unnerving. I found I liked Filtiarn better. He had a warm gentle smile, and a patient understanding. He was very solicitous to my health.

"Giolladhe performed a spell which bound the sword to Filtiarn, explaining that he could not perform the rest of the actions until the full moon. I confess, I do not know why the sword is bound to Filtiarn, I have never heard of that before, and neither had Filtiarn, but Giolladhe explained it was necessary for the rest of the spell to work effectively. Filtiarn was very cross and wondered why Giolladhe had bound the power of transformation to such a slow and restrictive cycle. Giolladhe explained – quite patronisingly – that transformation was difficult, and required a lot of power. The most effective way to do this was to draw on the moon, and the full moon

was the most potent. At this point the arguing became angry and Giolladhe said he was lucky to be able to transform at all. I think they had forgotten I was there. In fact I tried to make it that way — I hid at the back, pretending to admire Giolladhe's other work, whilst making notes for my book.

"Finally Filtiarn stormed off, without Galatine as Giolladhe was still perfecting it, and they made arrangements to meet in the glade in the forests of the shoulders of the mountain, to perform the ceremony under the Wolf Moon. I asked if I could attend, but Giolladhe was now in a foul mood and refused, and after that I left. However I have no intention of being denied the ceremony, and so I intend to find the grove.

"The Morning after the Full Wolf Moon

"I am in quite a state and I know not what to do. Last night I witnessed Filtiarn's transformation. I had spent several days trotting around the forest, becoming covered in twigs, dirt and dust, until I found a grove, not far from Giolladhe's, with a large flattened rock, which I deemed to be the outside area designated for magical happenings. Obviously I could not ask anybody, it would have given away my intent, but I was right.

"Last night I lay hidden for hours until they both arrived. Neither, it seemed, had quite forgiven the other, but they pressed on with the ceremony. I am obviously familiar with magic, but do not practise it myself. My own natural talents are eloquence, *written and verbal, and other abilities do not interest me. However, this was fascinating. The moon fell full upon the clearing, the yellow light bathing the spot in luminescent beauty. As Giolladhe performed the spell, the light seemed to grow brighter, stronger, until the grove dazzled. It seemed as if the moon had lowered herself directly over us. The sword was placed in the moonstone, and as the light hit, it glowed as if it were on fire. Filtiarn was kneeling in front of it, and it struck him clearly in the chest. I almost cried out at this point, because his whole body was consumed with light, and he screamed and fell to the floor writhing. And then the most monstrous thing happened. He turned into a great black boar. Not a wolf. And Giolladhe laughed and laughed until tears ran down his cheeks, and I could do nothing. Nothing. The young wolf howled and ran round and round the boar whimpering, and the boar seemed to lie as if dead. Giolladhe grabbed Galatine and ran, leaving the moonstone in the clearing.*

"For what seemed like an age, I sat and wondered what to do, but because the boar lay still, I crept to his side and sat there, stroking him, and saying soothing things, which of course I'm sure he couldn't understand. Or maybe he could. Could Filtiarn understand human speech? The wolf, sensing I was no danger, lay close to me, and I comforted it too. I realised there was nothing I could do. To tell anyone what had happened would mean admitting that I was there. I fear what Giolladhe would do. As time passed the boar seemed to

*recover and staggered to its feet, and at this point I fled the forest.
Boar can be killers.*

*"And all today I have debated my actions, and have
again decided there is nothing I can do. Clearly Giolladhe has
betrayed his brother. I can only hope that in a month Filtiarn will
return to his human form. In a few days I will visit Giolladhe and
ask his progress. I confess I cannot bring myself to go before. It will
be interesting to see his response.*

"The Waning Wolf Moon

*I saw Giolladhe today. He said the ceremony went well,
and his brother bounded into the forest with his wolf. I asked him if
he will return to human form in a month and he said, of course, just
as agreed. But his smile did not reach his eyes, and I fear what will
become of Filtiarn. I have decided to stay in the Hollow for another
month, and continue to write my book, whilst waiting for Filtiarn to
return."*

Finnlugh looked up to a spellbound room, all eyes fixed on
him. Even Jack and Fahey had roused slightly. "I shall flick
forward a few pages to a later entry." He skimmed through
some pages and then read again.

"The Morning after the Hare Full Moon

"Last night I did something quite rash. I went to the clearing where Giolladhe performed the spell and waited to see if Filtiarn would return. I again hid in deep shadows, squashed beneath some bushes. It was a good job I did, as Giolladhe also returned, sitting on the flat rock which served as the altar, his feet propped on the moonstone which was still there. I confess I was quite surprised, I would have thought he'd remove it.

"After waiting for some hours Filtiarn returned, in his guise as a great black boar. His eyes glowed a dangerous yellow, and this time he was alone; the young wolf was nowhere to be seen. He walked right up to the altar stone and sat in front of Giolladhe, waiting. And Giolladhe just sat and looked at him as the bright white light from the Hare Moon fell upon them. I feared nothing would be said at all, but eventually Giolladhe laughed. 'You can wait here all night, dear brother, there will be no transformation.' The boar grunted and snuffled and pawed the ground. Giolladhe laughed and said, 'What was that? I can't understand you. I locked you into the thousand-year Wolf Moon cycle, dear brother. Isn't that funny? You must wait a full thousand years until you transform back into fey. But you will only remain in that form for one month, unless you have the sword and the moonstone, and the knowledge to perform the ritual and break the spell. At the end of that month you shall again become a boar, and thus shall the cycle continue for another thousand years.' The boar howled and howled; I thought my heart would break. And Giolladhe just laughed. 'Good luck with *that, because I won't help you, you ungrateful cur.' And then he stood and shouted, 'This is what you get for questioning my skills!' And he turned and left, and Filtiarn just collapsed. It was obvious to me that he had understand everything and had retained his human intellect.*

"I waited sometime, and when it was safe I crept out from hiding place and fled the forest. And I am now leaving the Hollow. I cannot bear to be here any more, and I fear to see Giolladhe again as I may say something I regret and find myself in great harm."

Finnlugh took a deep breath as he looked up, and held his hand up to still any questions. "One more passage," he said, as he pulled another leather-bound book from his cloak and rifled through the pages. "This features Giolladhe's great deeds. One of many stories about fey heroes.

"The Forger of Light's reputation had spread far and wide. He was asked to create a sword for the Earth beyond the bright realms, in the shadows of the Otherworld; a sword to unite and lead, to deflect loss, to add glamour. The price was high, but willingly paid, and the sword Excalibur passed to the Lady of the Lake and then beyond the shores of Avalon. She returned to him seeking a second sword to give to a knight of this great king, but specified no attributes other than that it should be of fine

workmanship, and be possessed of fey engravings and glamour, so that all who should see it would never question the righteousness of the owner. Giolladhe declared that his brother must be dead, and that it would be a shame for such a fine sword to languish unused and underappreciated, and so he gave Galatine to the Lady and it passed beyond the Realms."

The room was quiet as Finnlugh finished.

"I know many tales," Fahey said, "but I have never heard of Filtiarn and Galatine and the transformation. Is your relative the only one to have known?" He looked puzzled, and a little annoyed.

"I think he must be, or him and maybe only a few others. He was obviously far too terrified to tell anyone," Finnlugh reasoned.

Bloodmoon spoke from where he sat by the fire, listening intently. "But Filtiarn transformed for one month every thousand years. If he had retained his wits he would have gone searching for the sword and his brother. He would have told someone. Family members. Friends."

"Well clearly the satyrs knew something at some point," Nerian said, "although they have forgotten how."

Tom nodded. "Maybe this is why Giolladhe eventually left Dragon's Hollow. He had to hide from Filtiarn."

"How did Vivian find him?" Arthur asked.

"I would imagine he'd disappear for just that month, and when the danger had passed he could return again, to continue his business," Merlin said thoughtfully.

"Until he upset the sylphs," Tom reminded them, thinking of their time at the Palace of Reckoning. "They didn't want to talk about him at all."

"By Herne! Is that great beast, the black boar in Inglewood, the one from the tale? Is it Filtiarn?" Arthur spluttered.

"What boar?" Finnlugh asked, amused to be the centre of so much curiosity.

"There's an enormous bloody great boar trampling around Inglewood, and I can't catch it," Arthur explained. "And it's always surrounded by wolves."

"But that's not the point!" Beansprout erupted from her chair next to Jack, who despite all the excitement was now dozing again, his head lolling on the pillow. "If that *is* Filtiarn, he's been trapped in that form for over a thousand years!"

"Closer to five thousand – the dragon wars were a long time ago," Nerian said. "The sword has been in your Earth for fifteen-hundred of your Earth years."

A collective gasped echoed across the room as the enormity of the spell and the injustice registered.

"We must help him," Brenna said, "not hinder him."

"We can't forget what someone's done to Jack and Fahey," Arthur said.

"Of course not, but how desperate would *you* be if you found the sword to set you free was within your reach?" Brenna said, looking at all of them.

"And a Wolf Moon was about to occur," Nerian said softly, from his place next to the fire.

Arthur whirled round. "Is it? I didn't know that."

"Yes, the full moon will be in about two weeks. I would imagine that wherever he is, he'll be turning any day now."

"So someone is helping him," Bloodmoon said. "A boar could not have knocked out these two and put them under a spell."

"Are we going to give them Galatine?" Beansprout asked, slightly confused.

"No!" Arthur said indignantly. "I will *loan* them Galatine to release the spell, and then I wish it to be returned. It was Gawain's, and it's now Tom's. It has value to me." He looked a little sad. "I've lost too much and don't want to lose any more. However, I want to know what's going on before I give the sword to anybody."

"But Arthur–" Beansprout started.

Arthur interrupted. "For all we know it could be used as a weapon against us. I won't let that happen."

Silence fell for a few seconds as they considered Arthur's words and realised he was right. They had no idea what the sword might be used to do.

"Elan." Woodsmoke sat deep in thought. "He fled to the wood. He must be a grandson, or great grandson, or something. And he's clearly been watching you, Tom." Woodsmoke looked at him, and a smile started to spread. "I think you need to carry Galatine again."

"You want me to be bait!" Tom was indignant and a little resentful. "What if he puts a spell on me, whacks me over the head and steals Galatine?"

Arthur was equally indignant. "Woodsmoke, that is underhand, dangerous, and ..." a note of admiration crept into his voice, "quite brilliant!"

"Will everyone please stop rejoicing in me as bait!"

Merlin held up a hand for peace. "May I suggest an alternative. I will glamour your old sword, so it looks like Galatine, and add a little extra protection to your bough. You still carry your talisman, Tom?"

"Yes, but …" Tom couldn't believe his ears. No-one seemed to be saying this was a bad idea. And then he realised he could get even with Elan. He grinned. "Oh, all right then."

11 To Catch a Spy

The next morning Tom, Beansprout and Woodsmoke were sitting on the top row of the wooden benches around the horse-riding skills arena, looking out across the racing tracks, jumps, ditches, and pools of water. Overhanging trees and bushes provided further obstacles, and the taller trees had viewing platforms in them, like miniature tree houses. A few fey were already making their way up their ladders.

To Tom, the competition ground looked like a death trap.

"This event is going to be so much fun!" Beansprout said.

"If you like risking life and limb," Tom said.

Woodsmoke surveyed the ground. "I must admit, I was tempted to enter, but it looks very tricky. Did Merlin help with this?"

"I think so, I saw him heading over this way yesterday afternoon. I believe there's a few surprises in there."

"He's had a busy few days, then," Woodsmoke said, nodding at Tom's sword where it lay in its scabbard.

Tom pulled it free and laid it on his lap, turning it over so that it flashed in the sunlight. It was his old sword, but it looked just like Galatine.

"That is such a cool spell," Beansprout said. "I can't tell the difference at all."

"Neither can I, and it's my sword!" Tom looked at its fine engravings and the large pair of yellow fire opals on either side of the hilt.

"And have you got the bough?" Beansprout asked.

Tom pulled it from an inner pocket. Vivian had given him the small silver bough when he'd first arrived in the Realm of Earth. It gave him a level of magical protection that had enabled him to wake Arthur, and had also saved him from becoming trapped in Nimue's spell. It was the length of his hand span, and fashioned into the shape of twig, with buds along it, as if it was ready to break into leaf. In fact, when Vivian had given it to him it had been a living branch that quickly turned to silver in his hands.

"Merlin's enhanced its protection," he said. "Don't ask me how. He just muttered something over it."

Woodsmoke grinned. "I'm sure it was more than a mutter, Tom."

"Well let's hope the sword draws some attention so we can catch whoever attacked us." He put the bough back in his pocket, reassured by its presence.

From their vantage point they watched as fey wandered over and found spots on the wide benches. The only other event on today was the wrestling, which was taking place in what had been the sword-fighting area.

"What exactly are we looking for?" Beansprout asked, scanning their surroundings.

"Anyone who looks like Elan, or who just looks suspicious," Tom said, taking a big bite of the wood-smoked pork sandwich he was having for breakfast.

"Just make sure you flash that sword about regularly," Woodsmoke said. "No-one can steal it if they don't know you've got it. We'll move around the different sections so that everyone can get a good look."

Slowly the benches filled up around them, a mixture of young and old – Aerikeen, Cervini, satyrs, fey, dryads, pixies, and even a few goblins. And then the half a dozen judges arrived, a mixture of the different races, Merlin amongst them, and headed to their posts around the ground and on the tree platforms.

"Who's competing in this?" Tom asked.

"Bloodmoon, most of Finnlugh's crowd, and Brenna and a few Aerikeen," Beansprout said.

An enormous blast from a trumpet resounded through the trees and the first competitor approached the start of the course, marked by a flag with a dragon on it. The rider was a fey on a large black horse, and after another short sharp blast of the horn he was off, galloping through the trees at a blistering pace. Within seconds he disappeared from view, reappearing seconds later, weaving effortlessly through the trees, over the obstacles and through the water. There were unexpected hazards too, like obstacles that moved, water that rose up, and mist that rolled suddenly across the ground. All things considered, Tom thought it was a miracle that the rider made it through the course at all.

As rider after rider competed, with varying success depending on which obstacles arose, Tom found he was forgetting all about his sword, until Woodsmoke prodded him. "Come on, time for a walk."

"Suppose so," Tom said, and he and Beansprout clambered down after him, through the crowded benches. There were lots of ooh and aahs, and a thud as a rider fell from his horse, and then the arena was behind them as they walked to the refreshments tent.

They found Rek sitting with Orlas at a long table, drinking a pint of Dryad's Pride.

"You should try one of these," Rek said by way of greeting, indicating the dark brew. "It'll put hairs on your chest."

"I don't want hair on my chest, thank you," Beansprout said archly.

Rek grinned. "Only for the men, my lady."

"Don't worry, I'll risk it," Beansprout said, as Woodsmoke brought three pints over from the bar.

"Where's Arthur?" Orlas asked.

"As it's the final day, he's taking part in the judging and getting ready for the awards," Tom said. "And watching for out for more unexpected visitors, probably."

Orlas nodded and extended his hand. "So, I think you should show me this amazing sword of yours, Tom. I haven't had a chance to examine it properly yet."

Tom handed it over, and Orlas made of show of examining it minutely and then holding it up to the light. He even got to his feet and swished it around a few times so everyone got a good look.

"Nicely done," Woodsmoke said, as Orlas sat down again.

"Thank you, I aim to please. And," he nodded discreetly across the tent, "quite a few are looking."

"Not surprising after all that," Rek said, rolling his eyes.

Orlas ignored him. "How are Jack and Fahey?"

"Not too bad, really," Tom said. "I just want to catch whoever did it."

"We all do," Rek said. "When you've finished your drink, we'll follow at a distance."

After chatting for a few more minutes Tom, Woodsmoke and Beansprout set off, keeping to the edges of the crowds and scanning for familiar faces.

The next couple of hours were spent sitting, walking and watching. By early afternoon Tom decided the plan wasn't working. "I need to be on my own."

"It's too dangerous!" Woodsmoke said immediately.

"Whoever it is isn't going to attack when I have bodyguards."

"You're right. Tom, I think we need to have an argument and then you need to walk off in a strop." Beansprout looked very pleased with herself. "If you head to the orchards, keeping in the open for safety, it also means you can be seen on your own. Enter by the massive old plum tree and head for the walnut. We'll circle round and meet you there."

"What do you mean, pick a fight?" But instead of replying, Beansprout started having a go at him about something to do with cheating and bad sportsmanship, and then Woodsmoke rounded on him, and for a few seconds he felt anger mounting before realising it was a ruse.

"I'm not sticking around to listen to this!" he yelled. "You can both go stuff yourselves." And he marched off across the grounds, trying not to smile.

He pushed through the crowds and past the stalls, scowling, people stepping aside to let him through. When he reached open ground he slowed to give the others a chance to get in position, and strolled across the manicured lawns until he reached the meadows bordering the orchards. As he walked he swung his sword, swishing it through the long grass, looking mutinous, as if to challenge anyone who crossed his path, watching out of the corner of his eye to see if anyone was following him. Once or twice he thought someone was, but when he turned he saw nothing except grass and trees and the pavilions in the distance.

He slowed further as he reached the orchards. Finding the gnarled old plum he plunged into the trees, singing loudly to advertise his presence. The sunlight fell through the leaves in dappled waves, and as he advanced towards the walnut tree he stopped singing and walked in silence, listening for the sounds of anyone following him, accompanied only by the murmur of the bees.

In fact the bees' hum almost caused him to miss it – a low whispering drone.

He whirled around to see a figure in a long, hooded cloak, camouflaged by the shadows. He couldn't see a face, but he could hear a voice, and it sounded like a spell.

"Why don't you come a little closer and say that?" Tom raised his sword and stepped closer.

The figure held its ground and raised its voice, at the same time as its hands started to weave strange shapes.

Tom advanced on the intruder. "Spell not working?" He waved the fake Galatine. "If you want this, you'll have to come and get it."

The figure turned and ran, and Tom followed, yelling, "You'll have to find more than spells to stop me."

The cloaked figure raced through the high grasses, and then turned swiftly towards the high boundary wall, the hood falling back to reveal long red hair falling across slim shoulders – it was enough to show Tom his attacker was a young woman.

He changed direction to intercept. "Come back and fight, you coward!"

Two stags, Orlas and Rek, thundered into view, cutting off the boundary wall, and Woodsmoke stepped out of the trees, bow raised. As the woman turned again, Beansprout appeared in front of her and she hesitated for a second, giving Tom time to catch up. He leapt on her from behind, and they both fell heavily to the floor.

She fought like a wild cat, throwing Tom off with surprising strength and leaping back onto her feet, her head held high and her eyes flashing with malice – but also with panic. She wasn't as confident as she appeared. And she was young, maybe the same age as Elan. Again she started to whisper spells, and as the others advanced she threw her arms wide and they all flew backwards, crashing into trees and branches and the wall. Tom felt the wave of power pass through him as he too flew backwards, hitting the ground behind him with a resounding thud. He lay winded, trying to catch his breath.

The woman glanced at Tom's sword, still clutched in his hand, as if weighing up whether to try and grab it. Then she thought better of it and fled over the wall in one mad scramble.

Groaning, they rose to their feet, clutching heads, shoulders, and backs.

"What the hell happened?" Rek yelled angrily.

"And who was she?" Woodsmoke asked.

"Did she take the sword?" Orlas asked, clutching his ribs.

"Please stop asking questions! And no," Tom said, standing on unsteady legs, looking at the patch of Tom-shaped grass beneath him.

"I think her knowledge of magic is very poor," Beansprout said, grimacing. "When she couldn't bewitch you she was stuck, and had to use that other spell. It was pretty crude."

"But effective," Tom said sarcastically.

"At least she didn't smack you across the back of the head, Tom," Woodsmoke said grimly.

Orlas sighed. "Well, so much for our trap."

"But at least we know who attacked Fahey and Jack," said Tom, turning back to the castle. "That's kind of a win."

12 The Wolf Moon Waxes

Entering through the side doors of the castle, they limped into the infirmary to report on the attack.

Nerian was sitting with Jack and Fahey in a patch of sunshine by the open window. He looked at their dejected forms and immediately said, "So I take it your plan failed?"

"You might say that," Rek said sarcastically, slumping into a chair.

"Have you got anything for a sore back?" Tom said. "I hit a tree root particularly heavily."

"I'm sure I have a salve here somewhere." As he reached into his bag, Nerian was unable to repress a grin at Tom's discomfort. "How did that happen?"

"We were attacked in the orchard by a witch," Orlas explained. He turned to the young fey who was helping Nerian. She had just finished redressing Jack's head wound. "I would be most grateful if you could bring us some refreshments," he said politely. She nodded and left, returning with jugs of water and beer, and a platter of finger food which she set on the table by the fireplace.

Jack came over to Tom and examined his back, where a large bruise was now blooming a rich purple. "I knew that was a risky plan, Tom. You shouldn't have done it."

"At least we know who attacked you, though," Tom said, smiling ruefully. Jack still had a dazed look about him from the assault, compounded by the bandage wound around his head. Tom was amazed he was even walking about.

"Had you seen her in the grounds before?" Nerian asked.

They all shook their heads. "No, but she was young, with long red hair," Beansprout said. "And she looked really worried."

"Worried enough not to attack again?" Nerian said.

"Yes, maybe," Orlas said, as he helped himself to some food.

"So what happens about Galatine now?" said Fahey.

"It depends. How long did you say until the Wolf Moon?" Beansprout asked, watching Nerian as he examined Rek's injuries.

"I believe it starts tonight," he said straightening up. "But it will be two weeks until it becomes full, and then wanes again. It depends if he turns at the very beginning of the month, or only on the full moon."

"It sounds like a werewolf," Tom said, brightening.

Jack laughed nervously. "Fahey tells me werewolves don't exist, Tom. This is different, isn't it?" He looked at Nerian, who chuckled.

"Yes, werewolves are different. They do exist, but Filtiarn isn't one. And besides, he's a boar."

"OK," Tom muttered, wondering what else lived here in the Other that he'd thought only existed in myths and legends. He guessed if there were dragons, werewolves and witches, then pretty much everything weird and wonderful must be here. And yet it always surprised him.

"When Finnlugh read from the Gatherer's diary," Beansprout said, "it seemed to suggest the full month, but maybe we should read it again." She turned to Tom. "Finnlugh gave you the book, didn't he?"

Tom nodded. "It's in my room."

"Good, check it again. But be careful where you put it, Tom. We don't want that to go missing too." She smiled and looked at Jack, Fahey and Nerian. "Well, seeing as you two look so much better, and Nerian hasn't had any fun at all, I think we should go and watch the end of the tournament."

Promising to catch up with them later, Tom returned to his room, deep in thought, while the others headed back to the finals. He was relieved to find the diary where he left it, on a burnished copper table next to his bed, along with two more books Finnlugh had suggested might offer further insights into the two brothers.

He picked up the diary and stroked the worn and stained leather cover. In places it was cracked, but considering its age that wasn't surprising. It was curious that so few knew of Filtiarn's story, but it was long ago, and maybe Filtiarn hadn't wanted anyone other than his own family to know of the curse. It would make sense. Wouldn't it be embarrassing to be cursed and duped by your own brother?

He thumbed through the pages, wondering what else the Gatherer had been up to, then settled back on his bed to read. It was only later, flicking through the back pages, that he discovered a pocket in the leather back cover. Inside were some old drawings and maps – and one of them looked like Dragon's Hollow.

The tournament was nearly over. The wrestling had finished and a winner was announced – a satyr from the woods around Aeriken. The final rounds of the horse riding skills were finishing; the stands were full, the crowds on their feet, cheering and shouting.

In front of the pavilions a podium had been set up for the awards presentation, and Tom found everyone lounging on blankets on the grass in front of it, soaking up the late afternoon sunshine. Arthur stood to the right of the podium, regal in a fine linen shirt, trousers and boots. Next to him stood Orlas and Ironroot, there to help with the prize giving, and a straggle of visitors who'd been involved with the judging. On a long table behind the podium was a row of cups, shields and plaques, ready to be given out.

Tom waved at the others and headed towards Arthur, who looked relieved to see him.

"I've been worried about you," said Arthur. "I haven't seen you for hours!"

"I've been reading, and I've found out some interesting things."

"I heard all about the incident earlier. Are you all right?"

"I'm fine, but after this I need to show you what I've discovered."

A long loud blast from a horn interrupted them.

"That sounds like the end of horse riding, Tom. We're nearly finished now. Don't go anywhere, you have a prize to collect." He grinned before turning to Orlas.

Tom groaned and joined the others on the grass, sitting next to Brenna.

"I thought you were competing," Tom asked, curious. "Shouldn't you be over there?"

Brenna laughed. "I was out in the early rounds – there's stiff competition in the horse riding." As she spoke the crowd erupted again, cheering and clapping, before slowly starting to disperse from the benches.

The grassed area started to fill up and eventually, as everyone finally settled with drinks and food, Arthur started the prize giving. Tom generally hated these things, but had to admit that Arthur did it with a certain panache. He was glad that his granddad was there to see him collect his award, and that he and Fahey could enjoy at least some of the tournament.

Tom found his mind returning again and again to the woman in the orchard. Who was she, and how was Elan linked to it all?

But Beansprout had decided the night was all about celebrating. "There's plenty of time to worry about Filtiarn, Tom," she said, noticing him brooding, "and this isn't it." She grinned. "Tonight is about celebrating friendships. Later …" she pointed to where Merlin was walking out to the edge of the field, "there'll be fireworks."

Tom laughed. "In that case, Beansprout, I'll enjoy the party."

And then Adil, the young Aeriken from the sword fighting round, sat next to him with a smile, and he thought the night might become even more interesting.

13 Planning the Hunt

By mid-morning, the sprawl of tents and stalls had been packed up, leaving in their place flattened grass and furrowed land. A team of servants was already at work on clearing the grounds and dismantling the pavilions. People dawdled out of the gates and on to the moors, back to their villages and homes, carrying tales of daring and courage.

Arthur had mingled amongst them, shaking hands and promising to put on the event again. Tom had watched, curious, wondering if this was how it had been in Arthur's time, with pageants and contests, and knights setting off on their quests and adventures. He had a sudden pang for what had once been. He liked Arthur's quiet informality, his ability to treat everyone equally. No wonder he had been a good king.

Finnlugh and the royal household were mounted on stamping horses that snorted with excitement, ready to be off. Finnlugh slipped to the ground as he saw Arthur and Tom.

"Well done, Arthur!" he said, shaking his hand. "Excellent event. I shall look forward to the next. Do you need me to help with the witch?" He grinned rakishly. "You know I always enjoy a challenge."

"Thank you, but no," Arthur said, smiling. "I think small numbers will be advantageous in this case."

"Well, you know where I am if you need me." Finnlugh turned to Tom and shook his hand. "Good to see you back. Make sure you stay this time."

"I'm not going anywhere!" Tom said, his heart skipping a beat at the thought.

Finnlugh swung himself up onto his horse. "Look after the books – it'll be a good excuse to come and see me when you've finished with them. I'll keep looking too; if I find out more, I'll let you know." And with a flash of white-blond hair and the gleam of sun on silver lances, bridles and stirrups, the royal household disappeared.

Tom felt a stab of sadness as Finnlugh left. He would miss him. But as he and Arthur headed back to the castle, he was cheered by the thought of the conversation they'd had with Brenna earlier, at breakfast. She had sent the other Aerikeen home, while opting herself to stay and help. Tom had teased her, saying, "I'm sure we could manage without you, Brenna. You must have lots to do."

With a glint in her eye, she'd said, "Thank you, Tom. When I need your advice I'll ask for it."

He'd scooted out of the way as she tried to cuff him on the shoulder.

Also at breakfast, Orlas and his wife had announced their intention of returning to the White Woods with the rest of the Cervini. "I'm sure you'll be happy to get your home back, Arthur," Orlas had said. "Rek wanted to stay, but I need him. I'm not sure he'll forgive me." He'd turned to the grizzled older warrior. "I'm sure they'll manage without you."

"I'm sure they will, but I'll miss out on all the fun!" Rek had moaned, his mouth full of sausage.

Tom smiled. They had got to know the Cervini well since moving into the castle, and had become good friends, especially with Rek. "We'll miss you," he'd said. "But Brenna can come get you if we need support."

Tom's thoughts returned to the present as he and Arthur entered the infirmary, where they had arranged to meet the others. Tom immediately felt soothed by its calm atmosphere. The windows were open and a warm breeze flowed through the room. The gardens outside were a vigorous green, and the walls blocked out the noise of the departing guests.

Nerian was standing by an open window, talking with Jack and Fahey, his bag in his hands. He turned as they entered. "I'm glad to see you before I go. These two have made a good recovery. I've left some of the healing brew, but otherwise there's nothing further I can do."

"Give me a few more years of that stuff, and I might feel young again," Jack said, grinning.

Fahey laughed. "I don't think even Nerian's that good."

"Good luck finding Filtiarn," Nerian added. "I'm glad Merlin's going with you. I have a feeling you'll need him." With a swing of his dreadlocks he left.

"You know you two can't come with us," Arthur said, "so don't even try to argue."

Jack nodded. "Don't worry, I know my limitations. And besides, my head still hurts."

"I think that may have been the beer last night," Fahey said with a grimace. "But it's all right, Arthur. We have no intention of coming."

Arthur nodded. "Good. It's only that I think we'll have enough to worry about."

They were interrupted by the arrival of Brenna, Woodsmoke and Bloodmoon, and then Beansprout arrived with Merlin.

Merlin had brought the real Galatine. "I cannot find anything else on this sword that gives a clue to reversing the spell. I presume all will become clear on the night of the Wolf Moon."

"And what if it doesn't?" Woodsmoke asked. "How do we break the spell?"

"I think the first thing we need to do is find Filtiarn," Arthur said. "Soon he'll be in human form, hopefully, and will be able to speak to us. He must know how the spell works."

"If he lets us help him," Woodsmoke said.

"If we can even get near him," Bloodmoon added.

"If Elan and the woman are helping him," Tom said, "I don't understand why they wouldn't just tell us what's going on."

"When you've been betrayed before," Merlin said, "it can be hard to trust again."

Merlin's tone was measured, but Tom wondered if that applied to him too, after all Nimue had done. But something else was tickling his brain.

"I found some maps in the back of that old diary Finnlugh found," he said.

"Maps of what?" Beansprout asked, intrigued.

"One looked like Dragon's Hollow, although it appeared much smaller on the map. And a few other places I didn't recognise."

"Dragon's Hollow?" Beansprout said, excited. "Was there anything about the Forger of Light?"

Tom shrugged. "I don't think so."

Bloodmoon grinned. "Old maps, Tom! Hidden treasure?"

"Is that all you think about?" Woodsmoke asked, looking at his cousin sceptically. "Are you sure you haven't got anything better to do?"

"No. And you know I can be very useful," Bloodmoon said, smiling at Woodsmoke's discomfort. He tapped his sword where it hung in its scabbard, "And I've still got my dragonium sword. It may come in handy."

Tom shuddered slightly, remembering their encounter with the lamia.

Arthur nodded thoughtfully. "Yes, it may! I think we should get moving. Let's head for Inglewood. And bring those books with you, Tom."

12 Back to Inglewood

Within the hour they had left to search for Elan, Filtiarn, and the mysterious woman. There were seven of them: Arthur, Tom, Merlin, Beansprout, Woodsmoke, Brenna and Bloodmoon, racing on horseback across the moors to Inglewood. They had no idea what to expect so were all heavily armed, and supplied with food, water and bedding.

The day was again hot, and they were relieved to enter Inglewood. As they descended into the valley the temperature dropped, and the black shadows beneath the trees hijacked the sunlight. Arthur rode ahead with Woodsmoke, while Tom kept to the rear with Bloodmoon. The trees thickened and they slowed their pace. Even though Tom hunted here regularly, he still found it a bewildering place. Large rocks and misshapen trees provided landmarks, but he still felt he could easily get lost in here.

Arthur was aiming for the place where they normally saw the boar. Elusive though it was, it seemed to favour a certain part of the wood. And it was close to where Tom had been surrounded by the wolves.

"I recognise this place," Arthur said. "But there's a path I don't remember seeing before." He pointed to where a barely-there path snaked into the undergrowth.

"It could be a trap," Brenna said, drawing her horse to a halt.

The others did the same, and Merlin moved next to Arthur, holding a hand up for silence. He sat silently, his head bowed, his hair covering his face. For a few moments he listened intently and then said, "Let me lead."

Woodsmoke was about to protest but Merlin fixed him with a piercing glare, and he fell into step behind him with a nod and a sigh.

They followed in single file, as the path eventually led to a clearing in which was a stagnant pool. Beyond it was a rocky mound with a cave in it, the entrance dark and overgrown with bushes.

"I don't recognise this place," Arthur murmured.

As they entered the clearing a strange green smoke started to rise from the ground, eddying across the rocks and bushes and the surface of the pool, reaching out towards their horses. In response Merlin raised his hands and started an incantation, his voice soft and seductive. Immediately the smoke stopped, as if it had hit an invisible wall. Beyond this, it thickened.

Instinctively they started to retreat, but after only a few paces the white wolves emerged from the trees behind them, bellies low and teeth barred. Goosebumps rose up Tom's neck as they were forced back towards the pool, weapons ready, bunching up behind Merlin.

Arthur turned to Merlin. "What's that smoke? Can we get through it?"

"No. And stop asking questions," Merlin muttered. He continued to chant, his hands raised, and the invisible wall moved away from them, pushing the murky green smoke back, allowing them to edge forward uncertainly.

A young woman emerged from the cave. Her long silky red hair snaked down her back, almost to the floor, and she wore a black velvet gown edged with sable. It was the woman from the orchard. Elan stepped out behind her.

"Who are you that brings such powerful magic to my grove?" she said, her voice loud and clear.

"I am Merlin; prophet, sorcerer and advisor to the court of Arthur Pendragon, Boar of Cornwall, Dragon Slayer, bearer of Excalibur." Although his eyes never left her face, his hands continued to weave his magic. "But I think you know that. And you are?"

"I am Rahal, Guardian of the Wolf Mage," she said. "You must be the one responsible for protecting the boy over there. There are faces I recognise from our encounter in your grounds."

"The Wolf Mage," Arthur repeated, nodding as their assumptions were proved correct. "So it *is* about him. I do not appreciate the games, Rahal. You have attacked us, grievously. What do you want?"

"Galatine. It belongs to us." She lifted her head, her eyes flashing.

"Why didn't you come and ask for it?"

"I shouldn't need to ask for it. It is Filtiarn's to take. And I will take it for him."

She again raised her hands as if to strike with magic, but in a flash Merlin launched a flaming arrow straight through the invisible wall towards her, dispelling the green smoke and causing Rahal to shriek curses at them.

The wolves hurtled towards them in a flash of fur and teeth. Tom swiped at the first one as it leapt at his throat, and sent it whirling backward. The others were also fighting frantically, arrow after arrow flying into the wolves, a few falling dead around them. Furiously fighting and trying to control Midnight, who was bucking with fear, Tom didn't at first realise he was getting cut off from the group. He tried to make his way back as Bloodmoon fought his way over, Woodsmoke next to him, yelling, "Tom, get behind us. They want your sword."

Tom heard a scream, and Elan shouting, "Stop, stop!"

He glanced round and saw Merlin standing over Rahal's unconscious body, Elan at her side.

"What have you done?" Elan cried.

Merlin was furious. "She was trying to kill us!"

"She was trying to protect Filtiarn," he said, leaping to his feet, sword drawn.

"No – she was trying to steal Galatine! Call the wolves off, Elan," Arthur said, his sword at Rahal's throat, "or I'll kill her right now."

Elan glared at Arthur, and then yelled something at the wolves in a language Tom didn't understand. Immediately the wolves withdrew, growling and snarling in a semi-circle in front of them. Elan continued Rahal's argument. "It's our sword; we have a right to it."

"You do not have a right to knock people unconscious for it!" Arthur said, towering over Elan. "Did you not think of asking, of telling us of your plight and the curse upon Filtiarn?"

Elan faltered, "You know of the curse? No-one should know that, it's a family secret."

"Well *we* know. Repeated attacks upon us made us look into Galatine's past. You should know right now, that I do not tolerate attacks upon my friends or household, and you should be very careful what you do in the future."

Elan stepped back a pace, but his expression remained mutinous.

Arthur turned to Woodsmoke and Bloodmoon. "Check around the back of this rocky mound, I want to make sure there are no more surprises."

They nodded and set off, swords drawn.

Arthur turned to Elan. "Where's Filtiarn?"

Elan nodded behind him. "He's in the cave." Looking nervous he raised his sword as if prepared to fight. "Do you mean to attack him?"

Arthur snorted. "Great Herne, no! We are here to help, you stupid boy. Although," he looked at Elan's sword, "if you keep pointing that at me I might change my mind."

Elan nervously re-sheathed his sword. He didn't look keen for a fight, and Tom didn't blame him. No-one in their right mind should want to fight Arthur.

"When will Filtiarn change form?" Arthur asked, returning Excalibur to its scabbard.

"Tonight, midnight as the Wolf Moon begins." Elan hesitated. "We think so, anyway. Neither of us was around the last time he changed form."

Merlin straightened and peered at Elan, Rahal still unconscious at his feet. "So you have no idea what to expect?"

Elan shook his head looking suddenly young and vulnerable.

"Show me to him," Merlin said, and Elan led him into the cave.

Arthur turned to Tom. "Go with him, I'll watch Rahal."

The cave was dark, and a small fire smouldered to the rear. The smoke wound its way up to a narrow vent in the roof, but eddies of it drifted around, and Tom's eyes started to smart.

Filtiarn wasn't far from the entrance. He lay on his side, his huge mass stretched out across the floor, an earthy musky smell emanating from him, adding to the stink of the cave.

"Have you been living here?" Merlin asked Elan, kneeling at Filtiarn's side.

He nodded. "For a few months, ever since we heard about Galatine." He looked at Tom and then the sword at his side. "Is that Galatine?"

"Yes."

"May I look at it?"

Tom glanced at Merlin. At his nod, he took it from its scabbard and handed it to Elan, who turned it over, examining it minutely in the dim light.

"Have you any idea how long we've been looking for this?" he asked, relief evident in his face.

"We have a rough idea," Tom said. "We're thinking close to four thousand years."

"Close enough. Long enough that we need to break the curse or he may not live another thousand years." He sighed. "My family history says that the last time he returned to human form he was wild, almost inhuman, and mad with grief." He looked at Tom. "Do I have to give it back?"

"For now." Tom took Galatine and returned it to its scabbard. "And why are *you* helping Filtiarn?"

"Every new generation, two guardians are assigned to Filtiarn. I'm one of them."

Tom couldn't help but notice he didn't look pleased with the job. "And who's Rahal?"

"My cousin. She was chosen for her knowledge of magic, and I was chosen for my skills with the sword. The old guardians died, and the new ones are always young. Rahal, however, is senior to me."

As much as Tom was mad at Elan for attacking him during the tournament, he felt sorry for him. "It must be a hard job."

"It's a thankless task," he agreed, annoyed and sulky.

"Do you know how to break the spell?" asked Merlin.

"Not really. Only that we need the sword. We hoped it would become clear when we had it."

Tom felt his heart sink. No-one seemed to know how to break the curse.

Merlin groaned, looking incredulous. "Haven't you any books or histories to refer to?"

"No!" Elan's voice rose in alarm and distress. "When it first happened, Filtiarn just disappeared. Of course no-one knew where he had gone. And then when he did return, after that first thousand years, he was so mad at his brother's deception that he didn't want to share anything. Apparently."

Filtiarn stirred and rolled in his sleep, and then his eyes fluttered open.

"I'm going to try something," Merlin said. In a flash he changed form, and now two boars were lying on the floor of the cave, snorting softly to each other.

Tom tried to reassure Elan, who if anything looked more alarmed than before. "It's what he does," Tom said, shrugging. "He shape-shifts. Tell me more."

"I don't know what more I can say. He lives in and around our family castle, roaming the woods and grounds, along with a pack of wolves. Every thousand years he changes form, returning only briefly to our home, and then he searches, endlessly, for Giolladhe. Guardians were assigned to watch over him, to help search for the sword with him, and to continue the search when he is in animal form. When he found out Giolladhe had given Galatine to the Lady of the Lake, he thought everything was lost. *We* thought everything was lost. But now it's back, you understand why we had to come for it …" Elan's voice trailed off.

"You should have come to us," Tom repeated.

Elan's voice dropped and he couldn't look at Tom. "To speak of the curse outside the family is to risk death. Both for us and you."

"Why?"

"Our family is proud. To admit that one brother double-crossed another is too embarrassing. Especially two very famous brothers whose deeds are well known across the Realms."

Tom gasped, trying to ignore the snorting and snuffling coming from Merlin and Filtiarn. "Are you kidding me? That's the stupidest thing I've ever heard. It was forever ago!"

"My father doesn't think so. Our family may have fallen on hard times, but the family pride remains. Things will change now we have the sword. We can pretend you don't know anything, and that we managed to steal it."

"But you don't know the spell. And neither does he by the sound of it. And there's nothing inscribed on the sword that will help break it."

"At least we have the sword!"

Tom felt his frustration growing. "Elan, I don't think you can do this without us. It may not look like it, but Merlin is one of the greatest sorcerers ever." They turned to look at Merlin and Filtiarn, as they shuffled to their feet and waddled out of the cave.

"Really?"

"Yes! You need him to undo the spell. Especially if Rahal can't do it."

"My father will kill us."

"I think he'd be angrier still if you let this opportunity pass. You said it yourself. Filtiarn may not survive to see another Wolf Moon."

Elan looked out of the cave, clearly wondering what he should do.

Tom patted him on the shoulder. "Come on, let's see what the others are up to."

15 Brother's Betrayal

Night was falling as Tom and Elan left the cave. Someone had started a fire in the centre of the clearing, and branches were stacked in a pile next to it. In the shadows at the far edges, the wolves sat and watched them, their yellow eyes glinting in the firelight.

A few logs had been pulled around the fire, and Beansprout and Brenna were sitting warming their hands, their cloaks pulled close. Lying next to them, where they could easily watch her for signs of movement, was the prostrate form of Rahal, wrapped in a blanket. After a warm day, the air was now chilly, and a few stars had started to spark in the night sky.

Tom and Elan joined Arthur where he stood talking to Merlin, no longer in boar form.

"How is he?" Arthur asked, looking in concern at Filtiarn snuffling in the edges of the fire.

"Confused," said Merlin. "There were flashes of comprehension, but mostly all he could say was that he was hungry and tired."

"Hungry?"

"It's a primal urge in animals as well as humans. I'm not sure if we'll get any more sense out of him once he changes."

"So his mind might have gone forever?" said Tom.

A sad smile flickered across Merlin's face. "Maybe. But perhaps not being able to reason with a human mind is a way of preserving his sanity, Tom."

"But you can think clearly as an animal?" Elan asked.

"Yes, but I only turn for a short period, and shapeshifters such as Brenna are meant to change. Filtiarn has lived as a boar for a thousand years, and more."

Arthur shivered. "I only turned for a short time in Nimue's spell, and all I can remember is trees and more trees. I don't think I had one logical human thought in my head."

Merlin nodded thoughtfully. "All being well, he will change form later and his human reasoning will return. Until then, we wait."

Bloodmoon and Woodsmoke had returned with news that they could find nothing else of danger in the surrounding area. They had shot rabbits and a pheasant for supper, and sat side by side, expertly skinning, de-feathering and gutting the carcasses, before chopping them into chunks and placing them in a large pot over the fire, along with water and herbs. The smell of cooking reminded Tom how hungry he was.

He left Elan talking with Arthur and Merlin, and sat next to Beansprout, nibbling on a piece of cheese. It was strange seeing her out of her long dresses. She was now wearing dark leather trousers, a shirt, and a leather tunic that doubled as some kind of body armour. "How're you, Beansprout?" he mumbled.

"OK, Tom. Just realising this is going to be harder than we thought." She turned her gaze from the fire to look at him. "I mean – we don't know anything! Just a few old stories. It would seem like a story if we didn't actually have proof in front of us." She glanced at Filtiarn.

Brenna leaned across. "Didn't you say you'd found some old maps?"

"Ooh yes!" Beansprout said, brightening. "Let's have a look, Tom."

He pulled the book out of his pack, carefully extracting the maps at the back. "This is the one that looked like Dragon's Hollow."

They stared at the map in the firelight, following the lines and contours. "Looks like it to me, but it's smaller," Beansprout said. "Look, he's marked a few places. That could be Raghnall's place, and there's the mines, and there's a mark on the hill behind Raghnall's."

Woodsmoke joined them, leaning over Beansprout. "I knew that path led somewhere!"

Tom looked up at him, confused. "You mean the one that leads up the mountain? We know where it goes. To the top."

Woodsmoke shook his head. "Tom, Tom, Tom. Subterfuge only! Convenient, yes. But I bet that's Giolladhe's place. The route to it must be off that main path."

Now Brenna looked confused. "But why would he hide it? What does it matter?"

"If Raghnall hid it, it's because there's something valuable there he didn't want anyone to know about," Woodsmoke reasoned. "He was a sneaky rat, remember?"

"Maybe," Beansprout said.

Tom had pulled some of the other drawings out and was examining them too. "He's drawn some people. Must be some of his famous fey." Underneath the drawings were names of fey he didn't recognise, but then he gasped. "Look! Giolladhe and Filtiarn."

On one page, tattered and worn like all the others, were pen and ink drawings of two men, one with light hair (or so Tom presumed – it had less ink than the other), and one dark. The blond one had short hair, thick and wavy, and a sharp chin and narrowed eyes, and underneath was written *Giolladhe*. The dark-haired one had longer hair, and a slight beard, and under him it said *Filtiarn*. Next to both was written, *The famous brothers*.

"How amazing," Beansprout said. "To see a picture of the Forger of Light! And Filtiarn, who's right here! He looks so young and handsome," she said with a wistful sigh.

By now Elan had joined them. Beansprout looked at him, comparing him to the picture. "He looks a bit like you, Elan."

Tom thought he detected a snort from Woodsmoke, who didn't seem too pleased at Beansprout comparing handsome men.

"I bet he doesn't look like that any more," Tom said, wondering what was going on with Woodsmoke. "And look, a drawing of Galatine." He pulled his sword free. "It's incredibly detailed. The Gatherer was a very skilled artist as well."

"Where did you get those from?" Elan asked, looking at the drawings with interest.

"A friend of ours found them, they were in a diary. Someone watched Filtiarn get cursed."

Elan looked shocked. "And they didn't help him?"

"He couldn't help him," Tom explained. "He was scared."

"What else is in there, Tom?" Brenna said.

Tom passed her some more papers, and she opened one and looked puzzled. "Galatine's moonstone." She looked up, startled. "What's this?"

Before anyone could answer, Rahal stirred and her eyes flickered open. Brenna pulled her dagger free and placed it under Rahal's chin, calling sharply, "Arthur, Rahal's awake."

"Don't hurt her!" Elan shouted. "She was only doing what she thought was best."

"So am I," Brenna warned with a sidelong glance.

Elan ran to Rahal's side. "Rahal, it's all right. You're safe."

Arthur stood over her, putting her in shadow, and she recoiled nervously. "Rahal, if you promise not to try anything stupid, Brenna will put away the dagger."

She glanced nervously at Elan, who nodded and said, "Honestly, we're fine. They want to help."

"All right, no magic, no tricks." She rested back against the log and put a hand to her head. "What did he do to me?"

"Only a little spell," Merlin called over from where he sat next to Filtiarn.

Tom reminded himself never to underestimate Merlin's hearing.

Arthur smiled before continuing. "As I said earlier, Rahal, we are here to help you break the spell. In a few hours Filtiarn will change form. We need you to tell us what you know of the spell, if we are to break it forever."

"It's our family secret," she said quietly. "It is not for others to know."

"That time has gone," Elan said. "They're right. In all these years no-one has come close to breaking the spell. In another month we may not have another chance." He grabbed her hand. "I've told them what I know, but it's not much. Do you know any more?"

For a few seconds she sat in silence and then came to a decision. Looking at Arthur she said, "I know where we've searched, and I know we found nothing in years. The old guardians had given up hope. They were old and I know they stopped looking, and if I'm honest we didn't know where to start.

"All the guardians keep records and I've read them all. When Filtiarn originally went missing no-one knew what had happened, and all Giolladhe said was that he had set off with his wolves to explore his new abilities."

"Who did he tell that to?" Arthur asked.

"Their family, and his wife and children, when they wondered where Filtiarn was. They knew Giolladhe was helping him to shape-shift, so that wasn't a surprise. What was puzzling was the fact that he never returned. Giolladhe denied having any knowledge of what he was doing."

"Fancy lying to everyone. About your own brother!" Beansprout said.

"Not everyone has your scruples," Woodsmoke said, squashing in next to her on the log. "Go on," he said, to Rahal.

"Many years later, after endless searches and speculation, the boar arrived on our land and wouldn't leave. He brought with him with a pack of wolves, and his wife had a flash of insight or something. Everyone thought it was a fancy at first. But she was convinced from the start that it was Filtiarn. She forbade anyone to hunt the boar, on pain of death. And eventually, after a thousand years, he turned back to his human form and revealed the story. His father was furious."

"So when he first turned he was himself again?"

"That's what I understand," she said. "Well, after a few hours of confusion at most. I think a burning anger kept him sane. From what I can gather, his father really didn't understand the deliberateness of the betrayal at first, and he joined Filtiarn on his search. Insisted in fact."

"When did he find out?" Arthur asked.

"When they found Giolladhe had fled, and no-one knew where to. Of course Filtiarn had to explain their argument – he'd kept quiet about it up to that point, probably hoping he was wrong, or that Giolladhe was exaggerating. His family was devastated. And then Filtiarn changed form. For years they kept searching for Giolladhe, but he kept a low profile, and then his father died, and his mother, and then his wife, and the hunt was forgotten, and then, finally, Giolladhe returned to Dragon's Hollow."

"Why didn't Filtiarn's children find him there?" Arthur sounded incredulous, and Tom knew that if it had been Arthur, he would never have stopped looking.

"Because no-one told the family he was back, and no-one knew about the curse. And by then I think the guardian who had been appointed was probably terrified of Giolladhe." Rahal dropped her eyes to her hands, which fidgeted nervously in her lap. "If I'm honest, I'm scared of him too."

Tom saw Arthur deflate a little, as he considered her words.

"Anyway," she continued, "we knew we needed Galatine. Filtiarn had told us that much, but we never found it. The next time he turned, the Guardians searched with him, but found nothing. And so it went on, until eventually Galatine passed to you, Arthur."

"I had no idea–"

"I know," she interrupted. "It's not your fault. But we have it now, and I still don't know what to do other than perform a spell we don't know on the night of the full moon."

"And you've never found the spell?"

"Never," she said, her face filled with regret. "Not one scrap of paper, whisper of a spell, a hint or a clue. Nothing. However, we have gathered a large store of knowledge about spells during the Wolf Moon, not specifically shape-shifting, but it's something."

"We need something else too," Brenna said, holding a piece of paper in her hands.

"Like what?" Arthur said, a hint of impatience in his voice.

"The moonstone. Don't you remember the story Finnlugh told? The moonstone the sword sat in, that was in the clearing on the night of the spell?"

Tom groaned. "Yes, I remember. It was at Giolladhe's feet during the spell."

"He's drawn it, right here. It must play a part in the ritual." She passed the drawing to Tom.

Arthur rubbed his face with his hands and took a deep breath before looking at Elan and Rahal. "Have you any idea what this could be? Or where it is?"

They looked at each other, and then at Arthur, shaking their heads. "I've never heard of it before," Elan admitted.

Arthur jumped to his feet and began pacing up and down. "This just keeps getting worse."

Bloodmoon interrupted from where sat tending the food and watching the events unfold. "Come on everyone, eat. It fuels the brain."

They were glad of the interruption, and for a few minutes sat eating and thinking about their dilemma, until one by one they wrapped themselves in blankets to get some sleep. As Merlin said, they would all be awake soon enough if Filtiarn changed.

16 The Wolf Mage Rises

A long groan, grunts, and a painfilled howl shocked them from their sleep. They were awake in seconds, weapons drawn.

Merlin called out, "Stand back, it's started!"

Tom's tiredness vanished in seconds and he rolled free of his blankets, retreating with the others behind the fire.

The wolves crept closer, sniffing the air and whining, sensing that Filtiarn was changing. Everyone was transfixed. Filtiarn's large solid form now became fluid, his body rippling as he began to change shape. His hairy coat began to melt and morph into white skin, and his huge head shrank. The dull glow of the fire exaggerated the unreal aspect of the scene, as Filtiarn's body cast grotesque shadows. Tom couldn't quite work out what was happening, but it was clear from Filtiarn's unearthly howls that it was a painful and brutal process.

And then it was over, and the long skinny form of a man lay motionless by the fire, his limbs looking almost wasted. Tom couldn't believe that the huge form of the boar could produce such an emaciated figure.

Arthur grabbed a blanket and threw it over Filtiarn's body, as Rahal and Elan rushed to his side.

"Filtiarn, can you hear me?" Rahal said softly.

He groaned, and moved slowly until he was sitting up, Elan supporting him. Filtiarn's face turned to them, shocking

Tom with its intensity. His dark eyes looked hollowed out and full of fear.

"It's all right," Rahal said, trying to reassure him. "I'm your guardian, you're with friends."

He looked at her, and the wildness in his eyes ebbed for a second.

Merlin intervened. "He needs quiet. Come on, let's get him to the cave until he's stronger. I'll start another fire there."

Arthur bent to help him to his feet, and Elan supported his other arm. Slowly, on shaking legs, Filtiarn made his way to the cave.

Beansprout looked at Tom. "It's a miracle he's still alive. I mean ... he looks terrible."

"A cruel fate indeed," Woodsmoke said, heading back to the logs by the fire, the others following.

Within minutes Arthur joined them, his face grave. "He won't survive another change, I'm sure of it. Come on, Tom, let's have a look at the rest of those pictures."

Tom handed the drawings round, and Arthur examined the one of the moonstone. "So, we need to find this, in order for the spell to work."

"Maybe it's in the weapon's room in the House of the Beloved?" Bloodmoon said.

"No, I'm pretty sure I'd remember that," Beansprout said, peering at the drawing over Arthur's shoulder.

"Is the room still locked?" Woodsmoke asked from where he sat on the ground, leaning back against the log, his long legs stretched out so that his feet were almost in the fire.

"Oh yes," Beansprout said, joining him, her blanket pulled close around her shoulders. "There's still all sorts of amazing, dangerous and valuable weapons in there."

Woodsmoke teased her. "Ever tempted?"

"Plenty of times, but I'll stick with Fail-not, thanks," she said, grinning. Fail-not was Tristan's bow, given to her by Woodsmoke. "Nimue is very protective of them, says they're a rich legacy of magical knowledge that must be kept safe."

Arthur snorted. "Yes, I'm sure that's why she keeps them locked up."

"It doesn't help us though, does it?" Brenna said.

"I think we need to go back to Dragon's Hollow, that's where it all began," Arthur said thoughtfully. "We need to find his old workshop and see if there're any clues in there."

"And see what's in Raghnall's library," Brenna added. "He must have one, and he'd have known Giolladhe."

Beansprout nodded, "The library's huge, full of arcane materials. I'm happy to do that."

"One thing's certain," Bloodmoon said. "Filtiarn won't be able to travel with us, he's far too weak."

"And it will take at least a week to get to Dragon's Hollow," Woodsmoke pointed out.

"But he could follow, at his own pace," Beansprout said. "Hopefully arriving in time for the full moon."

Merlin appeared out of the darkness and sat next to Tom.

"How is he?" Tom asked.

"Confused," Merlin said. "I'm hoping we get more sense out of him in the morning."

"Merlin," Beansprout said, "do we need to perform the spell on the full moon?"

"For the best possible chance, yes. In the Gatherer's story, he talks of drawing down the power of the moon for the spell – that means a full moon."

"So we have to find the moonstone and the spell, all within a few days?" Tom said. This was going to be almost impossible. "Presuming it's all hidden at Dragon's Hollow."

A collective groan sounded as they realised the seriousness of their position.

"We need to sleep," Arthur said. "Tomorrow's going to be a long day."

After a poor night's sleep, Tom woke with a groggy head to a mist-filled dawn.

He sat pulling his blankets around his shoulders, and moved closer to the fire, prodding it into life. And then he got a shock as he saw the wolves had surrounded them, or rather Filtiarn, whose hunched figure sat gazing into the fire. Wolves lay at his feet, nuzzled his hands, or lay with their heads on crossed paws, watching him. Tom studied him for a few seconds. His hair was still long, and it hung lank around his shoulders, matted in places, but it was no longer dark. Instead, streaks of grey ran through it. His skin was a deathly white, his face drawn, and his limbs were painfully thin. Tom recognised some of Woodsmoke's and Bloodmoon's clothes. He smiled; they must have loaned them to him in the night.

Tom looked around nervously, and then decided there was nothing to worry about. The wolves weren't interested in him at all. He built the fire up and put some water on to boil, falling back into the familiar routines of camping. Filtiarn glanced up at him and Tom smiled nervously, but Filtiarn dropped his gaze back to the fire, mute, apart from a hacking cough that made him shake uncontrollably.

It wasn't long before everyone was up, and the smell of bacon and eggs was drifting across the camp. Rahal put a plate of food in front of Filtiarn, and he ate ravenously. He looked old and fragile, but clearly his appetite was healthy. Tom couldn't help but wonder why they had brought bacon, when Filtiarn had been a boar, but as it didn't seem to bother him, he tucked into his own food with relish.

Rahal addressed them from where she sat amidst the wolves, petting them absently. "I've explained to Filtiarn who you are and how you want to help." She glanced at Filtiarn, who ignored her, and continued nervously. "He refuses your request, but asks to see Galatine."

Arthur nodded to Tom, and Tom passed it to Rahal who placed it on the floor at Filtiarn's feet. He put his plate down and picked Galatine up. His voice was barely more than a croak. "I didn't think I'd ever see this again," he said, turning it over in his hands. He looked up at Tom as if to challenge him. "I'll need to take this with me, to break the spell."

"And how are you going to find the moonstone?" Tom asked, incredulous that Filtiarn wanted to go on alone.

Arthur snorted in a very unkingly manner. "That's an excellent question, Tom, seeing as Filtiarn can barely walk!"

Filtiarn glared at Arthur. "I'll manage just fine."

"Yes, of course, that's gone so well for you over the last few thousand years," Arthur said dryly.

Filtiarn dragged himself to his feet, clutching Galatine, and the wolves started to growl softly. He was tall; he'd have been a handsome and imposing figure once. The tension around the camp shot up and everyone now paid full attention. "This is my business and I will deal with it."

Arthur refused to be baited, continuing to eat as he watched him. "How?"

"I have two weeks until the full moon, I'm sure I'll cope." But he looked unconvinced, and Rahal and Elan exchanged worried looks.

"Bravo," Arthur said. "Two weeks, fantastic. What's your plan? Or don't you have one?"

He glared again at Arthur. "I'm going to search Dragon's Hollow for the moonstone, and go back to my brother's workshop." His voice was resolute, but he swayed on his feet and Tom could tell it took a lot of effort to stay upright.

"You remember where it is, then?" Arthur asked.

"No, but I'll find it."

"Just like you found Giolladhe?"

"It is *not* your business."

"So you're happy to die as a boar," Arthur continued. "That's fine. We'll pack and leave you to it." He looked at the others as they stared back, wondering what was happening. "You heard him, start packing!"

Woodsmoke got to his feet. "It's OK, Filtiarn, you can keep my clothes." He looked at Tom and as he turned away, gave him a wink. "Come on, Tom, you heard Arthur."

Filtiarn started coughing and dropped to his knees, unable to stop. Galatine fell to the floor. Rahal rushed to his side and he shooed her away. "I'm fine."

"No, you are not!" she shouted. "How dare you let your pride get in the way of us finally breaking your curse!"

"My dear lady," Arthur said, in his most infuriating tone. "It won't be you who dies. Just think, your responsibilities will be over. You can do whatever it is you do, and I can go back to my castle and start planning my next tournament."

Tom was disappointed. If Rahal and Elan had seen sense, why couldn't Filtiarn?

Merlin finally broke his silence. He'd been staring into the fire for a long time, listening to the exchange. He looked at Filtiarn who now rose on shaky legs to sit again on the log. "That way lies death, Filtiarn. I have seen it. You will fail."

Filtiarn stared at him, fear in his eyes. "How do you know?"

"It is my gift, or my curse, whatever you choose to call it. But I have seen it. You will not survive another change, and will not find the stone alone."

"I always get stronger in the days after the change. Always."

"It won't be enough." Merlin closed his eyes regretfully, before opening them and fixing him with a piercing stare. "But it's your choice."

Elan pleaded with him. "This is the closest we've been in years! The most we have ever known! Filtiarn, please."

Filtiarn looked around at the camp as the others packed, and resolutely turned away, walking back to the cave. Rahal and Elan cast a pleading glance back towards them, and then ran after him, followed by the oldest wolf. Tom picked Galatine up, brushing the dirt from its blade.

"Keep packing," Arthur said. "We're leaving anyway, in one direction or another."

17 Return to Dragon's Hollow

While they packed up, the wolves padded around the camp, alternating between watching them and the entrance to the cave. Tom had just about got used to them, unnerving though they were. It seemed Elan and Rahal could communicate with them too, and Tom presumed they had reassured the animals about their intentions, because they were now almost friendly as they sniffed around, curious.

As they finished packing, Filtiarn returned with the wolf at his side, Elan and Rahal trailing behind, looking relieved. He stood in front of Arthur, lifting his head proudly. "I accept your help. You're right, I can't do it alone. Will you still come with me to Dragon's Hollow?" His belligerence had gone, but Tom could tell he wasn't happy about accepting help.

Arthur smiled and clasped his hand. "Of course we'll come with you."

Bloodmoon interrupted, already astride his horse. "You will slow us up, Filtiarn, and that's the brutal fact of it. You'll have to follow us there, that way we'll have a few more days to search."

The steel returned to Filtiarn's voice as he shot an angry look at Bloodmoon. "I won't, I'm a good horseman."

"I don't doubt it, but you're just not fit enough. I ride fast, and you won't keep up. And we need as much time as we can get."

"I agree," Arthur said, trying to reason with Filtiarn. He threw an appealing glance to Rahal and Elan. "You should take your time, gather your strength with your guardians, while we ride ahead. If you tell us what you remember, it will help us start looking."

Rahal stepped forward, putting a hand on Filtiarn's arm. "He's right, we can follow. We don't want to jeopardise this."

Filtiarn hesitated for a second and then nodded.

"Good," Arthur said. "What do you remember of that night, and Giolladhe's workshop? You need to tell us everything."

"If I'm honest, I remember very little now, it was so long ago. And the change I undergo, it strips the memories, a little every time." He looked at the ground, his shoulders dropping. "I can't even tell you with great accuracy where his workshop is. I couldn't even find it last time."

"Tell me what you can remember," Arthur said gently.

"I remember the workshop was on the right shoulder of the mountain, on the hillside above the dragon sorcerer's house. One evening as I was leaving, the sun was setting and as I opened the door, the sun dazzled me."

"That's good," said Arthur, nodding at Woodsmoke, who turned to Tom and whispered, "I knew it!"

"Go on, what else," Arthur prompted.

"The door was set back, under a slight overhang. It was made of beaten copper, I think. He knew the dragon sorcerer well, they talked often, shared ideas and spells."

"And the moonstone. Where did you last see it?"

"I suppose at the altar in the forest. When I first turned I kept my human thoughts for a while, and I kept returning to the clearing. It was just lying there on the earth. But I took little notice of it."

"Can you remember where the clearing was?"

"In the wooded slopes behind Raghnall's house. He had marked a path to it, with torches."

"Who? Raghnall?" Arthur asked confused.

"No, Giolladhe." Filtiarn closed his eyes in grief. "I was so excited at the thought I would join my brothers." He reached out a hand and stroked the head of the old wolf. "I still can't believe that he tricked me. He was ... so cruel." Filtiarn swallowed painfully.

"Why do you think he tricked you?"

Filtiarn looked confused. "I don't know. We'd had an argument about the spell being locked into the moon's cycle, but that was all. I do remember him laughing, though, and saying I should know better than to criticise him." He closed his eyes again, as if to block out the memory.

"Are you sure there wasn't something else?" Arthur asked.

Filtiarn looked up at him. "What do you mean?"

"It seems extreme. Did he want you out of the way for some reason?"

"I don't think so. And how could this help, anyway?"

Arthur paused for a second. "I don't know, but I have a feeling there's more to this. Just think about it. Try to remember what you were doing at the time."

Filtiarn started to shout, his voice breaking. "I can't think now. I'm too tired."

"It's all right," Arthur said, soothingly. "You'll have plenty of time to think on the road. We'll carry on, and will meet you at the Hollow." He pointed to Brenna. "Our friend here is Aerikeen, she can check your progress, and when you arrive we'll send someone to meet you at the gate."

Filtiarn nodded, and suddenly looked weak. "Yes, thank you."

That was Arthur's gift, Tom thought. He engendered such trust.

Arthur smiled at Filtiarn and shook his hand. "Travel safely and we'll see you again soon."

With a flurry of goodbyes, they mounted their horses and left for Dragon's Hollow.

After days of hard riding, involving long hours, short stops and little sleep, they arrived at the base of Dragon Skin Mountain. Brenna had already flown ahead and warned Nimue of their arrival.

Tom was more tired than he'd been in a long time. Arthur and the others were expert horse riders, and Tom had kept up with difficulty. He ached all over, but he smiled as they started on the path to the Hollow, feeling he was returning home, which was an odd sensation considering how little time he had spent there. Bloodmoon had been right, though. Filtiarn would never have managed the journey at their pace.

Bloodmoon and Woodsmoke had the led the way, across parts of Blind Moor that Tom had never seen before. As usual Tom rode towards the back of their group, and Beansprout rode next to him.

"You'll be pleased to know," she now said, smiling at him, "that our new housekeeper is very efficient. He fills the baths quickly, and he's an expert cook. And you can have your old room."

"Well I hope the bath is run, because I stink, and I could sleep for a week."

"We all stink, but you can't sleep, we've got a lot to do in a very short time," she pointed out.

He groaned. "I know, but just give me tonight. I'm going to be in bed early, and then I'm up and on it. I promise!"

She laughed. "Fair enough, I'm knackered as well. And I've got Raghnall's weird stuff to go through. His library is huge – can you imagine? Thousands of years of collecting books! And there's a separate spell room."

Dragon's Hollow looked as beautiful as ever. The damage caused by the dragons' attack a few months before had been repaired, and once again the fey serenely walked along the gilded paths and roads, and the enormous dragon fountain splashed water into the lake. Across the valley, the House of the Beloved gleamed in the afternoon sun, the black marble shining like a well-polished gem. As they strolled through the city Tom saw huge round golden lanterns suspended above the streets, and every so often they'd pass fey children chasing each other around wearing wolf masks. The celebration for the Wolf Moon had started.

Nimue greeted them at the door, her grin broad. She hadn't changed. Her long dark hair curled across her shoulders, her skin was pale, and her green eyes sparkled. "I knew you couldn't keep away, Arthur. Have you missed me?"

He laughed. "I'm not sure that's how I'd describe it." And then he corrected himself as he saw her indignation. "Of course, always!"

Beansprout ran to her, giving her a big hug, which shocked Tom. They'd obviously become very close. Nimue flashed a smile at the rest of them as she welcomed them into the house. She led the way up to the broad balcony overlooking the city, and Arthur introduced Bloodmoon, who she'd never met before. He swept into full charm mode, and Tom felt a little resentful of Nimue's appreciative smile. She never looked at him like that.

He noticed Merlin kept his distance from Nimue. Suddenly, all sorts of dynamics seemed to have entered their group.

As they helped themselves to drinks, Tom noticed a subtle change in the house. The furnishings were still opulent, but there seemed less formality than before. Maybe it was because it was less tidy than he remembered. Books were stacked on the table, scarves and throws were draped over chairs and the divan. Raghnall had clearly been a neat freak, and Nimue was not.

He was jolted out of his thoughts when Nimue said, "You've grown, Tom. You're a bit broader round the shoulders I think."

He felt suddenly self conscious under her gaze, and again was slightly mesmerised by her green eyes, which still crept into his dreams sometimes. He caught Woodsmoke trying to bury a smirk, and was grateful when he rescued him.

"We've been teaching him how to fight, Nimue. What you see before you is months of hard work. He came second in the beginner's sword-fighting competition."

"Well done, Tom!" She looked genuinely pleased, and Tom mumbled his thanks, relieved when she turned to Beansprout. "We need to continue with your training."

"I know, but Merlin's been helping me too."

"Good." She nodded at Merlin. "He's a good teacher." And no-one knew that better than Nimue, Tom thought uncomfortably.

Later that evening, after long baths and a rest, they met again before dinner. Nimue wanted to show them something. She led them along an upper corridor, into a room that led out onto the roof. Along one long wall was an astrological chart, embellished with gold and silver and other precious metals and gems. The lines and swirls of stars were faintly illuminated, and Tom couldn't help saying, "Wow, that's amazing!"

On another wall was a plan of the different moon cycles. There weren't any dates, but their succession was again marked out in a flowing script, in what looked like white marble on a black wall.

"It's amazing what I keep finding," Nimue said. "When Brenna told me what you were looking for, I started to search the house. It sounds ridiculous, but I've been so busy maintaining Raghnall's spells and establishing myself here, that I still haven't explored the whole place." She looked sheepish. "And the library and spell room occupy me for hours. Anyway, Beansprout's right, the moonstone is not in the weapons room. In the rooms I have searched, it's not on display, and as well as the rooms I haven't searched, there may be hidden rooms too. And then I found this."

Merlin stood absorbed in front of the star charts. "Raghnall certainly spent his time productively. The star chart moves?"

"Yes, too slowly to see, but when you come back here, there are changes. What you see now is how the stars stand at present." Nimue pointed to a line of stars that were almost aligned. "The Wolf Moon is unusual in that it occurs only once in a thousand years, aligning with certain other stars. It has long been held to be a powerful time to perform spells and rituals, and it has a certain reputation."

Bloodmoon agreed. "I have never lived through one, but certainly there are stories amongst those who have. Strange tales, weird magics. Fahey has a store of such tales."

"I can't seem to get a straight answer," Arthur said, frustrated. "Does the ritual have to be performed on the night of the full moon, or if we miss that, could it be performed at any time through the cycle?"

Nimue nodded. "In theory, yes, any time. But the full moon is always the most powerful."

"Unless the spell says otherwise," Merlin said, once again introducing confusion.

"Right," Arthur said decisively. "I suggest that Beansprout, Nimue and Merlin search the house, including the library, for signs of the moonstone and any spells, or old diaries. I will search the woods behind the house for evidence of an old altar, or clearing. Brenna, if you would join me?"

She nodded. "But after a few thousand years, Arthur, that will be hard going."

"I know." He turned to Tom, Woodsmoke and Bloodmoon. "Will you search above the house, on the mountain? We need to find the workshop."

They nodded, and once again Tom felt daunted by their task. Surely this was impossible. But then he thought of Filtiarn, and Rahal and Elan, and how he desperately didn't want to let them down.

18 Hidden Places

After an early breakfast, Woodsmoke, Tom and Bloodmoon
saddled their horses and headed up the path behind the
house. The last time Tom had been here was when he'd
returned from the Realm of Air, after their imprisonment and
near death by the sylphs.

For a while they were sheltered by the trees on either
side, and then they left the woods behind and were dazzled
by the sun, already warm despite the early hour. The
mountainside was covered in a mix of trees, scrub and bare
earth, huge stones littering the ground. Small animal tracks
snaked along the slopes, and insects chirped in the
undergrowth.

Woodsmoke and Bloodmoon looked very otherworldly
today. Woodsmoke always became more intense when
hunting; his eyes were dark with concentration as he followed
the path up and across the mountain, his focus absolute. His
hair was tied back, and he wore a sleeveless leather jacket
rather than a cloak.

Bloodmoon sat beside him, as blond as Woodsmoke was
dark. Bloodmoon had inherited the family colouring that
Fahey once described in his tale about Vanishing Hall. His
skin was a creamy white, and his eyes dark green. His long
hair was streaked with plaits, and it snaked down his back.
The huge hilt of his dragonium sword glinted as it caught the

sun. Tom felt that Woodsmoke and Bloodmoon had become his brothers, and the feeling gave him strength.

Woodsmoke pulled Farlight to a halt. "Let's push up to where the path levels out," he said. "We'll tie up the horses beneath those trees and continue on foot."

Tom groaned and Bloodmoon laughed. "All the best hunting is done by stealth, Tom."

"And remember," Woodsmoke said. "The doorway faces west."

The horses secure, they split up and left the main path, with instructions to shout if they found anything.

Hours later, Tom had found nothing. He was hot, dusty and sweaty. The paths he had followed led only to animal burrows and dead ends, some petering out to nothing. He poked under trees, around streams, and brushed overhanging branches back from near vertical stretches of mountain, feeling as if at any moment he would plunge down the side to his death.

Eventually he came across a small overhang, and shouted to the others that he was taking a break. He sat in the shade beneath it, swigging water which had become unpleasantly warm in his animal-skin bottle, and looked out over Dragon's Hollow glittering in the valley below.

A few minutes later Bloodmoon skittered to a halt beside him. His face was streaked with dirt, and he started to complain. "I could easily die of boredom doing this, Tom."

"But think of the rewards," Tom said, knowing exactly what would motivate Bloodmoon. "Who knows what Giolladhe may have left in his workshop."

They were disturbed by a shout, and a summons, coming from somewhere high above them. They scooted out of the shade and looked up to see Woodsmoke gesturing, and scrambled up to join him.

Woodsmoke was standing on a barely-there path, grinning. "I think I've found it. I heard a stream, and thought I'd find it and fill up my water bottle. There was an overgrown path, but I realised it was edged with stones, so I started to clear it." He pointed. "Look, it's paved, although covered in dirt now. Come on, there's more."

He led the way down the path, and they forced their way through bushes, getting scratched and smacked by protruding branches, until they came to a small shallow curve in the hillside. An overhang of rock cast some shade, and a stream ran over it into a small pool. Next to it was a door.

"By Herne's knobbly horns – you've found it!" Bloodmoon exclaimed. He ran his hands over the copper door, its shine dulled by the weather. In the centre was an engraving of a large flame below a sun.

"I had to clear it," Woodsmoke said, pointing to branches lying to one side.

"Well done," Tom said. He was grateful to be out of the sun, and put his head beneath the waterfall, gasping at its coldness. He shook his head like a dog. "Who's going in first?"

"I am!" Woodsmoke said, indignant. "I found it. But it's locked."

They lined up next to each other and pushed, trying to force the lock or hinges, but the door remained stubbornly shut.

"Hold on," Bloodmoon said, rummaging in his pack. "I have some tools." He pulled out a selection of skeleton keys and sharp-edged files.

"You've brought your thieving pack?" Woodsmoke said, affronted.

"I am not a thief! Sometimes I am recruited by thieves."

"Same thing," Woodsmoke said.

"Bloodmoon, you never cease to surprise me," Tom said, not sure whether to be impressed or worried.

Bloodmoon was on his knees, his eye to the keyhole. He sat upright with shock. "There's a key in it."

"How can there be?" Tom said, doubting him. Bloodmoon moved aside, allowing Tom to see a small blockage in the lock, caused by a key on the other side. "So someone's still in there?" he said, alarmed.

"No, someone's bones are in there," Woodsmoke corrected.

"Out of the way," Bloodmoon said. "I have work to do."

They stood silent for a few minutes as he wiggled his tools in the lock, and then tried a few keys, until they finally heard a click. He smiled with satisfaction. "Now, after three."

With an enormous effort they pushed the door open. Rusty hinges groaned, and there was an ear-shattering grating noise as the door caught on debris and the key that had fallen from the lock. Bloodmoon flattened himself against the floor and managed to hook the key out of the way, so they could push it open further.

Dust billowed out, followed by a musty smell. Dirt and small stones were strewn down a passageway which stretched away into darkness.

Bloodmoon stepped aside, saying, "After you," to Woodsmoke.

They each pulled a torch from their packs, and after lighting them, started down the hall. It was eerie; the air was stale, and their footsteps sounded loud in the confined space of the hill. The passageway was long, eventually leading to a door that opened into a large room, in the centre of which was a fireplace and chimney heading into the roof. Around the walls were broad work benches, shelves, and a scattering of tools, all covered in thick dust. Three doors led out of the room.

For a few seconds they were quiet, taking in their surroundings, as the dust of hundreds of years swirled around them. Tom grinned in the gloom. "We've actually found Giolladhe's workshop! Well done, Woodsmoke!"

"It was nothing," Woodsmoke said casually. "Just my skill and hunter abilities."

"Yeah, yeah. Now to find the moonstone," Bloodmoon said, lighting the lanterns that hung overhead.

Tom paused in front of one of the benches, examining the tools spread over it. He scraped his finger across the surface, clearing a thick covering of dust. "Wow, just think, we're the first people in here for hundreds of years."

"We won't find the moonstone," Woodsmoke said.

"Why not?" Tom asked.

"He's cleared the place out, or someone has," Woodsmoke pointed out. "Nothing except tools and dust."

"Maybe he was on the run from someone," Bloodmoon said, raking through the fire before moving on to the cupboards beneath the benches.

"Filtiarn?" Tom said.

"Or the sylphs," Woodsmoke reminded them. "Remember, something happened with them."

Tom drifted around the room, absently picking up tools and putting them down again. "Maybe he didn't hide the moonstone," Tom said thoughtfully. "Maybe he just lost it." He pushed open the other doors. "There's a set of stairs, and another room, so I'll start on this one."

Woodsmoke nodded. "We'll head up the stairs and search the upper floor."

The next room was smaller, lined on one side with floor-to-ceiling shelves filled with an assortment of boxes. On the other side, at the far end, was a large cupboard. Tom started on the shelves, moving methodically along, but the boxes contained only paper and packing material. Feeling despondent, he moved to the cupboard. It was large – much bigger than he was – with double doors. The door he tried was stiff, but he pulled it open and found another door in front of him, set back into the wall. Shelves had been dismantled and were stacked to the side, looking as if they had previously been in front of the door. A hidden room? Suddenly excited, he pulled the door open. There was nothing but blackness beyond. Without wondering whether to call Woodsmoke, he stepped through. Immediately he experienced a familiar sensation of floating, weightlessness and a pulling deep in his gut. He'd stepped through a portal.

19 Mountains of Fire

Tom panicked. What if he was going back to his Earth? This would be the absolute worse thing. Or what if it was the Realm of Air again? They might never let him go. Or the Realm of Water, where he might drown? As these thoughts were flashing through his mind he landed with a thump, feeling rock and sand beneath his fingers. He rocked back on his heels and sprang to his feet, pulling Galatine free. In his other hand he held his now extinguished torch.

He found himself in a shadowy room strewn with rubble and suffused with a warm orange glow. It was in fact another cave, with rough walls and stone shelves, similar to Giolladhe's workshop except that it was fiercely hot. The heat and glow were coming from a pit in the centre, and for a few seconds Tom couldn't work out what it was. Only when he stood over it did he realise it was bubbling lava.

Lava? Where the hell was he?

He thrust his torch into the pit and it flared to life. As his eyes adjusted to the light he saw that the cave was partially collapsed, a wall of rubble blocking some of it, while the floor was crunchy and blackened in places. At some point the lava must have erupted from this pit and covered some of the room, and if it had erupted once, it could do it again.

Lava could mean only one thing – he was in the Realm of Fire. His panic turned to relief. He was still in the Other.

Herne's Horns! Was he trapped here? He whirled round and saw that the portal entrance was behind him, the familiar rock archway filled with blackness. Interesting. Giolladhe had a hidden portal that led to the Realm of Fire. A fixed portal too, which suggested he had passed through frequently. Well, Tom wasn't going back yet.

He examined the wall of rubble ahead of him, and saw a small hole at the top, a faint red glow illuminating its edges. He wedged his torch upright and scrambled up. Within seconds he was filthy and scratched, but was soon able to stick his head through the gap.

On the other side was a much larger portion of the cave, and beyond that was an entrance to an underground cavern. Tom glimpsed rock archways and rivers of lava. But something else caught his eye. A glimpse of white stone on a workbench, partially covered in debris.

The moonstone.

He was so shocked he cried out and hit his head on the roof. He'd found it! Giolladhe must have hidden it here all those years ago.

He eased backwards and started to pull the rocks away to make the entrance bigger, but as he did the roof started to slip and crumble, and in seconds the hole had vanished. Tom fell backwards, landing with a thump. He held his breath as he watched the roof, but after a few seconds the slip stopped and he breathed again.

He had to find another way round – if there was a way out of here.

He leapt to his feet and grabbed the torch, and spotted a shadowy archway in the corner of the room. Passing through it he found himself at the bottom of a flight of steps that rose steeply above him, illuminated by a weak red light pouring through a hole in the smashed door and roof at the top. He rushed up the steps and pushed aside the ruined door, entering a huge cathedral-like building made of dark red sandstone. It was a ruin; a few columns stood upright, the rest had fallen and lay broken and crushed on the floor. Above him, through the fractured roof, he could see a bright sun blazing in deep blue sky.

The place was deserted, his only company the strange faces of unknown beings carved into the walls, watching him through cracked eyes.

He scrambled over the fallen rocks of masonry, taking care not to slip into the gaps between them where he could easily be crushed, and eased his way through a hole in the wall. He immediately shielded his eyes from the intense glare, squinting until his eyes adjusted, and found he was standing on a low rise of a rocky hill. In front of him, all he could see was orange sand, rising and falling in huge dunes, interspersed with rivers of blackened molten rock and the remnants of buildings.

What had happened here? Immediately Tom wondered if it was dragons. He remembered Merlin telling them about the dragon wars, and how the dragons had left the Realm of Fire because of the djinn. He paced round the edge of the massive building he'd exited, stopping in shock when he saw the range of volcanic mountains, so close that Tom was almost on the slopes. They were still belching smoke into the air. Maybe it wasn't dragons after all.

Nothing moved in this barren landscape. Could this be where Giolladhe had disappeared to? That would have been hundreds of years before. Was that why the key was in the lock? Could he still be here somewhere, alive? If Raghnall had lived that long, maybe Giolladhe had too.

But it seemed nothing could be alive here; the destruction was too absolute. Somewhere below him was the other side of the cave, so somewhere out there was another entrance. As Tom squinted, he thought he saw a shadow on the ground, or a rather a black spot, sharp against the red sand. That must be the way down.

20 The Secrets of the House of the Beloved

Beansprout stood at the entrance to the library in the House of the Beloved and sighed. It was a sigh of pleasure, but also of trepidation.

The library was a large room set into the top two floors of the building, the upper floor being a mezzanine. A stained-glass roof cast jewel-like shades of colour onto the room. Both floors were lined with bookshelves filled with conventional books, as well as rolls of scrolls and pamphlets. In the centre of the lower floor, under the square of light, was a large table.

Beansprout headed to a section tucked in the corner under the mezzanine, where it was protected from daylight. It was here that Raghnall had stored some of his oldest books and scrolls, and she presumed that if anything referred to Giolladhe and the curse of Filtiarn all those years ago, then it would be here.

Starting methodically at the bottom shelf, she worked through the texts, finding old treatises on magic; maps, and family histories. Dust rose in clouds as she pulled the books off the shelves, and she was soon smeared in dust, print and cobwebs. She put anything of interest in piles around her, only shelving things that seemed of no relevance at all. But she quickly became side-tracked, also putting things aside for examination at her leisure.

She sighed again. She had to keep focused. Filtiarn's life was at stake.

Hours later, she moved on in exasperation, using a finding spell that Nimue had taught her, tailored to find mention of Giolladhe and Filtiarn. The spell made the books wriggle and rustle on the shelves, leading her to a shelf of history books. They were all about the dragon wars and the founding of Dragon's Hollow – this was interesting, but it didn't tell her about the curse. Maybe Raghnall had known nothing about it? Maybe it was just between the brothers.

She hoped Nimue and Merlin were having better luck searching the rest of the house. Nimue was searching Raghnall's old room, which both of them had avoided following his death, and Merlin was studying the moon cycle charts.

She was distracted by books rustling in a corner where she hadn't looked before. As the rustling became more insistent, she headed over and saw a scroll wriggling in the middle of a tightly packed shelf. The shelf was labelled *Maps and Plans*. Intriguing.

She eased the scroll free and it immediately unfurled, revealing several sheets of paper – the floor plans of the House of the Beloved. One rustled free and fell at her feet. It was the plan of the lower floor. Why would Filtiarn or Giolladhe be mentioned here?

The ink was faded and difficult to read, but the paper itself was in good condition, looking as if it had been barely touched in years. She took it to the table and examined it under the daylight.

It took her a few minutes to get orientated, but then she saw a passageway leading from the lower floor to the mountain behind the house. The end of the passage was just marked *Giolladhe*.

She gasped. It must be the workshop.

21 The Citadel of Erfann

Tom scrambled down the shattered paths of the hillside, wishing he was wearing sunglasses. The Realm of Fire was hot and relentlessly bright. And eerie.

It was strange being the only one here in such a vast and empty landscape. Black lava flows ran across the desert floor, and he walked over them warily. But they were cold and hard, some covered with layers of sand.

Stopping for a look round, he was shocked to discover he was standing on what looked like a roof. These weren't the foundations of a ruined city – this was a buried city. Everything beneath him was filled with sand, which gave him another unpleasant thought. He could be swallowed up by sink holes. But how filled up with sand was it? The other side of the cave had been intact, so potentially, areas of the city were still accessible.

Trying to ignore his misgivings he was careful to walk only on solid rock, slowly making his way to the shadowy area that marked the cave entrance. Every now and again the hard edges of the city disappeared, swallowed by sand dunes, and he lost the dark shape completely as the dunes rose above him. Finally, sweating heavily, he saw the area of blackness ahead, and edged his way towards it. When he was only a few feet away, the ground gave way beneath him and he shot downwards on a chute of sand, bumping against hard angles of stone, until he landed on a platform below.

As he waited for the dust to subside, he held his breath, rolled onto his back and looked up at what appeared to be a large rectangular entrance high above him. A skylight, perhaps, long since broken by the weight of sand. There was no way he could get out through there.

Rising to his feet, he brushed sand away and tested the ground. It seemed to be made of solid slabs of stone. On the far side was a balustraded area, and he peered over to see stairs leading down into the gloom. He still carried his torch, although the flame sputtered and smoked heavily. He'd felt stupid carrying it across the sand in the burning sunshine, but was glad he had it now.

Tom made his way downstairs onto a landing, where a long passage partly blocked by stones and piles of sand led off to his left. He was tempted to explore it, but was sure the cave he wanted to access was deeper than this. He headed down another two flights of steps, passing more partially blocked passages, until he arrived on what must have been the ground floor.

A doorway led into a passageway with a cracked stone roof, flanked by a row of columns, between which were more entrances offering glimpses of dark spaces. Tom tried to orientate himself, and headed in what he hoped was the right direction. He followed the passageway until it ended at a wall of rubble, and then retraced his steps back to what had looked like the biggest opening. He stepped into another dark, half-collapsed room. His flaring torch showed the remnants of furniture and destroyed furnishings. It was a city of the dead. Nothing moved, except for the odd whisper of sand settling. He could be buried alive at any moment, but he also couldn't wait to see more. Or to find the moonstone. He was sure that was what he'd seen.

Tom plodded along through a series of linked rooms, until he came to one with a domed roof high above, pale red light filtering through what looked like areas of glass covered in a thin film of sand. The roof was supported by thick columns of red stone, and on the far side another entrance yawned.

He was halfway to it, his feet echoing on the stone, when a voice called out, "What brings a stranger from the Realm of Earth here to the edge of the desert?"

Tom whirled around, pulling Galatine out as he sought the source of the voice, but the space was empty. "I'm trying to find Giolladhe's cave, the Forger of Light," he shouted, his heart thudding painfully in his chest.

The voice laughed. "Giolladhe! You have travelled a long way to find a dead man."

Tom's heart sank. "I don't care if he's dead. All I want is to find his workshop. Will you tell me what you know? It's important. His brother's life is at stake."

Again the voice laughed. "And what's his brother's fate to me?"

"It might be nothing to you, but it means a lot to me!"

"You should leave, boy, there is nothing for you here."

Tom was exasperated. It was infuriating talking to someone he couldn't see. "At least show yourself! Or are you scared!"

The sand shifted beneath him, knocking him onto his back. He immediately rolled onto his feet, and could barely believe his eyes as the sand rose in a whirling cloud before him, filled with fire and darkness, two flame-filled eyes glaring at him from the centre of the mass. The sand reassembled into a huge, bronze-skinned, man-shaped creature, with flames instead of hair. Two black horns protruded through his flame hair, and his fingers and toes ended in long talon-like nails.

Stunned, Tom stepped back. "Are you a djinn?"

"You may call me that – I prefer it to demon."

Tom could see why the djinn might be called a demon, but swallowed his fear and asked, "Did you know Giolladhe?"

"You think I'm old?" the djinn asked, amused.

"Well, you've obviously heard of him," Tom shot back, annoyance replacing his fear.

"So have you. Did you know him?"

"No!" Tom stopped and took a breath. "No," he said, more calmly. "But I've met his brother, who he trapped in a spell for thousands of years. We want to help him break it."

The djinn didn't appear to be listening, instead looking at Tom's sword. "You have Galatine. How did you come by that?"

"You know my sword? I got it from King Arthur; it belonged to Gawain, one of his knights. Well, actually, I got it from Raghnall."

The djinn's amused tone disappeared, the flames in his eyes roaring to life. "Raghnall! And how is that old devil?"

"Dead. Killed by my friends Arthur and Woodsmoke." Tom gripped his sword tightly, wondering if the djinn was a friend of Raghnall, though from his tone he didn't think so.

"Ha! Then you are welcome here. But you risk much to venture this far into the centre," the djinn said with a grin, exposing fine white teeth with sharp points, like a shark. "Do you seek to awaken your sword?"

"Awaken my sword? What do you mean?" Tom asked, looking at Galatine in confusion.

"Its powers have been muted, probably by Giolladhe before he gave it away. It wasn't like that when he made it, I can assure you."

"But how do you know?"

"The stone here," he said, pointing with a shiny black talon. "It does not move. The centre should swirl with motion. The stone is a djinn's eye opal."

"But we thought it was a fire opal."

"You were wrong." The djinn smiled again – it wasn't a pleasant smile. Tom was beginning to feel very uncomfortable.

"But why would he mute it?"

"Powerful swords should be wielded only by those who deserve their power. No doubt Giolladhe did not wish someone to benefit from such a great gift."

Tom wasn't sure he believed this explanation. He thought it more likely that, should Filtiarn ever find it again, Giolladhe didn't want it to work.

"Some spells and metals require great heat for their completion," the djinn continued, "and that heat must be maintained for a very long time. The best way is to use the heat of the fire mountains and their lava flow. Hence Giolladhe made another workshop here, within the city. A workshop *we* permitted him to build; he promised weapons of power in exchange for his place here."

This djinn seemed to know a lot about how Giolladhe worked. It couldn't be a coincidence that he was here. "How do you know so much about him?"

"His story is well known. It has passed through the generations, and carries the thick smell of deceit," the djinn said with a low growl.

Tom skin pricked with goosebumps. "What did he do?"

"Dark murky secrets, boy," the djinn said. "He betrayed us in many ways. His workshop was an evil seed in the heart of the city." He lowered himself until he was at eye-level with Tom, and fixed him with a piercing stare. "He betrayed many who knew him, eventually. It is rumoured that Giolladhe made the sylphs a weapon as a gift of protection, but it turned out it sent the dragons to their door. When they found out, his life was forfeit and he fled here."

Things started to fall into place for Tom; it explained the sylph's loathing of Giolladhe.

"Why are you here?" Tom asked. "Alone in a deserted city."

"Many reasons." The djinn's eyes flared with flames. "Best not to ask."

A rumble disturbed their conversation, and the city creaked around them, sand swirling down from above.

"What was that?" Tom asked, alarmed.

"The fires in the mountain. If you want to find that workshop, you'd better hurry."

"Can you take me there? I don't know where I'm going. It could take me hours."

The djinn grinned his shark's smile again. "I like you, boy. I like that your friends killed Raghnall. And I will help you wake the sword, because it is exactly against what Giolladhe would want. You want to wake it, I presume?"

Tom's thoughts whirled as he wondered what to do for the best. "I suppose so," he said finally, thinking that if they were to rescue Filtiarn, it had to be awakened. Tom wondered if the djinn knew about the sword's ability to turn Filtiarn into a boar. "But what will happen?"

"The opals will awake and the blade will sing again."

"Does that mean I'll hear animals speak?" he spluttered, not at all sure that would be a good thing.

"Maybe," the djinn said. "It will activate whatever spell Filtiarn wove into it.

Tom experienced a flash of fear as he realised he had no idea of what he would he awaken in the sword, or its consequences. But the djinn had turned away.

"Come then, friend of slayer of Raghnall. Once again Giolladhe's pit will ring with the magic of light."

22 Beneath Dragon's Hollow

Merlin and Nimue stood next to Beansprout, examining the plans she had spread across the central table.

"Where did you find these again?" Merlin asked.

"Over on that shelf, using a finding spell," Beansprout said with pride.

"Well done," Nimue said, smiling, before turning her attention back to the plans. "I bet there's all sorts of hidden rooms and passageways here. I can see a couple of markings in rooms I thought I knew well." She shook her head. "What else was he hiding?"

"Time enough for that, Nimue," Merlin said. "What are we going to do about this passageway? Should we wait for Arthur?"

"No," Beansprout said quickly. "We should search now. Arthur could be hours yet. And it might be nothing."

"I agree," Nimue said. "Let's go." She rolled the plan up and led them down the stairs towards the kitchen. "From the look of this map, the passageway should lead off one of the cellars."

They passed through the kitchen and into the storage room beyond. From there a small passageway led off to more rooms. Beansprout had only been in here once before, and all she remembered was stores of dried foods, and Raghnall's fine wines. Nimue led them to the middle room, lined with racks filled with plates, bowls, cooking utensils, glasses and garden lanterns.

"Anyone would think he was running a hotel," Beansprout said, pulling a plate off a pile. "This has actual gold on it!"

Nimue took a quick look. "Porcelain too, probably the best money can buy. So if that's up here, who knows what's in the passageway."

The walls were made of polished granite, solid and unyielding, and although they examined them in great detail, there wasn't the slightest hint of a break in them.

Merlin turned to the floor, made of thick timbers. "Maybe it's a trap door?"

Once again Nimue studied the map, turning it this way and that, while Beansprout and Merlin tugged at the floor boards and tapped them, listening for a change in sound.

"Try the far corner," Nimue said.

Beansprout crouched down and ran her hand under racks loaded with heavy pans, serving platters and glasses. She gasped. "I can feel a draught!" She knocked the floor and it sounded hollow. "It's here!"

Within minutes they moved equipment off the shelves and onto the floor in teetering piles, and then pulled the rack away from the wall. The only discernible change in the flooring was that the planks looked a little shorter and made an uneven square. Grabbing a large serving spoon off a shelf, Beansprout wedged its end into the gaps and levered the planks up. As they started to lift in one solid mass, Nimue and Merlin grabbed the edges and pulled, and the entire trap door swung upwards and back, landing with a thud against the wall.

Underneath, steps led down into darkness.

They grinned at each other. "Me first," Nimue said, "then Beansprout. Merlin, you'll go last."

They each grabbed a lantern and Nimue said, "Beansprout, you can light them for us."

Beansprout concentrated her energies and repeated the short spell she had been taught. A small flame appeared in the centre of her palm, which she directed to the lanterns. Within seconds they were burning strongly.

As they made their way down the dozen or so steps, the temperature dropped and they found themselves in a low-ceilinged passageway with walls of rough rock and ancient bricks. Before long it turned a corner and started climbing upwards, and then opened into a small square space with several exits leading from it. Beansprout's heart sank. They could easily get lost down here.

"Damn it," Nimue said, pulling the map out again. "There aren't any other passages marked on here."

"I suspect the one we want must go up, if it leads to the mountain with Giolladhe's workshop," Merlin reasoned.

"But where else could the others go?" Beansprout asked, nervously looking around.

"Other buildings, maybe?" Merlin said, thoughtfully stroking his long white beard. "Or to caves. Dragon hoards?"

"Hidden spells?" Nimue added.

"Please don't suggest splitting up," Beansprout said.

"Not a chance, dear girl," Merlin said, patting her shoulder. "Let's find the workshop first." He examined the entrance to each passage. "Only one leads up, so – after you, Nimue." He gallantly stood aside as she led the way, Beansprout close behind.

23 Galatine Awakes

The djinn led the way into another series of passageways and rooms. He didn't so much walk as lope on all fours, barely marking the sand. Tom found him unnerving, and tried not to focus on his long black claws, which looked as if they could rip Tom's innards out with ease.

Tom stumbled on the uneven ground, and as he was regaining his balance a shake and a roar shattered the silence. The djinn turned and shouted, "Move boy, the mountains may erupt at any moment!"

Staggering to his feet, Tom ran after the djinn, fearing that if they didn't get there quick enough, not only would the moonstone be gone, the portal would be destroyed too.

Tom sweated as he scrambled after the djinn, stumbling into a sand dune piled across a room, and sinking up to his knees. Within minutes the djinn had disappeared ahead of him.

After a few seconds of panic, Tom pulled himself free and for the first time thought of Woodsmoke and Bloodmoon. He hoped they hadn't followed him. It was so weird here – Tom had the feeling there was more to this place than he was being told.

He stumbled after the djinn, winding around towering piles of stones and along tightly woven paths between broken buildings, the way lit by the smoky light of his torch. The city was a warren here. Occasionally, a broken wall revealed a glimpse into a courtyard, or a room, still partially furnished.

He stopped suddenly when the djinn reappeared.

"We must tread carefully now," he said. "Or rather *you* should. There are crusts of river fire here; if they are too thin …" His words hung in the air.

"I get it," Tom said, just wanting to find the moonstone. How he would get it through the fallen ceiling and rubble wall was another matter.

The djinn led Tom to a large stone archway. Beyond was a large chamber with a flat roof that had withstood tons of sand, lava, and volcanic eruptions. Broken windows leaked in rubble and sand, and through one a river of lava oozed like a living being, splitting into tributaries across the floor, bubbling and licking in the channels it had carved over hundreds of years. Beyond that, Tom recognised the other side of Giolladhe's cave.

He took a deep breath. If he got this wrong he would be burned alive, and not even his bones would remain. Was that what had happened to Giolladhe? Were his bones now ashes?

He tentatively set off, stepping gingerly on the stone floor, until he came to the lava rivers. The first few were narrow, and he stepped over them, hoping the ground beyond was firm. The djinn bounded away in front of him, leaping easily over the fiery pits, each time looking back at Tom with a vicious grin.

Ignoring his spite, Tom kept going, until he found a larger river ahead of him. He headed left to where it narrowed, enabling him to jump again. But it was getting more difficult. Thick crusty blackened lava made lumpy islands in the middle of flowing rivers, and at one point Tom was blocked, a blackened lump the only way across. He leapt with a spring, knowing he couldn't linger. As he dropped to the ground, the crust started to snap, and Tom leapt again, terrified he would fall in. He landed with a thump on the other side, his nose almost in the lava.

He stood breathing heavily. Sweat stung his eyes and he wiped it away with his shirt, blinking furiously, ready to jump again. With relief he saw he was almost there. Just as he made ready to jump again, another huge rumble ripped through the air, and lava started to bubble and ooze furiously; the smell of sulphur was suffocating. Without stopping to think, Tom leapt again and ran into Giolladhe's cave.

The djinn smirked. "Well done! I didn't think you'd make it."

"Thanks for the vote of confidence," Tom said, annoyed and exhausted.

"It's not personal. I have little faith in humans."

Ignoring him, Tom quickly found the shelf he had seen earlier, and with relief saw the white stone, covered in ash. It was bigger than he'd expected. He pulled it to the edge of the shelf and then lifted it down, staggering slightly under its weight.

The bottom was flat, but the top was domed with a slot in the centre. He placed it on the floor, brushing away the ash. Underneath the dirt, seams of gold and silver wrapped around the moonstone in an intricate pattern.

"Now I just have to get it through there," he said, gesturing to the rubble wall. "After you wake Galatine."

Another rumble followed, and Tom's stomach started to knot. "Can we hurry please!"

The djinn smiled. "Give me the sword."

Tom wondered if this was a trick – he could lose the sword and the stone. But no, the djinn could easily take it from him. And besides, what choice did he have?

Tom pulled Galatine free and handed it over.

The djinn stroked it reverently. "This was made using fire magic, and the inscription was burnt in by djinns' tear diamonds, you know."

"No, I did not know," Tom said, wishing he'd just get on with it.

"Few fey make weapons like this any more."

Another rumble made the cave tremble.

The djinn ran a long talon across his own palm, producing a stream of green blood. Holding his hand in a fist he squeezed the blood onto either side of the blade, rubbing it into the engravings. He said something Tom couldn't catch, then a flash of black flame engulfed the sword and the engravings glowed. The djinn smiled with satisfaction. "Now, put the sword in the stone."

Tom took Galatine and gently pushed it into the opening in the moonstone. It sank in, halfway up the hilt.

Immediately the moonstone started to emit a soft white light, and the silver and gold metalwork started to glow red as it heated. The glow spread up through Galatine, the blade turning white with heat, and as it reached the hilt the stones either side blinked open like eyes. The glow intensified until a blinding flash engulfed the sword and stone and a screech echoed through the cave.

Tom scrunched his eyes closed and covered his ears for a few seconds, and then tentatively peeked at Galatine. Both the sword and the moonstone had returned to normal, although the opals now swirled with an inky blackness.

"Can I touch it now?" said Tom.

But the djinn looked past him towards the door beyond, and the rivers of lava. "You'd better go, boy. We have woken the dragon."

Tom grabbed Galatine, the hilt warm to his touch. And all of a sudden he heard it. A low guttural growl that made the floors shake, and the word, "Galatine."

"Did you hear that? Did the dragon just speak?"

"It spoke to you," the djinn said, still watching the entrance. "I only heard the growl."

Tom looked at the sword in amazement. It had worked. He could hear the dragon's thoughts. And then an enormous crashing sound reverberated through the chamber, and a burst of flame erupted in the room beyond. "I have to get the moonstone out of here!"

"Make a wish, boy," the djinn said. "Quickly. Before I become too distracted."

Of course, djinns granted wishes. Tom scooped up the moonstone. "I wish to be on the other side of this wall, in front of the portal to Earth."

As he spoke a blast of flame shot across the room beyond, licking the workshop entrance. With a flick of his wrist the djinn produced a long black whip with multiple tails that flickered like smoke and flame. He cracked it into the room beyond, and with barely a glance to Tom said, "Safe travels, boy."

In a flash, Tom was on the other side of the wall, and the portal was in front of him. He could hear the now slightly dulled roar of the dragon. Hoping the djinn would be all right, he hugged the moonstone tightly, checked Galatine was safely in its scabbard, and, before anything else could happen, stepped into the portal.

24 The Door in the Dark

They travelled in silence, plodding upwards in patches of lamplight, until they arrived at a dead end.

Beansprout couldn't hide her disappointment. "It doesn't go anywhere!"

Nimue grinned. "I bet it does! A hidden door, Merlin?"

"Of course," he said. "Only an amateur wouldn't hide it."

Beansprout's hopes lifted as Nimue placed her hand on the wall and murmured a spell.

Nothing happened.

She frowned, and tried another. Again nothing happened.

"Let me," Merlin said. "What did you try?"

"The reveal spell and an invisibility spell."

Merlin snorted. "It must be something more relevant, Nimue."

Nimue raised an eyebrow. "I was starting with something simple," she said huffily and stepped back. "Your turn, Merlin."

Beansprout suppressed a smile at their banter. It was amazing, considering their history, that they could stand to be so close now – it was as if old friendships had returned. Although Nimue remained a little aloof from Merlin, Beansprout could see she cared about him, and that they respected each other. And Merlin certainly minded his manners around her, and never outstayed his welcome, often keeping to his own company. Knowing how much his attentions had smothered her in the past must have made him modify his behaviour.

"Do you remember that obsequious king who threatened Arthur, Nimue?" he asked as he examined the wall.

"Many kings threatened Arthur; you'll have to be more specific."

"That little one, from across the sea. He arrived on a black ship with gulls' wings on the side. He turned up in court one day with an ultimatum and I banished him to a room with no doors."

She looked thoughtful. "Vaguely. Why?"

"Because I think it was the same spell that Giolladhe has used. Or Raghnall." He muttered softly under his breath and a faint line started to spread from the floor upwards, until it made the shape of a door. "I thought so, just a 'say please' spell."

"And what happened to the king?" Beansprout asked.

"We found him a week later, dead. He never could find his manners, even when his life depended on it."

Before Beansprout could say anything else, Merlin pushed the door open and they all heard a yell and the distinctive whisper of swords being drawn. Then, as the door opened fully, Merlin found a sword tip under his chin.

"Woodsmoke! It's me!" Merlin shouted, as Nimue raised her hands to attack.

"That's an excellent way to get yourself killed, Merlin!" Woodsmoke said, annoyed, as Bloodmoon sighed behind him and sheathed his sword. "Welcome to Giolladhe's workshop."

"Where have you come from?" said Bloodmoon.

"The House of the Beloved, of course," Beansprout said.

"Of course!" Woodsmoke said snarkily. "That's so obvious."

She grinned at him. "Oh hush, Woodsmoke. So, we're actually here – in the workshop!"

They filed into a dimly lit room with a low roof. The only things in it were a wooden chair and a huge wooden bed that took up most of the space. In the wall opposite the hidden doorway was another door.

"Have you found anything?" Nimue asked, looking around. "I presume there's more to the place than this?"

"There's a lot of rooms here," Bloodmoon said, "all layered on top of each other. We think some are natural caves, and others were made by magic. But there's nothing here, other than old furniture and tools."

"It's odd," Woodsmoke added. "The place has been cleared as if he was ready to leave, but there was a key in the door, locking it."

A shiver ran up Beansprout's spine. "You mean it was locked from the *inside*? But there's no sign of him?" She looked around the room as if she might see his bones in the corner.

"No sign. Not even under those rotten bed covers." Woodsmoke gestured towards the pile on the unmade bed.

Merlin stalked around the room, feeling the walls. "Any suggestion of magic?"

"Not that we can tell," Woodsmoke said. "We certainly couldn't see that door you've just come through. Although seeing anything here is difficult in this dim light."

Nimue walked over to the lantern hanging from the centre of the ceiling. "Let me see if I can improve this," she said, and with a murmur the light flared brightly and the whole room emerged from the shadows.

They spent a few minutes checking there was nothing they'd missed, before Woodsmoke said, "Come on, we'll give you the tour. You might see something we haven't."

As they followed him downstairs, Beansprout said, "Where's Tom?"

"We left him searching boxes in the downstairs storeroom. I suppose we should check on him, he's been very quiet," Bloodmoon said, a note of worry in his voice.

"Better take us there now," Merlin said.

A sudden urgency drove them down the warren of steep stairs and past open doorways until they came into the main workshop. They followed Woodsmoke into the storeroom and found it empty.

"Where is he?" Nimue said, voicing everyone's concern.

"Have we passed him somewhere in another room?" Merlin asked.

"He'd have heard us, surely?" Beansprout said, her heart sinking.

"Perhaps there's another doorway?" Woodsmoke said, now looking confused. "He can't have gone far."

"Oh yes he can," Merlin said, from in front of a cupboard. "There's a portal here."

"What!" they exclaimed as one, rushing over.

Then there was chaos as they argued about what could have happened and where Tom could be. They had to physically restrain Woodsmoke from plunging in after him.

"I *must* go!" he yelled. "Tom could be in trouble!"

"But where would you end up?" Beansprout said. She agreed Woodsmoke should go, but was worried they'd lose him as well.

As they argued, the blackness in the portal swirled and Tom fell out, bringing Beansprout down with him in a tangle of legs.

Tom gasped. "Wow! I'm back! Awesome." And then he realised who he'd crashed into. "What are you doing here, Beansprout?"

"Great Goddess, Tom!" she said, the wind knocked out of her. "Where have you been? You're filthy! And you reek of sulphur."

It was twilight, and they were sitting outside enjoying the heat after the dark dampness of the caves, listening to Tom's story and examining the moonstone.

Woodsmoke was angry. "You should never have gone in alone, Tom!"

"I didn't plan to," he reasoned. "I thought it was another room." He looked at Beansprout with guilty delight. "I met a djinn – he granted me a wish!"

"Tom, you could have been killed," she said, excited and cross at the same time. "What did you wish for?"

"Gold? Jewels?" Bloodmoon asked, his eyes lighting up.

"No! I just wished to be in front of the portal."

Bloodmoon sighed. "What a wasted opportunity."

Merlin shook his head. "Arthur will not be happy at you going alone."

"Will everyone please calm down?" Tom said, beginning to look grumpy. "I'm fine, and I've found the moonstone. That's good, right?"

Bloodmoon gave a sly wink. "I'll make a fine thief of you yet, Tom."

"No, you will not," Woodsmoke said, with a glare.

Tom interrupted them. "And look at Galatine." He showed them the swirling djinns' eye opals.

"What's happened to it?" Merlin asked, examining it.

172

"The sword now lives … or something like that," Tom said. "The djinn said it was muted before. Inactivated by Giolladhe before he passed it to Vivian." He paused for a second. "I think it was another way of Giolladhe trying to prevent Filtiarn changing."

Woodsmoke sighed. "My head hurts and I'm starving. Let's head back. We need to talk to Arthur, see if he's found the grove." He looked at Beansprout. "Did you find anything to break the curse?"

"Not yet, but we will. There are a few more passages to search."

"I'll seal this end," Merlin said, stroking his beard, "and we'll return above ground. I think we should explore the caves later. With one hidden portal to contend with, who knows what's down there. I feel we should be properly prepared before we look again."

25 The Clock Ticks

Tom wallowed in his bath, washing away the ash and black marks left by the fire and lava, and the smell of singed hair and sulphur.

The moonstone sat on the bathroom floor, Galatine propped next to it. Both seemed to give off a faint glow, but Tom wasn't sure if he was imagining that. Ever since the sword had woken – as he called it – he felt it, reverberating through him, like a tremor.

He hadn't heard any more animals speaking to him, but he felt aware of them, like a subtle presence on the edge of his perception. It was a strange feeling. But not as strange as hearing that dragon. He was sure it had spoken. Did that mean creatures could sense the sword? All Tom could think of was Dr Doolittle, and he sank beneath the water, trying to banish it from his thoughts.

By the time he got out of the bath it was dark and late, and he was starving. He carried the moonstone down to the long balcony overlooking the city, and placed it on the edge of the table for everyone to see. He was the first to arrive, and he helped himself from the platters of cold meats and cheeses, olives, sweet dishes and soft breads laid out on the table, nibbling on food and sipping wine as he gazed at the city, wondering what had happened here so many years before. He tried to remember what the djinn had said, but his time in the Realm of Fire already felt like a dream. He just felt lucky to be back here, and not back at his grandfather's cottage.

In a short time Arthur arrived, looking disappointed. He threw himself on the divan with a large glass of Satyr's Delight and complained, "I was clearly an idiot for thinking I would find the clearing. How did everyone else …" And then he stopped as he saw the moonstone. He looked at Tom. "Is that *the moonstone*?"

"Yes it is," Tom said with a grin.

"How? Where?" Arthur leapt to his feet, his energy returned, and looked at it from every angle as if it would disappear.

Tom felt a little sheepish. "I crossed to the Realm of Fire – accidently!" he added quickly as he saw Arthur's expression.

"Woodsmoke let you go alone?"

"Woodsmoke didn't know! And I'm fine – I'm not a child, Arthur. And I got the moonstone!"

Arthur's frown quickly turned to a grin. "Well done, Tom. That's my boy."

As Tom relayed his experience in the Realm of Fire, Arthur continued to prowl around the moonstone. "What's this slot for?" he asked, gesturing to the top.

"It's where Galatine goes." He pulled Galatine free and placed it on the table. "Look at the stones. The djinn helped me wake the sword."

"So you had to pull the sword from the stone?" Arthur asked, a smile hovering on his face as he looked fondly at Tom.

"Yes, I suppose, sort of," Tom said, and then realised what he'd done. "Oh! It's like your old legend – with Excalibur."

Arthur hugged Tom. "I think that means something, Tom." His voice sounded gruff and Tom peered at him closely. Arthur wasn't usually an emotional man.

"It does? What?"

"I don't know, but I feel we're linked, more than we were before," Arthur said, gripping him by the shoulders. "Galatine was never 'awake' with Gawain, maybe that's because it was never meant for him."

"That's because it was meant for Filtiarn!" Tom said, trying to deflect whatever Arthur was trying to say.

"But I think it's now meant to be yours, Tom."

Before Tom could comment further, the others appeared and they changed the conversation, Tom trying to cover his confusion.

"We're getting closer," Arthur said, smiling.

"You've found the grove?" Nimue asked.

"No." Arthur's face fell. "I meant the moonstone. We have more searching to do."

Brenna leaned back against the balcony, drink in hand. "I think it's impossible. Even in a hundred years a wood will grow and change, obliterating a clearing. In a few thousand it would change *everything*. But there's an area that might be worth looking at again tomorrow. I want to look closer to the mountain, closer to Giolladhe's place."

"We could create a new grove," Nimue said. "In fact, it's something I've been meaning to do. Merlin and Beansprout could help. But we still need to try and find the original spell, and that means exploring the passages between the house and the hill."

Tom was confused. "What do you mean, a new grove? Does it matter?"

"It needs to be sacred ground, Tom," Merlin explained. "A quiet space, prepared for magic. You can do magic anywhere, but big spells require a special place. It enhances the power of the spell."

"How long would that take?" Arthur asked.

"Not long, really. A day or two. But we're already short on time," Nimue said.

"Have we any idea where Filtiarn is? He should be here soon," Woodsmoke said.

"I flew out beyond the city today," Brenna said. "They're on the moors now, and should be here late tomorrow." She looked worried. "I stopped to speak to them, and Filtiarn looks exhausted. I hope he survives the spell."

News of Filtiarn seemed to energise Arthur. "So, we search again for the original grove, on the rise that Brenna saw, and if not we make a new one. We have a few more days until the full moon." He looked out, to where the moon was edging above the mountain. "Look, it's getting closer to full."

The slight curl of the moon seemed to grin down at them, bathing them in its yellow glow, and Tom felt a tug in the pit of his stomach.

"But first we search the caves, and I suggest that's something we do together," Arthur said, his voice excited. "Tonight."

26 Guardian of the Daystar Sapphires

They headed in single file down the steps into the dark stone corridor beneath the House of the Beloved, carrying smoking torches, lanterns and weapons. Arthur led the way, with Nimue and Merlin close behind.

Soon they came to the small space with three other passages leading off it, and Merlin pointed out the path to Giolladhe's.

"I wonder how often they used this?" Beansprout said.

"Depends on what terrible secrets they were trying to keep," Woodsmoke suggested with a grimace.

"Let's try this one first," said Arthur, indicating one of the other two passages. "Can we mark it so we know where we've gone? Things could get very confusing down here."

"Excellent idea," Merlin said. With a flourish of his hand, he scrawled *House of the Beloved* in shining writing on the tunnel they had come along. He marked Giolladhe's passage, and then the one they were about to take, saying, "I shall call this number 1."

"Inspired," Bloodmoon said, sarcastically. Merlin ignored him.

For some minutes the passage wound onwards, until it eventually began to widen, and a pale light seeped around them. Arthur called out, "Stop!"

"What's happened?" Woodsmoke called.

"Come forward – very slowly. We have reached an edge," Arthur said, sounding nervous.

They shuffled towards the light, and Tom gasped. The passage had opened out, and they were on a narrow shelf, looking out across a large cave that twinkled with a faint blue glow. Far below them was a lake lit from beneath, reminding Tom of Ceridwen's Cauldron.

"Where's the light coming from?" Tom asked, as he craned round to look at the cave. It was almost circular, and although the lake was a long way down, the roof seemed far above them too.

"Great Goddess!" Nimue murmured. "It must be coming from daystar sapphires." She pointed. "There are hundreds set into the cavern walls."

"What are those? I've never heard of them," Brenna said.

"Very rare stones with strong magical properties," Nimue replied. "Only those who practise magic use them, and they're very hard to get." She gazed around with wonder.

"And yet Raghnall seems to have had his own enormous supply," Arthur said.

"I wonder," Merlin said, "could they have been used in Filtiarn's spell?"

A narrow walkway ran off to their right before petering out, and Merlin felt his way along, heading towards where a smattering of stones came within reach.

"Maybe," Nimue murmured, deep in thought. "They have the ability to enhance any spell, but the power actually makes them dangerous. I have never used them, even when I had some. If they're used incorrectly, they can cause what I can only describe as a magical explosion."

"That's a long way down," Bloodmoon said, peering over the edge. He picked up a stone and dropped it. It was several seconds before they heard a faint splash. "I think there's something down there."

"Like what?" Tom said, alarmed.

Beansprout dropped to her knees, better to look over the edge. "Can you see that black shape against the blue? It looks like it's circling around."

"It's getting bigger," Woodsmoke said. "Is that because it's getting closer?" He looked at Bloodmoon, annoyed. "Have you woken something?"

"I only dropped a stone in!" he said, indignant. "Whatever it is, it's a long way down. You worry too much, Woodsmoke!"

Before anyone else could comment there was an enormous splash and the black shape emerged from the water, silhouetted against the blue. The shape kept coming, and then a spurt of fire emerged from the blackness, followed by the familiar roar of a dragon.

"It's a bloody great dragon," Arthur yelled, pulling Excalibur free with a hiss. "Run!"

But Merlin was still at the end of the ledge, examining the stones.

"Merlin, get a bloody move on!" Arthur yelled, preparing to fight as they stood mesmerised by the dragon's approach.

And suddenly Tom was aware of Galatine, trembling, its hilt warm to the touch. "How can it live in water?" he shouted as he pulled Galatine free, its opals now swirling furiously.

"Water dragon," Nimue yelled above the roar, "very vicious, and territorial."

A blinding white light emitted from her hands, held palms forward, forming a wall in front of them just as the dragon drew level and released another stream of fire.

They instinctively ducked, but the shield held, turning into a wall of flame as the fire hit it. Beyond, the dragon flapped its enormous wings and fixed them with a vicious stare before flying round to circle back, its huge wing span creating a rush of air.

"Wow!" Tom said, rising to his feet and looking with new appreciation at Nimue.

Merlin stumbled, and Arthur ran to him, helping him to his feet. Woodsmoke and Bloodmoon had already drawn their arrows in case the shield failed.

"Get a move on, Merlin," Nimue commanded icily. She turned to Beansprout. "Join your hand to mine, and hold your other hand out, like me."

Without hesitating, Beansprout did as she asked, and Tom saw her stiffen as a wave of power travelled through her, strengthening the shield.

Tom watched the dragon turn back towards them, dripping with phosphorescent water, like a sheen of blue fire racing along its wings and dripping down its jaw. It was magnificent and terrifying all at the same time.

Arthur rejoined them, Merlin with him, panting heavily. "Run, now!" Arthur said, pushing them one by one ahead of him into the passage.

The dragon attacked again, closer than before, its wide jaws showing its sharp cruel teeth, just before a powerful stream of flame poured out. Despite the shield, Tom could feel the heat licking closer, buffeted by the enormous wings. Its roar was enraged, and only when it turned again did Nimue drop her hands, grab Beansprout by the arm and run, Arthur following closely behind.

They kept running well beyond the turn in the passage, Arthur yelling, "Don't stop!"

Another roar echoed down the passage and for one horrible moment Tom thought the beast had somehow followed them. Glancing behind he saw flame coming towards them. "Duck!" he yelled, throwing himself to the ground. Beansprout landed next to him. A flash of flame passed overhead, bringing its own roaring crackle which seemed to last forever, and then it was gone.

He rolled over to see Beansprout looking at him wide-eyed in shock. He scrambled to his feet and grabbed her hand, pulling her up. Behind him, Arthur was lying on top of Nimue, shielding her from the flames. Ahead the others struggled to their feet.

"Keep going," Woodsmoke said, and they ran the rest of the way, only slowing down when they reach the other passages.

"That was close!" Bloodmoon said with a wry grin, and he sank to his knees breathing heavily.

"It's not funny!" Woodsmoke said. "We could have been killed!"

Brenna was the only one not breathless, having flown ahead of them. "You really should think things through first, Bloodmoon," she said, a note of disapproval in her tone. Tom knew she had a soft spot for Bloodmoon, and she couldn't help a small smile escaping; Bloodmoon gave her a wink which she tried to ignore.

She turned to Merlin. "Are you all right, Merlin?"

Merlin leaned against the wall, clutching his chest. "I think so. At least I'm alive."

Nimue was cross. "Bloodmoon! I didn't even get a chance to get some stones. Now I'm going to have to go back when the damn dragon has calmed down."

"Dear lady, fear not," Merlin said. He opened his hand to reveal a clutch of stones. "I prised them free before Bloodmoon nearly killed me."

Arthur smiled and patted his shoulder. "Well done, old friend." He turned to Bloodmoon. "Had enough excitement, or shall we carry on?"

"Always onwards, Arthur," he said, getting to his feet. "After you."

The next passage snaked downwards, and then split into two.

"Which way?" Tom asked.

"Left," Arthur said, decisively.

This passage was short and ended in another cave, but this one twinkled in the light of their lanterns.

"Herne's hairy hooves!" Bloodmoon said, incredulous. "It's a huge pile of gold and jewels!"

"And weapons, shields, and ornaments," Woodsmoke added, holding up a helmet. Although it was tarnished, it still reflected a gleam of torchlight.

"Dragon hoard," Nimue said. "But where's the dragon?"

She circled the pile of jewels, and called out, "There's another exit. Bigger this time."

Joining Nimue, Tom saw she was right. "I guess a dragon needs a much bigger passage than the one we came down."

"So do we explore it?" Woodsmoke asked.

They gathered around the entrance, but it was impossible to see more than a few feet ahead.

"It could go for miles," Nimue said, shaking her head.

"But what if the spell is hidden down there somewhere?" Tom said.

"Let's check out the other passage first," Arthur said. "If we have to we'll come back here."

"I could fly down, see where it heads?" Brenna suggested.

"It's too dangerous," Woodsmoke said.

Arthur nodded. "I agree. I don't want us splitting up."

"Look at this," Bloodmoon said. He stood at the edge of the hoard, where he had been pulling objects aside, rummaging in curiosity. He held up a sheet of translucent scales. "Dragon skin."

"Oh, that's disgusting," Beansprout said with a grimace.

"But useful for spells," Merlin added. He took it from Bloodmoon, carefully folded it, and put it in his cloak.

They headed back to the last passage, and it again led downwards, a mixture of winding path and rough steps, until eventually they came to a thick wooden door. Arthur tried it, but it was locked.

"Who locks a door down here?" Tom asked, exasperated.

"Someone who wants to hides something," Arthur answered.

With a flick of his wrist, Merlin unlocked the door with magic.

"Can you teach me that?" Bloodmoon asked.

"No!" Merlin said. "You cause enough trouble."

They pushed the heavy door open and their lanterns showed a small square room. All along one wall were alcoves, filled with candles, bones, artefacts and scrolls. Along another wall was a roughly hewn wooden table. Beansprout, clearly wanting to practise magic, lit the candles from a flame she produced in her hands.

"This must be it!" Arthur said. "Where else would you hide a spell you don't want anyone else to find?"

They fanned out around the room, and started to pull objects from the alcoves.

"Gently," Merlin called to the others as he extracted a scroll, "the paper's fragile."

"What animals are these from?" Tom asked, pulling down a skull with a sharp snout and huge hinged jaw.

"Marsh snakes?" Woodsmoke suggested.

"A marsh snake? It must be huge!" Tom said, turning the skull over.

"They'll eat you in one big gulp," Brenna explained.

Tom put the skull back on the shelf with a grimace.

Merlin and Nimue had pulled several scrolls out and carefully unrolled them on the table.

"These look like contracts," Nimue said, puzzled.

"Between who?" Arthur asked, looking over her shoulder.

"The sylphs and Raghnall. And this one," she said, unrolling another, "is between the sylphs and Giolladhe."

"For weapons, I presume?" Woodsmoke said.

"A design for an amulet, a large one by the look of it. To go on one of their towers, I think." She squinted in the light, and held the lantern closer. "I think it's to repel dragons."

Beansprout interrupted from the far end of the table, where she stood with Bloodmoon. "I think we've found it." In front of them on the table was a wooden box, an image of a wolf engraved on the top.

"The only thing is," Bloodmoon said, "we can't open it."

Merlin hurried over. "It could be it, I suppose," he said, turning the box over, examining it carefully. "It's either been sealed by magic, or just some clever lock."

"It's the best lead we have for now," Nimue said. "Nothing else here suggests the spell."

"But what if it isn't?" Tom said, not liking the idea of coming back down here again.

"Let's take anything of interest," Woodsmoke suggested, casting an appraising eye over the room, "including those contracts. And then let's get out of here."

27 The Wolf Mage Arrives

Tom sat with Woodsmoke at the entrance to the tunnel leading to Dragon's Hollow, looking out over the mountain below them. The rose gold gates were partially open behind them, glittering in the sun.

It was late afternoon, and they were in the shade of a towering tree, leaning back against the trunk, each sipping a bottle of Red Earth Thunder Ale.

"I really hope we don't have to go back into those tunnels," Tom said. "They were creepy."

"I felt like I was inside Raghnall's grimy little mind," Woodsmoke agreed. "All those twists and turns and hidden secrets."

"There's probably a maze of tunnels beyond the dragon hoard. It's weird to think that beneath us all sorts of things may be hidden away."

"And things we don't really want to find," Woodsmoke said. He pointed to the path, to where a pocket of dust swirled. "I think that could be Filtiarn."

Woodsmoke and Tom had volunteered to come and welcome Filtiarn, Elan and Rahal. Both were glad to leave the preparations behind. Nimue and Beansprout were out searching again for the grove, and preparing to start a new ritual place in the woods behind their house if needed, helped by Brenna and Bloodmoon, who was not good at being cooped up in the house. Merlin and Arthur were in the library, trying to open the box.

"Do you think we can do it?" Tom asked. He looked at Woodsmoke who reclined against the tree, his legs stretched out in front of him, and wondered if he would ever be as calm or composed. Woodsmoke took everything in his stride, and if he was worried about anything, he rarely showed it.

"I'm not sure, Tom," he said, his expression sombre. "It's a big ask after so many years."

"We got Merlin out of Nimue's spell."

"With Herne's help. There's no god to help us now."

Tom looked at Galatine. "I feel sort of responsible. And I know it's stupid, but I do. I mean, I have the sword that performed the curse."

"Oh come on," Woodsmoke said. "It has nothing to do with you. Neither you nor Arthur had anything to do it with it. And at least the sword's *'awake'* now. Filtiarn has a better chance than he's ever had before."

As he finished speaking the three figures rounded the bend in the path, followed by a dozen wolves, and they stood to greet them. "But you know what?" he added, before the others came within hearing. "I think there'll be another twist before this is all over."

Before Tom could question him further, Woodsmoke turned and waved. "Welcome back to Dragon's Hollow!"

Filtiarn looked tired, but better than when he had become human again. The haunted look behind his eyes remained, and Tom wasn't sure if that would ever go. Filtiarn managed a slight smile. "It's good to finally be here."

Tom looked nervously at the wolves that padded around them, sniffing at their feet. Rahal reassured him. "It's OK, Tom, they accept you as friends now."

They were beautiful creatures, their fur thick and white, their eyes intense. Tom held his hand out and one sniffed it cautiously, and then nuzzled under it, allowing Tom to pat it.

Rahal and Elan slipped off their horses, Rahal saying, "I have to confess, I need a good freshen up." She ran a hand across her face. "I feel very dusty."

"You can rest and change at Nimue's," Tom said. "We have rooms for all of you."

Elan smiled with relief. "Good, the ride has been hard on Filtiarn. Have you found anything to help us? We've found the moonstone, and have activated Galatine." He pulled the sword free and pointed to the stones swirling in the hilt.

"But we haven't found the spell yet," Woodsmoke added. "We think we're close, though."

"Wow!" Elan said, impressed. "You've found more than we have in years."

"But we had your knowledge to build on," Tom said.

"And a lot of luck," Woodsmoke added.

"Even so ..." Elan said, and he looked at Filtiarn. "Good news, yes, Filtiarn?"

Filtiarn didn't respond. Instead he stared down at his horse.

Tom held Galatine out to Filtiarn. "Do you remember the stones doing this?"

Filtiarn shook his head. "It was my sword for many years, but it never had the djinns' eye opals until my brother modified it."

Woodsmoke nodded. "Let's get to Nimue's where we can talk in comfort. Will the wolves follow us? They may unnerve the fey of the Hollow."

"I'll send them around," he said. He spoke a series of what sounded like barks and growls, but the wolves seemed to understand him, and they loped off beyond the gate, heading onto the steep mountain paths.

"Have either of you been to Dragon's Hollow before?" Woodsmoke asked Rahal and Elan.

"Never," they replied together.

"Well, you're in for quite the experience. Come with me, Rahal," Woodsmoke said, courteously. "I'll tell you all about it."

He mounted his horse and waited for Rahal, then led the way back through the tunnel, leaving Tom to follow with Elan and Filtiarn.

"Does anything look familiar to you?" Tom asked Filtiarn.

"A little. I recognised the moors we crossed, they have changed very little, but I'm pretty sure the gates were not of rose gold when I was last here." He smiled wryly. "They have obviously had good fortune."

"When were you last here?"

"Two thousand years ago. I could not bring myself to come here the last time I changed. I'm not sure I want to be here now." His hands trembled slightly as he gripped the reins of his horse, and Tom tried not to show he'd noticed.

"In that case, you'll probably find it's really different inside."

Tom had got used to the splendours of Dragon's Hollow, but Elan was quiet as they rode up towards the lake, looking around at the houses and the people. Once there, he gazed up at the huge dragon fountain in the centre of the lake. "This place is amazing."

"I certainly don't remember the fountain," Filtiarn said. He looked around, taking everything in. "The city has grown, and the houses are more decorative. I don't remember them being so richly embellished."

"Do you remember that?" Tom asked, pointing towards the House of the Beloved in the distance.

Filtiarn's eyes darkened. "Yes. I remember that. Raghnall's place. Although it wasn't as big." He looked up at the shoulder of the mountain beyond. "That's where Giolladhe's workshop was."

"We found it," Tom explained, wondering if he should mention the portal. He decided not to, things seemed complicated enough. "And we found the underground tunnels."

"What underground tunnels?" Filtiarn asked, looking puzzled.

Was it possible that Filtiarn couldn't know? It seemed Raghnall and Giolladhe had many secrets between them. "Let's keep going," Tom said, spurring his horse onwards, "and I'll explain."

Tom sat next to Beansprout at dinner, Brenna on his other side. They were again on the long balcony overlooking the city, seated around the table, chatting as they ate. Nimue and Beansprout had done their best to make their guests feel welcome, and the table glittered with silverware and candlelight. However, there was none of the Raghnall's ostentatiousness, and everyone was relaxed and laughing. Tom was oblivious to the decor, tucking into roast chicken with relish.

Beansprout watched him eating. "Where on earth do put it all, Tom?"

"What?" he said, indignant. "I'm very hungry. Hard work does that, you know?"

"Try making a sacred glade in this heat," she said sarcastically. "That's hard work."

"Is it done?" he asked, taking a breather and sipping his beer.

"We think we may have found the original," she said with a slow smile.

"Really?"

Brenna joined in. "As I thought, we were looking too close to the house yesterday. The place I saw was on a rise, and now I know where Giolladhe's workshop is, it makes sense. It's his grove, not Raghnall's. Well," she qualified, "we think it is."

Beansprout continued. "It's off the path up the mountain, the one you used to find the workshop. But you turn off it, before it becomes too high. Off to the right. But we couldn't have found it without Brenna. The path is completely overgrown."

"I had to work back, from the grove," Brenna said. "It looked less dense than the rest of the woods."

"So is that easier? Less work to do?" Tom asked, excited.

"You'd think so, but no," Beansprout said. "We've still got a good day's work ahead of us. And we need to prepare the path from the road."

"And set up lanterns to help us find the way," Brenna added. "Although the moon will be full, it will be dark beneath the trees."

"How are you clearing the trees?"

"A combination of magic and brawn," Brenna said, with a grimace. "Guess who's helping us tomorrow."

Tom looked at her suspiciously. "Do you mean me?"

"Yes," she said, "there's lots more to do."

Arthur joined in. "I am feeling more positive about this already."

"Why?" Beansprout asked. "Have you opened the box?"

"No," Merlin answered quickly, his glass halfway to his lips. "I don't want to risk it breaking. Whatever's locking it is powerful."

"It has a wolf on it, you say?" Filtiarn asked. He ate like a bird, picking at his food slowly, and pushing it around on his plate. He looked very pale.

"Yes, a wolf's head actually," Merlin explained. "I can show you later if you like."

"Maybe tomorrow," Filtiarn said. "I'm not sure I will be up too much longer."

"Yes, yes, of course," Arthur said. He looked at Filtiarn with concern. "You must rest. Tomorrow's fine. How many days until the full moon, Nimue?"

"Two."

Only two days. The table fell silent for a second as the news sank in.

"And I would like to ask you more questions about the ritual," Nimue said. She had been silent for some time, listening to the others and watching Filtiarn. "And a little about the arrangements with the sylphs at that time, if that's all right?"

Filtiarn looked startled, as did Rahal. "Why does that matter?" she asked Nimue, slightly aggressively Tom thought.

"It all matters," Nimue said sharply, her green eyes flashing. "Understanding what went wrong then may help us put things right now."

Filtiarn, Rahal and Elan soon pleaded tiredness and excused themselves, but not before the Wolf Moon appeared over the mountain. It was bigger again, and it seemed to Tom that the yellow hue was increasing as the moon grew in size, casting a sickly light over the city. As it rose, the wolves in the forest beyond the house loosed their unearthly howls and

Tom felt goosebumps rise on his skin. Filtiarn stood watching the moon for a brief second, before he turned and almost fled the balcony.

28 The Altar Stone

Tom wielded the machete with brutal determination, hacking it back and forth, creating the path to the ritual place as if there were sprites attacking him. Sweat poured into his eyes and stained the front of his thin cotton shirt, and he was covered in small twigs, leaves and dirt.

Woodsmoke was next to him, and together they moved at a good pace. The path started flat, but soon rose upwards towards the grove. It was on a hill – part of the mountain shoulder. Tom wasn't entirely sure what Beansprout had been on about; there was no original path left at all.

Brenna had flown ahead of them earlier, leading Beansprout, Bloodmoon, Nimue, Arthur and Rahal to the grove. They had slipped through the trees and bushes, hacking small branches away to mark their path, leaving Tom and Woodsmoke to create the path properly. Elan and Filtiarn had remained at the house with Merlin so Filtiarn could rest.

A flurry of wings interrupted them and Brenna appeared. She laughed at their appearance. "You two look like you're having fun!"

Woodsmoke had tied back his long hair, and a strand had escaped, hanging in front of his face. He pushed it back, smearing his face with dirt. "Yes, we're having a great time! Having fun flying around watching the rest of us work?"

"Yes, actually. It's especially fun watching Bloodmoon labouring away in the grove."

That cheered Woodsmoke up. "Good. Glad to hear he's not dodging work."

"No chance. Nimue won't hear of it."

Tom laughed as well. "So much for *protecting the ladies*."

"Yes, Nimue really needs his protection," Brenna said with a smirk. She added, "They've found the stone altar in the centre of the grove, and some of the trees around the edge – well, the original edge – are oaks, yew and elder."

"Is that important?" Tom asked.

"Apparently yes. They will add protection to the grove and enhance the spell."

Magic stuff he would never understand, Tom thought.

Brenna continued, "I'm heading back to Nimue's, to see how Filtiarn is. Do you need anything? You're heading the right way."

"No, we're fine, thanks. How far have we to go?" Woodsmoke asked.

"You're about halfway."

Woodsmoke and Tom groaned, but before they could say anything else, Brenna flew off.

When they finally arrived at the clearing, they found Nimue and Beansprout sitting on the altar stone in the middle. Arthur lay on the floor gazing up at the sky above. All three of them looked hot and bothered. Beansprout, who now usually followed Nimue's style of long dress, instead wore a cotton shirt and the loose trousers she'd travelled in, tucked into boots. Nimue remained in a dress, having announced she was far too old to change her ways now. Tom didn't believe that at all, but decided against arguing with Nimue. If he was honest, he was still a little overawed by her.

A ring of old gnarled trees edged the clearing, demarcating it from the rest of the woods, and although some of the larger trees still stood in the centre of the glade, they had managed to fell many smaller ones, and saplings lay strewn across the ground.

"What do you think of our hard work?" Beansprout asked.

"Impressive," Woodsmoke said, sitting beside them. "Almost as impressive as ours."

Beansprout laughed, and a tendril of hair escaped and brushed against her cheek. "I think we'll all need baths later."

Arthur spoke from where he lay on the floor. "So have we done now?"

"No!" Nimue said, throwing a twig at him. "We need to clear away everything and burn what we don't need."

Arthur sat up slowly, picking the twig from his hair, which fell around his shoulders looking knotty and wild. "I knew I should have stayed in the house today."

"You know you'd have gone mad."

He poked his tongue out at her playfully, reminding Tom of the fact they were old friends who were very comfortable in each other's company. Nimue laughed, looking like a teenager.

"Where's Bloodmoon and Rahal?" Tom asked, looking around.

"Trying to find a path to Giolladhe's workshop," Beansprout said. "We think it must be in that direction." She pointed to the far side of the grove, where the side of the mountain reared in the near distance.

"I suppose you want us to help here?" Tom asked with a sigh.

"No rest for the wicked, Tom," Nimue said. "You can help us gather the wood up."

"Is the fire for tomorrow?"

"Yes," Nimue answered, "and hopefully Merlin is making progress on the spell."

"So we're sure this is the grove where it happened all those years ago?" Woodsmoke asked, looking around with interest.

"Fairly sure. The trees on the perimeter are clearly ancient, and aren't native to the area," Beansprout said.

"Which means," Nimue said, "that this was planned. And this," she patted the altar stone, "was brought here for magical purposes. The stone has an unusual red vein running through it. It's not from here."

Arthur looked interested, "How do you know?"

"It's from Avalon."

"What?" All of them looked at Nimue in shock.

"I have no idea how it's here, but the stone is all over the island. It has strong conductive properties. It holds energies – of the elements, plants, growth ..." She laughed at their shocked expressions. "It's why the island is so magical. It's one of the things Raghnall used to complain about." Her face fell momentarily.

Tom jolted with a memory. "You had an argument, sort of, with Raghnall, about Avalon."

"Yes. It was an old argument. He believed Avalon shouldn't be hidden. He was wrong. It is powerful, too dangerous, even for the magical place of the Realms. It was the original crossing place between the Realms and Earth. And as Tom knows, things are buried there that should never see the light of day."

Tom nodded, remembering when he woke Arthur beneath the lake. "I guess it was quite a privilege to be there."

"And for me to be *sleeping* there," Arthur said.

Nimue nodded. "It was. It healed you, Arthur. And it was a difficult decision for me to leave."

"But you can go back?" Woodsmoke asked, puzzled.

"I can never go back. Not to live. Besides, there is too much to do here."

"Why can't you go back?" Woodsmoke persisted.

"You should never go back," she said enigmatically.

"So how is the stone here?" Arthur asked. He leaned forward, all tiredness forgotten.

"Raghnall or Giolladhe must have been to Avalon. Or a priestess arranged it."

"How long have priestesses been on Avalon? It can't have been Vivian."

"No, not Vivian," Nimue agreed. "But there were others before her. We priestesses, witches, are of an old order. We serve the Goddess. She has been here forever. Like Herne. Beansprout – we really must revert to your original name," she said, looking at Beansprout with a shake of her head. "One day, you must go there to complete your training."

"I must?" she replied, clearly excited. "To Avalon?"

"Of course. Anyway. However it happened, the stone is here. It explains why Giolladhe was such a success with his skills. This stone would have enhanced them. He must have used it many times. And I presume Raghnall would have used it too, when he needed it."

"It's fortunate we've found it," Arthur said. "It is meant to be."

"Maybe," Nimue said. "Maybe."

But Tom thought she wasn't convinced.

When they finally returned to the House of the Beloved it was dusk. They all ached, were filthy, and stank of sweat. Rahal and Bloodmoon had rejoined them, having found traces of a path up to the mountain workshop.

They were accosted on the stairs by Merlin. "There you are!" he said. "You need to come to the library now." In comparison to them, he looked refreshed, clean and dry. Tom thought he had washed his robe, but his beard was still wild, as was his hair. His appearance in many ways mattered little to him. However, his bright blue eyes sparkled.

"Why, what's happened?" Nimue asked, worried.

"We've opened the box. Or rather, Filtiarn has."

He refused to say any more, instead leading them up the stairs, past their bedrooms, which Tom gazed at wistfully as he passed, and on into the library.

The setting sun cast a warm rosy light over Brenna, Elan and Filtiarn, who were gathered around the table in the centre. In front of them lay the open box, its contents spilling onto the table. Tom saw a scroll, filled with tiny writing, and items that looked like stones, bone, skin and feathers. They turned as they entered, every one of them looking serious.

"What's wrong?" Nimue asked, striding towards them.

"We've found the spell, but the curse has a kick," Brenna said.

"What sort of kick?"

"A stone from Avalon has powered the spell. How do we get one of those?" Filtiarn asked. He was agitated, his dark eyes troubled, his gaunt, hollowed cheeks exacerbated by the soft light.

Nimue broke into a broad smile. "Is that all? We have found the grove; the altar stone is from Avalon. I'd know it anywhere."

"Really?" Filtiarn was so excited he started coughing, and Elan passed him some water.

"Are you sure?" Elan said, a doubtful look on his face.

"She's sure," Arthur said. "By tomorrow night this could be all over."

Merlin shook his head. "I'm not so certain."

"Why?" Nimue turned to Merlin. "How complex is it?"

"Very. Part of it involves a potion that Filtiarn must drink – and that we must make. There are a number of items we need to gather (some common, others not), and conditions must be right in order for it to work, which they are – the stars are aligning and the Wolf Moon is waxing. But the trouble is the language. It's archaic. Some terms are clear, others aren't. Which means although I understand some things," he shrugged, "some I don't understand at all." He looked tired and frustrated.

"Surely you must understand the language, Filtiarn?" Arthur asked.

"Yes, regular words and phrases, but there's an item listed called *Arach Frasan Fuil*. I don't know what that is, and neither does Merlin."

"What? I don't know what that is either. Rahal, Nimue?" Arthur asked, perplexed.

"No. Sorry," Rahal said, flustered. "I don't feel I'm helping at all."

Nimue looked thoughtful. "I've never heard of it either, but we have plenty of old texts. We just have to check and double check everything."

Silence fell as they understood the implications. And then a troubling thought crossed Tom's mind. "You know when we were trying to break your spell, Nimue, I was told that only the witch who cast the spell could break it. Or that death could release it? So how does that affect us?"

"Because this spell was designed to be broken. It is time bound, linked to the Wolf Moon cycle. Filtiarn's change depends on it. Regardless of who is around, he changes form every thousand years for the space of one month. Once in his human form, if we perform the ritual correctly, he will remain as human."

Merlin agreed. "Part of the curse is the knowledge of the change, and its time sensitivities. What better way to extract maximum torture than to know you are so close to being human, and yet aren't." He shook his head. "It's very cruel."

"But if the curse is still going, surely that means Giolladhe must be alive, somewhere?" Tom reasoned. "Or why is Filtiarn still changing?"

29 Arach Frasan Fuil

Night had fallen, and Tom leaned on the balcony watching the city lights twinkling. The dragon fountain was lit up from below, and it glowed red, green and gold. Around the rim of the lake, Tom could see the jugglers' fire clubs being thrown high into the air, and he watched the spectacle, mesmerised. He hadn't been into the town yet, and hoped that he'd have time to visit the market tomorrow. He looked up at the Wolf Moon, now almost full. Its sickly yellow glow was getting stronger and it chilled his blood.

The table had been cleared after dinner, and the wooden box containing the spell was now sitting on it. Nimue had rolled out the scroll and was making notes on a pad next to her. She sat at one end of the table, Beansprout, Rahal and Merlin next to her, reading and asking questions, and consulting several books stacked on the table – books on herbs, gems, and metals. Tom smiled to himself. Three witches and a wizard; he certainly kept unusual company these days. Beansprout looked animated, excited to be learning more magic, but Rahal seemed worried, despite her clear regard for Nimue and Merlin. She'd been asking questions ever since she'd arrived, and particularly this evening. And they still hadn't worked out what *Arach Frasan Fuil* was.

Arthur and the others sat at the opposite end of the table. Tom was the only one standing. He had grown suddenly restless, and could only put it down to nerves. Tomorrow night they would be making their way to the sacred grove, and they had to find out what some of the words meant, or it would never work.

Bloodmoon was examining something he'd found in the box – it looked like a tusk. He held it up. "Does this belong to a boar?"

"I think so," Rahal said, taking it from him. "The spell needs something to anchor the boar, and the change." She handed it back and then reached into the box, taking out a feather. "This is a raven's, it signifies change too."

"I must admit," Nimue said, squinting at the scroll, "this is proving harder than I thought."

Arthur interrupted, addressing Filtiarn. "How *did* you open the box?"

Filtiarn lifted his shoulders and spread his hands wide. "I merely touched it."

Arthur looked shocked. "Is that all?"

"Quite clever, really," Merlin said. "Only Filtiarn or Giolladhe could open it, and most of the time Filtiarn would be in boar form anyway. It ensures no-one else could rescue him."

"I wonder where he is?" Filtiarn said, looking down at the table. It was clear he was referring to Giolladhe.

"Does it matter?" Arthur asked. "We can break the spell without him."

"Yes, it does matter. He did this to me." He looked up and glared at everyone, suddenly furious. "Me. His brother! And I have no idea why!"

"It does seem a bit overkill, just because he thought you'd insulted his spell," Beansprout said.

"He was always quick to anger," Filtiarn explained. "But yes, his response seems *unreasonable*." His eyes flashed, but Nimue intervened with another question.

"What exactly was going on here five thousand years ago, Filtiarn?" She looked at him curiously. "I mean, the city didn't exist like this. It was overrun with dragons; traders were trying to mine for the rich seams of metals and gems, and they were battling with dragons and sylphs. And the sylphs found their city under attack as well. This would have been a battle zone. I've read accounts, but they are dry and dusty and probably don't contain the real history."

Filtiarn looked uncomfortable. "Just as you've said. It was a battleground for riches. Fey were here before the dragons."

"No they weren't," Bloodmoon corrected. Tom had forgotten he had an ear for stories, like Fahey. Bloodmoon leant forward, cupping his wine glass. "Dragons have always been in the Hollow. It was named after them. Where there's gems, there's dragons. Those are the rules of the Realms. But the fey wanted their wealth."

"Well yes, true," Filtiarn said. "But they were manageable, almost. It was when the dragons started arriving from the Realm of Fire that things became dangerous."

"Yes." Merlin nodded. "It started the Dragon Wars. What led you to ask for the spell?"

"I arrived with the early fey and attempted to negotiate with the dragons – I failed. Not long after, Giolladhe arrived – it was the best place for him to get precious metals and gems for his forging. And Raghnall had arrived too. Probably for the same reason. Raghnall immediately set up his spell, but with limited success. It was clear the dragons were stronger." He shrugged. "They're dragons, after all. I left for a while, and then thought I'd try again. And I'd decided I wanted to hunt with the wolves. I've always had a bond with them, something I can't explain."

"So you can speak dragon?" Tom asked.

Filtiarn looked at him and smiled. "Of a sort. Their language is guttural and difficult, even with my skills. I was trying to broker peace – I was a bit of a diplomat," he said modestly. "I had achieved success elsewhere where animals and fey had clashed. Sometimes just for small villages on the edge of wild forests, or for the Realm of Water where they waged daily battles with some of the fierce creatures under the sea."

So far, so true, Tom thought, remembering what the Gatherer had written in his diaries, and some of the other books Finnlugh had loaned them.

"When it was clear the fey wouldn't leave the Hollow and the dragons wouldn't stop attacking, I thought I'd try again, to help prevent more bloodshed," Filtiarn continued. "That's when I asked my brother to strengthen my sword so that I could enhance my skills. Galatine was one of his early creations, and I had owned it for a while. I was proud of it, and of him for making it. As you've seen, it is a work of great beauty. I thought he could concentrate energies within it, and that those energies could have another action – one of transformation that could help me run with my wolves, my companions of old."

"But he wasn't keen, was he?" Merlin asked, narrowing his eyes speculatively.

"No, not initially. How do you know?"

"While you were all busy with the grove, I spent some time reading those contracts we found, and it seems he and Raghnall were making a lot of money from protecting the town and the sylphs. Giolladhe had made the sylphs an amulet to protect them from the dragons. They paid a lot of money for it – I saw it in a contract. My guess is that the spell could have worked a lot better, but it suited Raghnall and Giolladhe to have it fail sometimes. It gained them protection money."

"That makes sense," Nimue added. "A few months ago a contingent of fey arrived here to present me with the annual gift to Raghnall for protection of the city. The gift that of course transfers to me, now I protect the city."

Beansprout looked at her in shock. "I didn't know that!"

"I was so disgusted, I couldn't bring myself to speak of it," Nimue said, annoyed. "Of course I refused. I don't take protection money. I do this to protect the city, as anyone with a conscience would. I confess I thought this was a later arrangement. I had no idea it had been going on for millennia."

Arthur said, "So that's why everyone looked so uncomfortable around Raghnall. He was holding them hostage."

Woodsmoke agreed. "And when we killed him they thought we had condemned them to death by dragon attack, and more extortion."

"Is that why we've getting gifts lately?" Beansprout asked. "And the occasional freebie at the market?"

"Probably," Nimue said. "They were so pleased I didn't want their money – it was a huge amount – that they are showing their gratitude in other ways."

"Have the sylphs forgiven you?" Bloodmoon asked Nimue, referring to the time when she had outwitted them at Arthur, Woodsmoke, and Tom's trial.

"No, not really. Although they are civil," she said with a smile. "But to go back to you, Filtiarn, you were about to disrupt the flow of money. You had to go."

Filtiarn looked at her and then Merlin in shock. "He cursed me because I could have ruined their protection racket."

"I think so," Merlin agreed.

"So where is Giolladhe now?" Elan asked. He looked agitated, as if he wanted to go searching for him right then.

"He hasn't been seen since after Excalibur was made. It was one of his final works," Merlin said.

"He had to flee," Tom said, recalling his earlier conversation. "The djinn said the amulet he made for the sylphs didn't confer protection – it drew the dragons to the Realm of Air, and eventually, somehow, they found out."

Merlin nodded. "That's true. I've been looking into the history of the Hollow in one of Raghnall's many books, and it seems he disappeared at the same time the sylphs discovered his deception. I think Raghnall blamed him completely to save his own skin, and Giolladhe had to run."

Beansprout tapped the scroll. "What if whatever this thing is in the spell, doesn't exist any more? You know, like an extinct plant, or something."

Rahal had been quiet for a while, carefully reading through a large black leather-bound book, and now her head shot up. "I've found it!"

"You have?" Beansprout asked, craning to read the passage.

Rahal groaned and covered her face with her hands. "*Arach Frasan Fuil* means Dragon Blood Jasper."

Nimue looked alarmed. "Are you sure it's not just Blood Jasper?"

Rahal looked up at Nimue, her eyes wide. "No, it's definitely Dragon Blood Jasper – that's what *Arach* is."

Nimue had gone white. "I've never heard it called that before." She looked at Merlin as if he could produce one from under his robe. "I know I haven't got one. Where in the Realm can we get one from? In time for tomorrow!"

"Slow down," Arthur said. "We are surrounded by markets selling gemstones. Why can't we just buy one?"

"Because Dragon Blood Jasper is found in one place only – in the skull of a baby dragon," Rahal said. "And we need that too."

"That's disgusting! What exactly are we supposed to do with it?" Arthur asked. He was leaning over the table, gripping the edges, his knuckles white.

Rahal read from the spell: "Take *Arach Frasan Fuil* and add whole to the potion exactly four hours after the brew has started. The following line says we are to grind the anchor to powder." She looked up. "The anchor *must* be the bone."

"This just gets worse," Nimue said, leaning back in her chair.

Tom interrupted, confused. "We're in Dragon's Hollow. Dragon central in fact. Surely a baby dragon's skull is easy to find?"

"Dragons guard their young more fiercely than their gold. How easily do you think you could get one, Tom?" Nimue asked, fixing him with her piercing stare.

"I didn't think of that," he said sheepishly.

"And that potion needs cooking time," Merlin said. "We need it in the next six to eight hours. I need to start the potion tonight." He grabbed the spell from her, and pointed out the line. "This refers to a potion that needs twenty-four hours brewing. We need to start this by eleven o'clock tonight latest."

"Oh, great Goddess. I thought we had a little more time," Nimue said, her calm demeanour shattered.

"Do we need anything else?" Brenna asked.

"I'm pretty sure we have everything else we need. Maybe more Wolfsbane?" Nimue said, checking her list.

Tom noticed Filtiarn had fallen silent, watching them debating back and forward. He had screwed his napkin up in his palm, and squeezed it again and again, wringing it out until it looked like a piece of rag.

"Maybe we need to search the passage again?" Woodsmoke suggested. "Although that could take days."

"I'm leaving you to worry about that," Merlin said, rising to his feet and rolling up the scroll in one swift movement. "We're going to the spell room up on the roof. We need to start assembling the ingredients now, and start the brew in …" He looked at the clock ticking on the wall – it was already nine o'clock. "Two hours. We need to weigh, grind, and prepare."

"So we have until three in the morning to get the Dragon Blood Jasper – and skull," Arthur said, jumping to his feet and starting to pace up and down. "Great. Just great."

"I'll help," Brenna said to Merlin. "I'll be your runner, for anything you may need."

Bloodmoon stood suddenly. "I have an idea. I'm heading into the Hollow. Anyone coming?"

"To do what?" Arthur asked, intrigued.

"Find the stone and skull of course," he answered with a grin.

Tom realised his whirling thoughts wouldn't settle for a few hours, and the thought of walking through the city at night excited him. "I'll come."

"Well I'm not leaving you with Bloodmoon. Herne knows what you'd get up to," Woodsmoke said, his tone mildly appalled, but clearly eager to be out of the spell-making.

"Great," Bloodmoon said. "Strength in numbers. And Arthur, we need you."

Arthur looked torn between helping Merlin and going with Bloodmoon. "Why?"

"You're the money. Bring lots of cash."

"I'm coming too," Elan said. He placed his hands over Filtiarn's, stopping their constant wringing. "We are going to do this. I promise you."

30 Smuggler's Retreat

The central streets of Dragon's Hollow were crowded with all manner of fey enjoying the cool evening air and entertainment. Jugglers and acrobats were performing under the Wolf Moon on the lakeside; huge spherical lanterns made of paper and metals that imitated the Wolf Moon, hung along the streets and by the water. They glowed yellow and orange and were etched with the snarling faces of wolves. The dragon fountain loomed above everything, and water shot from its mouth, frothing across the lake.

The Wolf Moon was almost full, and it looked enormous as it hung over the city, casting a malevolent eye over the activities. Tom felt the expectations of the next night weighing on him.

Bloodmoon walked ahead with Woodsmoke and Arthur, navigating through the crowds with a certain assurance. Every now and then he nodded at someone he knew – it was clear he was well travelled. Woodsmoke and Arthur kept up an easy stride next to him, glancing back occasionally to check Tom and Elan were still behind.

Tom pointed to where the water ruffled and something moved on the surface. "What's that in the lake?"

Elan dragged himself out of his reverie. "Mermaid, probably. Although I think they prefer salt water. May be a nymph?"

"That's so cool! I can't believe you're not looking at everything – this place is amazing!"

"Sorry, I'm distracted. We have twenty-four hours, and we haven't got everything we need." He slumped against a balustrade and looked over the lake, despondent.

"We'll do it. I know we will," Tom said, wishing he was as convinced as he sounded. "I can understand why you attacked me now – you know, at the tournament."

Elan fidgeted with his leather jacket. "I'm sorry. I was feeling pretty desperate. Stupid, I know. I wasn't thinking clearly. Like that would have solved anything."

"People do stupid things when they're desperate," Tom said, thinking of Nimue and her curse on Merlin. Although Nimue's act was a very calculated one.

Elan finally looked at Tom. "I'm worried that either we can't break the curse, and that would be devastating, or that the curse will shift to me."

Tom felt a knot form in the pit of his stomach. "Why do you think it would shift to you?"

Elan shrugged. "I don't know. But I just feel it can't be that easy."

Tom spluttered. "Easy? How is this easy? It's taken thousands of years just to get this far. And we haven't even broken it yet!"

"All right, not easy. But you know what I mean? Assemble the ingredients, and break the spell."

Tom was now frustrated. "But everything was hidden! It's only through luck and hard work that we've got this far. Stumbling into the Realm of Fire wasn't easy – I was nearly destroyed in a lava flow."

Elan sighed. "I'm not explaining this very well."

"You're just worried, understandably. It's weird to think something that's been hanging over your family could be over in a day."

Elan nodded. "You're probably right. We'd better go, before we lose the others." He headed back into the crowd. Tom hurried after him, remembering what Woodsmoke had said about a twist still to come. He hoped they were both wrong.

They caught sight of Bloodmoon and the others just as Bloodmoon turned down a side-street. It was narrow and winding and led back behind the markets, past a few small shops. Then they turned to the left and disappeared under a sign that read, "Smuggler's Retreat." Tom and Elan followed them down a flight of steps and pushed open a heavy wooden door, entering a low-ceilinged room – or rather, a cave. In fact several caves, all connected, shadowy in the low light. Smoke filled the air and the sound of music drifted from another room.

Bloodmoon stood at the bar, drink already in hand, while Arthur and Woodsmoke admired the enormous range of beverages. Tom had never before seen so many different colours and styles of bottles. There was wine, beer and spirits, and half a dozen hand pumps lined up with names in front of them.

"So what's your poison, Tom?" Bloodmoon said, grinning.

One caught his eye – Nymph's Nectar. "A pint of that, please."

"Good choice," Arthur said. "I'll join you."

Nymph's Nectar turned out to be a caramel-coloured beer, rich and sweet and malty. Tom sipped it appreciatively.

"Nothing like a good beer to clear the head," Woodsmoke said, as they settled themselves onto stools around a small round table in the corner. "This was a good idea, Bloodmoon, but aren't we supposed to be finding the stone?"

Bloodmoon seemed completely at home, looking animated and relaxed at the same time. "It is possible to combine business with pleasure, you know!"

"So who are we looking for?" Arthur asked, leaning back against the wall and surveying the room. "With a name like Smuggler's Retreat, this place must be about more than a great choice of beer."

"This is *the* best place for information on interesting goods," Bloodmoon said. "Many years ago it was used to store all sorts of things – gold, gems, weapons, art – all making their way out of the Hollow by slightly underhand means."

"And it still seems to have an unsavoury atmosphere," Woodsmoke added, although he didn't seem the least bit perturbed. "It worries me that you know this place exists."

"Well –" Bloodmoon started, but Woodsmoke stopped him with a shake of the head. "I don't want to know."

Woodsmoke was right about the atmosphere. Tom glanced around the room, trying not to stare, but there were some very interesting characters. A group of satyrs were talking loudly over a table full of glasses, the discussion becoming heated, and there were numerous shifty looking fey hunched over tables, deep in conversation, avoiding eye contact with anyone else as they exchanged packages and money. There were goblins, a couple of sprites, and even some sylphs, who looked huge in the low-ceilinged cave. There was a tenseness in the air that Tom hadn't noticed when he first came in, but he noticed it now and felt increasingly uncomfortable.

"Is this safe?" Elan asked in a low voice.

"Of course," Bloodmoon said breezily. "And we're all armed, aren't we?"

"That's not really reassuring me," Tom said.

"Anyway, I had a quiet word with the barman when we came in, and the fey we need to speak to is over there." He nodded towards the next cave, linked to theirs by an archway. "He deals with rare artefacts and interesting esoteric items. Are we ready if I go and fetch him?"

"Ready for what?" Tom asked, confused.

"Negotiation." He looked directly at each of them. "Leave the talking to me."

Woodsmoke and Arthur exchanged a long glance as Bloodmoon headed off, returning a few minutes later with a small immaculately dressed fey who reminded Tom of a car salesman. He was dressed in a black velvet jacket, slim trousers, highly polished boots, and a dark blue linen shirt with embroidered cuffs and ornate cufflinks.

He took a seat and looked expectantly at the others. "Good evening. I understand you need my assistance." He placed a glass of what looked like port on the table in front of him.

Bloodmoon slid back into his seat. "Carac, your reputation precedes you. May I say how much I admire your work."

Carac nodded, looking smug. His little finger was raised as he sipped his drink. "So does yours, Bloodmoon. I have followed your career with interest."

Bloodmoon smiled and lowered his voice. "We are looking for an *Arach Frasan Fuil*, complete with its anchor, and we believe you are the man to find one for us."

Carac's feline grin disappeared. "If you know what that is, you'll know what you ask is impossible." He started to rise as if to walk off.

Bloodmoon leant forward, hand on Carac's drink, and said in a low voice, "I know what it is, and I know you can get one. Money is not a problem."

The fey narrowed his eyes at Bloodmoon and sat down again. "The object you speak of is extremely rare. And very expensive."

"But you have one?" Bloodmoon stared at him, refusing to look away.

"No. But I know someone who has." Carac stared back at Bloodmoon, ignoring everyone else at the table, and Tom felt his breath become shallow.

"Here in the Hollow?"

"Maybe. But he won't give it up."

"Who has it?"

Carac hesitated. "He would not like strangers to know."

Bloodmoon leaned forward until he was inches from Carac's face. "I. Don't. Care."

"He won't sell it to you," the fey persisted.

"That's not for you to worry about."

"And what will I get out of this?"

Bloodmoon named a sum that had Tom almost choking – Arthur too, judging by the look on his face. "And our silence of course – your name shall not be mentioned. And this conversation never happened." He raised a quizzical brow at Carac.

Carac took only seconds to decide. "Your offer is generous." He dropped his voice to a whisper. "The most royal councilman, head of the city council, Finbhar of the House of the Fireblade."

Even Tom had heard of him. Finbhar owned a palatial building on the opposite side of town to the House of the Beloved. It was a vision of white marble, pink granite, and silver inlay. He remembered meeting him at Raghnall's funeral. He had long blue hair and small neat beard.

Bloodmoon sat back in his chair, looking thoughtful. "Tricky."

Carac grinned unpleasantly. "Very. My money, please."

Arthur reached into his cloak and pulled out a small leather bag. He checked the contents under the table, and removing only a few gold coins, slid it across to Carac.

With a nod the fey grabbed the bag and tucked it into this jacket. "Have an excellent evening gentlemen," he said, leaving them.

Arthur exploded. "Great Herne! Did you have to offer so much? I haven't got enough cash to buy the damn thing now."

"Arthur," Bloodmoon said quietly. "We aren't going to buy it. We're going to steal it."

31 An Audacious Plan

They stood in the shadow of a large tree close to Finbhar's house. The mansion loomed above them, its white marble a dull yellow under the Wolf Moon. It was now midnight, and they had three hours in which to get the skull and take it to Nimue and Merlin, and for them to prepare the potion.

"We shouldn't have stayed so long in the bar," Arthur said, looking anxiously at the house. A single light burned steadily on the top floor.

"If we'd come any sooner, the whole house would have been awake," Bloodmoon said.

"It's still lit up," Tom pointed out. The paths, trees and bushes were prettily illuminated by garden lights, making their approach difficult.

"I'm not proposing we walk up the path," Bloodmoon said, a look of incredulity on his face. "Have you never broken in somewhere before?"

"No, actually! I'm not a delinquent," Tom said. "You get arrested for that sort of thing where I come from."

"You get arrested here too," Woodsmoke pointed out crossly. "I can't believe we're actually considering this."

"Have you a better suggestion?" Bloodmoon asked.

"Yes. Ask him to sell it!"

"But if he says no, which he will, we're stuck."

"You don't know he'll refuse."

"Those things are hard to come by, and he's a collector. I know the type, trust me. He won't sell," Bloodmoon insisted.

Elan interrupted. "I'll do it. It's for my relative, after all."

"No!" Bloodmoon, Woodsmoke and Arthur said at the same time.

"Obviously I will do it," Bloodmoon continued. "I'm good at this. You will be my lookouts."

"You'll need someone in the grounds," Woodsmoke said. "As much as I hate this, I'll come with you."

Arthur tried to disagree, but Woodsmoke stopped him. "I'm much quieter than you. You'll have to get us out of trouble if anything happens."

"He's right," Tom said, wishing he had Woodsmoke's skills. "He's nearly invisible when he wants to be."

"Excellent," Bloodmoon said. "Let's find a way in. If someone's coming, give three owl hoots, and make sure it's close enough to the house for us to hear once we're inside." He took a small strip of leather from around his wrist and tied his hair back with it. His cocky sureness had been replaced with serious intent. "Elan, you stay here and watch the approach from the street. Arthur, there's another large tree further along. You stay there in case someone comes from the other direction. Tom, come with us."

Woodsmoke protested. "Why is Tom coming with us?"

"We need someone just inside the grounds with a clear view of the house. And he's smaller than Arthur. Tom, if you see lights going on in the house, three short hoots too."

It was fortunate, Tom thought as they edged up the street in the shadows, that this road was so exclusive. The houses all had large grounds, so none were close to the councillor's, which meant less foot traffic.

A low stone wall enclosed a hedge of thick shrubs and trees on the garden's perimeter. Bloodmoon paused where a large tree leaned over the wall, casting the path in shadow.

"I'll try here," he said, "and if it's clear I'll whistle once."

He vaulted the wall with ease and disappeared through the hedge.

For a few seconds they heard nothing, and Tom's heart pounded in his chest. He looked up and down the street, but nothing moved except for leaves trembling in the light breeze. Then they heard a whistle.

Woodsmoke offered a last word of advice. "Don't put yourself in danger, Tom. I want you to run and leave us there if anything happens." He then disappeared over the wall, and Tom followed, fighting his way through the hedge, getting scratched and slapped by leaves and whippy branches. Feeling like he'd made huge amounts of noise, he finally broke free and stood in the grounds next to the others.

A beautifully manicured lawn stretched ahead of them to the house, broken only by flower beds and shrubs, and a large pool covered in water lilies. The house was surrounded by a deep veranda, on both the ground floor and first floor. It was idyllic and silent except for the tinkling of running water.

"It's huge," Tom whispered. "How are you going to find it?"

"I have made discreet enquiries," Bloodmoon whispered back. "His collection is on the first floor at the back of the house. I don't just sit and drink, you know. There." He pointed to the left side of the house, where a small waterfall cascaded down a bank into a shallow pool. It was in shadow, blocked from the Wolf Moon by the bulk of the house. A stream meandered from here into the larger pool.

"Woodsmoke, follow me."

Tom watched them run around the perimeter, disappear for a few seconds, then reappear on the other side of the small pool, close to an ornate bridge. In a blink they had gone again, then Tom spotted them under the veranda. If he hadn't known where to look, he would never have seen them.

He looked nervously across the grounds. Nothing stirred. He looked back and saw a shadow move on the first floor veranda, and a door open. He presumed Bloodmoon was now in the house. He couldn't see Woodsmoke at all. And then he heard three hoots. *Crap.*

His heart started racing and he repeated the hoots, wondering who was coming as he heard the signal repeated low and soft on the balcony. A few seconds later he heard the rattle of hooves on the road, and the sound of a carriage. With luck they'd be passing. They came closer and closer, and then the worst thing happened. The carriage rolled up the driveway and made its way sedately to the front of the house. A light sprang on in the entrance and the door opened, illuminating the front steps. Tom stepped further back into the hedge, wishing it would swallow him up.

A servant helped a tall fey and a woman out of the carriage. As they walked up the steps and into the light, Tom saw the blue hair of the councilman. The woman must be his wife. She turned towards Finbhar and laughed, the light illuminating her beautiful face and dark hair. They must have been to a party – both were wearing elegant evening dress. The door shut behind them and the carriage trundled around to the back of the house, where Tom presumed the stables were located.

Tom looked back to the veranda, but there was no movement. Lights appeared in one of the ground floor rooms, and then another on the second floor. Tom gave three more short hoots. They sounded shrill in his ears. Again the signal was repeated, low from the veranda. And then came three short hoots from the road, urgent this time, and another rumble of wheels as two carriages rolled into the grounds. Herne's horns! They were having a party. This couldn't be happening. The front door flew open again and laughter drifted across the grounds as the fey exited their carriages and entered the house in high spirits.

Tom's heart was now pounding in his chest and he willed Bloodmoon to get on with it. He wondered whether to leave, but didn't move – he had to make sure they were coming. Then he saw a light flare on the first floor, and hooted again, feeling conspicuous and uncomfortably hot. A stiff breeze rustled through the trees and then the entire house fell into shadow. Tom looked up. Thick black clouds had passed across the moon, and a rumble of thunder reverberated for several seconds. This at least was in their favour.

Tom watched the veranda. After a few minutes he finally saw movement, then shadows were racing across the grounds towards him. For a horrible second Tom thought they were dogs, and stepped further back into the trees, but then the shapes materialised into Woodsmoke and Bloodmoon.

"Get out, now," Bloodmoon said, pushing Tom ahead of him.

As Tom was scrambling over the wall, he heard a howl and a shout and raised voices. He almost fell onto the road, where Elan and Arthur pulled him to his feet as Bloodmoon and Woodmoke landed with enviable grace.

"This way," Arthur said, setting off at a run.

They raced down the street, fortunately now in complete darkness. Thunder rumbled again, covering up the sound of their footsteps. Arthur headed down a side street, and they didn't stop running until they reached a main street leading to the lake, where they slowed to a stroll. Here late revellers laughed and talked, and they mingled in the thinning crowds, nodding in greeting as they passed, as if they hadn't just robbed one of the most important fey in the Hollow.

Bloodmoon glanced behind. "That was close."

"Have you got it?" Elan asked

"Of course. Never doubt a master."

32 The Spell

As they reached the House of the Beloved, the wind grew stronger, buffeting their cloaks around them. They headed up the stairs until they reached the spell room that looked out onto the roof through a wall of glass windows and doors. This was Nimue's doing. Raghnall's spell room had been in the centre of the house, but Nimue had brought all his spell books, and her own, into this room that reminded Tom of a conservatory.

Lining the back wall were shelves loaded with books and the usual jars and bottles of potions, herbs, bones, feathers, skins, gems and metals. Both outside and in were pots and troughs filled with herbs and other plants, and a long table ran down the middle of the room. In a fireplace, a small cauldron hung over a brightly blazing fire. Merlin sat next to it on a stool, patiently stirring whatever was in it. An unpleasant sickly-sweet smell filled the room.

Nimue, Rahal, Beansprout and Brenna were clustered around the table, chopping and preparing various ingredients. In the centre was the scroll, pinned at each corner.

"Well?" Nimue asked as they entered, her face etched with worry.

"My dear ladies, did you ever doubt me?" Bloodmoon said, producing the skull from his cloak with a flourish.

They grinned, and then whooped with relief. "Bloodmoon, you are quite amazing," Nimue said. "Where in the Realm did you get that?"

"We stole it," he said bluntly.

"You did what?" Beansprout said, eyes wide. She looked at Tom. "Did you help?"

"We all did. I was a lookout," he said, realising he had actually quite enjoyed it.

"And I had to go into the damn place after him!" Woodsmoke said indignantly.

"Another few minutes and we'd have all been on trial again," Arthur added. "You cut it fine, Bloodmoon."

"You should have seen what he had! That place was full of relics and all sorts of precious objects. I admit, I was distracted," he said sheepishly.

Brenna grinned. "You manage to sneak anything else out?"

"Of course not," Bloodmoon said slyly.

"Well, put it on the table," Nimue said.

Bloodmoon ceremoniously placed the skull under the lamplight where they could see it clearly. It was about the size of an adult human's, but with a long snout and jaw full of sharp teeth. The bone was old and dark brown in colour, but it still looked menacing. The thing that caught the eye was the green jewel in the centre of its forehead.

"So that's what all this fuss is about? It's actually quite cool," Tom said admiringly.

"Take a good long look, because we're about to smash it to pieces," Beansprout said, a small hammer in her hands.

"All of it?" Arthur asked, admiring it from all angles.

"It does seem a shame, doesn't it?" Rahal said, looking at it sadly. "I doubt any of us will ever see one of these again."

"That explains why I've spent a small fortune on it," Arthur muttered.

"We've been doing some reading about it while you've been gone," Beansprout said. "As we know, the dragon transforms after death into all sorts of metals and gems. But for a short time, a young dragon has a stone in the centre of the forehead – the Dragon Blood Jasper. This is only present for a few months, then it changes and becomes a regular skull. To have a baby dragon's skull is a great rarity; to have it with one of these in is even rarer. The stone is one of the greatest symbols of transformation. Youth to adulthood, naivety to wisdom, weakness to strength."

Nimue deftly leaned forward and prised the stone free with a small knife. "I'll take this."

"And the other ingredients of the spell?" Tom asked, curious.

"They all have properties necessary to aid transformation. Or in this case, banish it," Nimue said. "There are two spells on this scroll. One to cast the curse, one to end it. They're almost identical, apart from the incantation. And this skull."

Brenna picked up the skull, idly examining it. "The thing I really can't work out is, why have a spell to reverse it? Why not just curse Filtiarn forever?"

Merlin looked across from the fire. "I told you before. Power. It's a taunt. To know it exists and to constantly search for it, is psychological torture."

Brenna looked unconvinced.

"Where's Filtiarn?" Tom asked, realising he wasn't in the room.

"In bed. He's too tired for these late nights. And I think it's too depressing," Beansprout said. She reached across to

Brenna, taking the skull from her and placing it on a sheet of paper. She raised the hammer.

Bloodmoon turned away. "I can't watch. It's like burning money."

"My money at that," Arthur added with a glare.

Beansprout brought the hammer down on the skull with a sickening thud, and it cracked down the middle. At the same time an enormous rumble of thunder erupted overhead, shaking the room, and a flash of lightning illuminated the sky and the roof beyond the window. Within seconds heavy raindrops started to fall.

"I hope that's not a sign," Tom said, peering through the windows.

Nimue grinned at him. "Superstitious, Tom?"

"We're about to break a curse, this makes it very creepy," he reasoned. "And I happen to be carrying a cursed sword."

"The sword is not cursed, Tom," Arthur said. "It was magical aid, or something like that."

"Yes, something like that," Nimue said, with a note of impatience. "Please leave the magic to us."

Beansprout continued to smash the skull until it was in tiny pieces, and then she poured the pieces into a mortar and ground them with the pestle.

Merlin looked at his pocket watch. "Nearly time to add the skull. Measure it carefully, Nimue – we only need a thimbleful."

Bloodmoon was horrified. "Is that all? You've crushed that priceless artefact for a thimbleful?"

"All for a good cause," Beansprout said. "And besides, we'll keep it safe for other spells."

"Best it's gone, anyway," Rahal said. "The less evidence of your night-time activities the better, surely?" She looked at

Bloodmoon mischievously, and Tom was suddenly aware how pretty she was. Her dark red hair, snaking down her back and across her shoulders, seemed to glow in the firelight.

Bloodmoon seemed to think so too. He winked, and said, "Well thank you, milady, for thinking of me."

Merlin interrupted. "Come on, bring me the crushed bone, the boar's tusk and a dawnstar sapphire."

Nimue placed them carefully on the small table at his side, and the room stilled as everyone watched, Tom wondering if the dawnstar sapphire would cause a magical explosion. One by one Merlin added the ingredients, swirling the potion all the time. The smell of burnt hair filled the room and everyone coughed.

"Is it supposed to smell like that?" Tom asked, in between coughing. He opened the door onto the roof, and warm, muggy air flooded in, adding to the general soupiness of the atmosphere.

Merlin tutted, rubbing his hands across his face and down his long beard. "How do I know? I've never made this before. I am following the instructions to the letter, and now the liquid needs to reduce. The final addition will be the stone."

"Don't you grind the stone?" Arthur asked, watching the preparations with interest.

Nimue answered. "Apparently not. According to the spell it will just dissolve."

Merlin looked up, the lines on his face accentuated in the firelight, adding years to his already great age. "This will go on all night. I suggest you all go to bed. By the morning it will be done, and then it needs to rest all day. We must hope I have done it correctly."

33 After the Storm

Tom lay in bed listening to the rain lashing against the windows. It was mid-morning and he had slept fitfully, interrupted by the thunder and lightning, which had continued for hours. Now there was only the odd rumble in the distance. He hoped the rain would ease by tonight or they would get soaked, and he wasn't sure if cloud covering the Wolf Moon would affect the intensity of the spell. It was going to be a weird day.

Tom sat up and read the Gatherer's account again, ensuring they had missed nothing important. Tonight they would recreate that event. He pulled Galatine free of its scabbard and examined the fine engravings. It really was a beautiful sword, and he didn't want to give it up. It was his now, bound to him once it had been reactivated. He rubbed his hands across the djinns' eye opals, feeling their warmth. He'd heard no animals speak after that first time with the dragon – all he had was a subtle awareness of other creatures nearby. It seemed Galatine's ability to enhance communication with animals had not passed to him, and he felt a bit disappointed.

Shaking off his gloomy mood he dressed and went in search of the others, first trying the spell room. Despite the full-length windows, the room was dim. The fire had gone out, and a dark green liquid that Tom presumed was the potion sat on the table in a small glass flask with a stopper.

No-one was there, so shutting the door carefully behind him, Tom headed down to the kitchen where he found Beansprout, Brenna, Woodsmoke and Arthur sitting around the table, the remnants of breakfast in front of them.

"Morning," Tom said, heading over to the range, where covered dishes were being kept warm. "I'm starved."

"Morning, Tom," Arthur said, leaning back in his chair. "We're trying to decide what to do today."

Tom sat down next to him with a full plate of eggs, bacon and fried mushrooms, and a mug of coffee. "There's not much we can do, is there?" He looked around the table. "You all look very serious."

"Just worried," Beansprout said. "If it all goes wrong tonight, well …" She shrugged. "We'll have failed, won't we?"

He nodded and swallowed a mouthful of breakfast. "I was looking at that old diary this morning, just in case we missed something, but I couldn't see anything else. Where's Filtiarn?"

"I'm here," a deep voice said from behind him.

Everyone turned as Filtiarn entered the room, Rahal and Elan by his side, and a young white wolf pattering along beside him. "I've been told I need to build my strength, so I'm here for some breakfast." He looked better than he had in days, and his eyes had lost their wildness. With a shock Tom realised it was because Filtiarn was cheerful.

Arthur obviously agreed. "You look good, Filtiarn. Are you feeling better?"

He nodded and sat down, while Elan brought him a plate of food. "Having a good bed and lots of sleep has done wonders. And good food helps too," he said, tucking into his breakfast. Now that the lines on his face had softened and he was starting to fill out, Filtiarn was looking a lot more like the picture the Gatherer had drawn. "And Rahal tells me you have made the potion."

Rahal sat next to him. "We can't thank all of you enough. The support you've given us over the last few days has meant everything." Her eyes filled, and she brushed away a tear. "The strain of the last few months has been huge."

Arthur leaned forward and took her hand. "It is our pleasure, Rahal. I couldn't stand by, it is against my nature," he said earnestly.

"But we attacked you –" She faltered, looking down at the table.

"Not your finest moment," Woodsmoke said with a frown. "If you'd killed Jack or Fahey it would have been a different matter."

Arthur shot him a look of annoyance, but Woodsmoke stared back defiantly.

Beansprout intervened, shooting a comforting smile at Rahal and Elan. "Fortunately they're all right. Although it seems like a lifetime ago now."

"I'm so glad they're well. And I'm glad we're here now." Rahal smiled at all of them and Tom found himself smiling back. It was hard not to like Rahal and Elan. He wondered what would he have done in their situation.

Rahal pressed on. "In anticipation of success, we're taking Filtiarn into town to buy some clothes."

"Yes, I feel I should return my borrowed clothes," Filtiarn said. "And I'm curious to see how the Hollow looks now. It's certainly different to how I remember it."

"I admire your positive attitude," Arthur said. "Aren't you worried we'll fail?"

Filtiarn pushed his plate aside. "I have failed since I was cursed. This is the closest I have ever got. We have Galatine, the moonstone, the spell and the potion. I have to allow myself some hope today. I'm going to pretend it is already over, and this is the start of the rest of my life. After all, by tomorrow I could be cursed forever and I shall have to end the curse another way."

He spoke with such finality that Tom and everyone else knew exactly what he was talking about.

"I can't imagine you would kill yourself," Arthur said, looking at him with incredulity. "Not after enduring what you have for so long."

"But I always had hope." Filtiarn's expression was deadly serious. "After tonight there will be no hope if we fail. I refuse to live like this. In fact I can't. I think one last change will kill me. But *I* will choose how I die. Not Giolladhe."

If anyone hadn't understood the importance of their task before, they did now.

Arthur was insistent. "We will not fail. I will not accept defeat. I never have."

"You are fortunate, then. I hope that continues. For my sake as well as yours."

Tom asked a question that had been bothering him for some time. "Do you still talk to animals? I mean, can you hear them, understand them?"

Filtiarn looked at Tom curiously, and then patted the head of the wolf sitting next to him. "No. I hear only my wolves, my constant companions. The curse affected me in other ways. I cannot hear any other animal now. Why do you ask?"

"Now I'm carrying Galatine, and it's awake, I thought maybe I would hear something, but I can't." Tom was going to explain about the dragon, but that sounded too weird, so he kept it to himself.

"I can only presume it's because it was to enhance my own powers," said Filtiarn. "You have never had them, and therefore …" He shrugged, his meaning clear.

"So if we break the curse, your full powers will return?"

"Maybe, Tom. Maybe."

Tom was dreading asking his next question, and he knew Arthur didn't want him to. But he had to. "If you had the sword back, would that help?"

Filtiarn shook his head. "I do not want the sword. It is yours now. I do not even wish to look at it."

Tom nodded, relieved. He loved Galatine, despite its origins. After all, it had belonged to Gawain. And it made him feel closer to Arthur.

Woodsmoke gave Filtiarn the ghost of a smile. "Enjoy your day, Filtiarn. Leave the preparations to us." He turned to Tom. "You're helping me – we're going to finish the clearing and build the fire."

"I am?" Tom said, surprised. "But it's raining!"

Woodsmoke gestured towards the windows. "It's stopping. Besides, the Wolf Moon doesn't stop for the rain."

"Don't worry," Brenna said. "I'll come and help. I'd like to keep busy. It will take my mind off tonight."

"I'll be spending the day with Merlin and Nimue," Beansprout said, barely suppressing a grin. "More magic stuff."

"And then I suggest we rest," Arthur said. "It's going to be a long night."

34 Releasing the Beast

The path from the road to the sacred grove was lined with torches that spluttered and flared in the warm breeze. The rain had long since stopped, and now scudding clouds passed across the sky, occasionally blocking the Wolf Moon.

Tom looked up at the full yellow moon that blazed above them with a feral light, and again experienced a sinking in his stomach and a creep of dread he couldn't fully explain. The feeling had been growing all day, and Galatine seemed heavy at his side. He presumed the others felt the same – apart from Filtiarn, who had a bright air of anticipation.

Merlin, Nimue and Beansprout walked ahead with Filtiarn, and the rest followed. The dozen wolves that accompanied Filtiarn had gathered close, and they slipped through the trees on either side, like ghosts, their yellow eyes glinting like tiny beacons in the darkness. Tom had got used them, and found their presence oddly comforting.

Tom was carrying the moonstone. It was awkward and heavy, and it made his arms ache. Woodsmoke and Bloodmoon had wanted to help, but Tom had refused. He had found it, and he felt he had done little since, this was his contribution. He stopped and put it down for a few seconds, shaking his arms to return the blood flow.

Woodsmoke and Bloodmoon waited with him. "Are you sure you don't want me to carry that?" Woodsmoke asked.

"No, I'm fine," Tom repeated, slightly breathless.

"It was good of you to offer to return the sword," Woodsmoke said, his expression invisible in the darkness. "I know you didn't want to."

"No, I didn't, but it seemed right. I'm quite relieved." Tom gestured up the path, towards where Arthur walked with Rahal and Elan. "And besides, Arthur wants me to have it."

"Well, Arthur can't always get his own way," Woodsmoke said. His response reminded Tom of when Woodsmoke had disagreed with Arthur when they were searching for Nimue.

"It's just Arthur's way. He means well," Tom said, wanting to defend him.

Bloodmoon agreed with Woodsmoke. "He's a good man, but he's still a king in his head. You will always need to stand your ground with him, Tom. Old habits are hard to break."

Tom sighed. "I know, but it's OK." He bent to pick up the stone, to deflect further discussion. "We should get on."

When they arrived in the clearing, torches were flickering all around the perimeter, and the fire was burning in the centre, next to the altar stone.

Nimue called, "Put the moonstone on the altar stone please, Tom."

He struggled over, and placed the stone in the centre. "What about Galatine?"

Nimue looked to Merlin. He had unrolled the scroll and was squinting to read it under a torch held by Beansprout. "Merlin?"

He nodded. "Yes, place it in now, Tom."

Tom withdrew Galatine and carefully placed it in the moonstone. He immediately felt a tingle run along his arm and through his body, and at the same time a soft glow seemed to emanate from the centre of the stone, shining up along the blade.

Tom released it quickly, and stepped back.

"Are you all right?" Arthur asked.

"Fine, just nervous," Tom said, feeling bad for lying to Arthur.

Before he could ask anything else, Merlin marshalled them into position. "I want all of you standing well back, against the tree line. Only Filtiarn needs to be in the centre, next to us." He turned to Beansprout. "Stand next to Nimue."

Arthur looked worried. "Why do you need Beansprout?"

"There is power in three. And this is a powerful curse. And there's a line in here I don't fully understand. I'm worried about what it means."

Arthur looked aghast. "Is this a joke? We're about to perform the spell and you don't know what a line means?"

Merlin met his gaze evenly. "No. No-one understands it, not even Filtiarn. But we have to go ahead."

"But why does no-one understand it?" Arthur's voice was raised and impatient.

"Because it's an ancient document, and the language is archaic, as we've explained before." Merlin pointed behind him. "This is no time for arguments, Arthur. Now step back."

Arthur stood his ground and was about to speak again when Nimue interrupted. "Arthur. Step back. We need to begin."

Arthur glared at both of them and retreated to the edge of the grove, standing alone in a brooding silence.

Tom stood next to Elan, who had been quiet all evening and now looked pale and worried. "Are you all right?" Tom asked.

"Not really," he said. "I just want this to be over." He fixed his gaze on those in the centre and refused to say anything else.

Merlin started to speak, but it was in no language Tom could understand. Nimue handed Filtiarn the potion, and when Merlin nodded he drank it down in one long gulp. A shudder ran through him and he coughed. Merlin turned to face the altar stone and Galatine. Nimue and Beansprout joined Merlin's chanting, their voices rising on the air.

The Wolf Moon cleared overhead, filling the grove with a pallid yellow light. As the chanting continued the moon seemed to grow larger and larger until it was pressed over the grove like a gigantic eye. Tom looked up and gasped, not believing what he was seeing. This had to be an illusion. He felt dizzy, and he shook his head as if to clear his vision.

At another gesture from Merlin, Filtiarn stepped forward and grasped Galatine. Immediately a ball of light engulfed Filtiarn and shot up into the sky, straight at the Wolf Moon. Nimue, Beansprout and Merlin stepped back, but continued to chant loudly. Then Filtiarn flew backwards and landed on the ground, seemingly unconscious.

The sword, the stone and the moon remained connected in one blazing beam of light, and a shape rose from Filtiarn's body. The wolves howled around the grove, and Tom's skinned prickled all over. He was so tense he could barely breathe. And then the form rising from Filtiarn became clear. It was the shape of a boar, glowing red, and pulsing as if it had a life of its own. It stepped out of Filtiarn and onto the ground next to him, turning to where Tom and Elan stood.

It fixed its hollow eye sockets on them and charged across the clearing. Tom was vaguely aware of shouts all around him. He looked at Elan in shock. Was Elan right? Was the curse about to move to him?

Before Tom could do anything Elan had stepped in front of Tom as if to protect him, holding his arms wide as the boar rushed at him. But the form passed through him and on to Tom, its hollow eye sockets getting bigger and bigger, and then it was on him and in him, and he felt the strange sensation of something settling within his blood and bones and mind.

Tom fell to the floor wondering who was screaming, before realising it was him.

And then he passed out.

35 Possessed

Tom lay on his back staring at the Wolf Moon, which had now returned to its normal size. He ached all over and felt strange. People clustered at the edge of his vision, and he heard Arthur yelling, "This is your fault! I can't believe you have been so stupid!"

Merlin and Nimue replied, but he couldn't tell what they were saying.

Beansprout leaned over him. "Tom, Tom. Thank goodness. You're awake."

Woodsmoke was on his other side, leaning over him too. "Let's help you sit up, Tom."

Tom was dazed, but saw him exchange a worried look with Beansprout as he reached out to squeeze her hand. Woodsmoke put his arm under Tom's shoulders and sat him up.

Tom's vision swam for a few seconds and then everything focused. The fire still burned in the centre of the grove, and Galatine sat in the moonstone, the firelight flickering along the blade. He could even see the stones swirling lazily in the hilt. He could see Rahal sitting by Filtiarn who still lay prone, surrounded by the wolves who sat and whined, or lay next to him on the ground. But Elan sat at Tom's feet looking at him, ashen.

Arthur was standing arguing with Nimue and Merlin, Bloodmoon and Brenna either side of him, Bloodmoon with a restraining hand on Arthur's arm.

Tom looked beyond them into the trees and realised he could see further than normal. The night was less dense. He could see the shapes of leaves and bushes, the tiniest details that should be impossible for him to discern. And he could hear things in the undergrowth – the scuttle of small things, the presence of dryads who remained firmly out of sight, and birds ruffling feathers in their nests. He could smell things too. Everyone had a distinct scent. He turned to Beansprout. "You smell of blossom. It's pretty."

"Blossom?" She looked confused.

"And you smell of some sort of musk," he said to Woodsmoke. "And pine."

"Do I now?" Woodsmoke said, a worried look on his face.

"And I can smell Brenna. She smells of mountain air, with a hint of snow."

As if she'd heard her name, Brenna turned and saw him sitting up. She smiled, relief washing across her face, and prodded Arthur. "Arthur, he's awake."

Arthur broke off and raced over, dropping to his side. "Tom. How are you? Are you all right? Can you feel that … thing inside you?"

"I'm fine Arthur, slow down." Tom felt a weird calm settle over him, despite the knowledge that some kind of supernatural boar was inside him.

"You're not fine. You are far from fine," Arthur said crossly.

Woodsmoke cut him off, "Arthur, stop it. We don't need this right now."

Arthur glared at Woodsmoke. "What do you suggest?"

"Some rational thinking. And you can stop glaring, it won't work with me." Woodsmoke turned back to Tom. "Let's get you to your feet, shall we?"

Tom nodded, and with Beansprout's help, stood up on slightly shaky legs. Elan remained with him, silently watching.

Tom shook off their help. "I'm OK. I'll stretch my legs for a few minutes."

He took a few faltering steps, and quickly felt stronger, a rush of adrenalin coursing through him. He headed to Rahal's side. "How's Filtiarn?"

"Still unconscious," she said, looking up at him, her eyes bright with tears. "But his breathing's stable. I think he'll be all right."

"We should put him by the fire," Tom said. And without thinking he picked him up as if he was as light as a feather, and carried him to the fireside, throwing his cloak over him. Rahal and the wolves followed, settling around Filtiarn again.

"How did you do that?" Woodsmoke said from behind him.

Tom turned to find everyone watching him. "I don't know. I just did."

Elan spoke. "It's the boar, of course. It's given you extra strength."

Tom looked up at the Wolf Moon. He felt it was laughing at him, and the realisation hit him. "When will I turn?"

Nimue answered, her face drawn. "Two weeks, when the cycle ends, unless we can do something."

The arguing started again.

"We'll make another potion," Arthur said angrily.

"The curse is bound to Galatine," Merlin said. "Which is bound to Tom. To make it leave Tom, Galatine must be bound to someone else. It's a never-ending curse. I think that's what this phrase must mean."

"Oh! Now you know what it means!" Arthur spat. "Well done Merlin."

Beansprout started to cry. "Please don't, Arthur. Today is bad enough. It's my fault too."

Woodsmoke wrapped Beansprout in a hug, and she buried her face in his shoulder.

Arthur looked stricken. "No, I didn't mean …"

"All of you stop. Right now," Tom said. "This isn't helping."

Bloodmoon pulled a small flask from his pocket, removed the stopper and took a long drink. He passed it to Arthur. "We need to think this through. Let's sit."

Arthur looked as if he was going to argue again, but instead raised the flask to his lips.

Tom shot Bloodmoon a grateful look and threw more wood on the fire. He pulled Galatine free from the moonstone and sat on the Avalon stone, warming his feet.

"What do you want to do, Tom?" Bloodmoon asked, sitting on the ground next to Filtiarn and Rahal.

"Find Giolladhe. It seems to me that's my only way out of this."

"I agree. Where do we start?"

Tom smiled. He liked that Bloodmoon was letting him lead rather than telling him what to do. "Good question. There are four realms to find him in, and only two weeks in which to do so." He laughed dryly. "That's not so hard, right?"

"There are places he'll be known to have favoured. We can start there," Woodsmoke suggested. He had stopped comforting Beansprout and they both sat near the fire, passing another flask back and forth. The two of them were so comfortable together, it was as if something was unspoken between them. Woodsmoke looked at Beansprout in a different way to anyone else. Tom turned away, suddenly feeling he was spying on them.

The rest of his friends, realising there was little else they could now do, joined them around the fire, except for Brenna who sat next to Tom on the Avalon stone, nudging him gently along to make room. The moon had retreated to its normal place in the sky – if it had ever moved – and a pale yellow light illuminated the grove. It was an oddly comforting scene. Looking round at them all, Tom realised how much they meant to him. They weren't just his friends, they were his family. To lose them so soon was unthinkable.

"But first we should celebrate," Tom said, desperate to cheer himself and the others up. "For Filtiarn, it's over."

As he spoke Filtiarn blinked and stretched, and Rahal sighed with relief. She eased him upright. "Welcome back," she said, giving him a shy smile.

"I feel different," he said, sounding slightly incredulous. "I can't feel the beast any more."

The joy faded from Rahal's face. "No, it has left you, but moved elsewhere …" Her voice trailed off.

Filtiarn immediately looked at Elan, but he shook his head and nodded towards Tom.

"No. It can't be," he stammered. "How can this have happened?"

"It doesn't matter how," Tom said, reluctant to have the argument start again. "Did the beast make you stronger? You said you could feel it."

Filtiarn looked bewildered. "At first, but then it just ate at me, using my strength. Now it's gone, I feel lighter." He couldn't help grinning. "I can't believe it. You've done it. But the cost –"

"Forget it," Tom said, genuinely pleased to see Filtiarn looking so happy. "You've carried the burden enough. Enjoy your freedom, Filtiarn." Suddenly he knew where he needed to be. "I should rest, I'm going to bed." He stood, and when Woodsmoke went to stand too, said, "No. I want to be alone." He squeezed Woodsmoke's shoulder as he passed. "Goodnight everyone."

And he left the clearing, leaving them talking over his fate.

36 The Forger of Light

Tom didn't waste time sleeping, or even heading to the House of the Beloved. He was going to the Realm of Fire and the dragon.

The second he'd heard the dragon say "Galatine", something had triggered a warning in his head. He could hear it for a reason. It had recognised Galatine. Why would a dragon recognise Galatine unless it had seen the sword before? Unless it had made it.

He had no idea how Giolladhe had become a dragon, but he knew beyond doubt it was him.

Tom still couldn't understand animals, even now he was possessed by a supernatural boar, but he had inherited its strength, and its ability to hear and see far beyond normal human abilities, and this gave him an advantage. He aimed to make full use of that.

He passed down the path to the main road behind Raghnall's house, and then up on to the shoulder of the mountain, avoiding the short cut they had found on the other side of the grove. He had deliberately said nothing to the others. This was his fight, and he didn't want them helping. Even his closest friends. Every single one of them would have insisted on coming, but he didn't want them to. A dragon was deadly, and no-one else should risk their life for him. He wondered if this was the bravado of the boar.

He was worried that he wouldn't find the workshop in the night, but he shouldn't have doubted himself. The Wolf Moon gave him good light, and his eyesight and sense of smell quickly identified the path to him. Soon he stood in front of the copper doorway, looking black in the shadows. Tom opened it – it hadn't been locked – and passed down the passage and into the workshop. He didn't even need to light a lamp, his ability to see in the dark was so good. He carried on past the chimney looming huge in the centre of the room, and through the door at the back, until he reached the cupboard and the hidden portal.

He paused for the briefest of seconds, wondering if the lava had swallowed the room and he would be passing into a fiery death, and then stepped through anyway, arriving with a thump in Giolladhe's other workshop.

Tom felt the beast surging within him, straining against his physical dimensions, as if it couldn't wait to burst into its natural form. He breathed deeply in an effort to subdue it, almost choking on the smell of sulphur, and took his bearings.

The lava pit still bubbled in the centre of the room, the blackened pools around it showing where it had overflowed, but the floor was otherwise undamaged and he could walk over it. He sighed with relief. So far, so good. But best of all, a huge hole had reappeared in the collapsed rock wall, high up towards the roof. The rumbling eruptions must have dislodged the rock. Either that or the djinn had made it.

He scrambled up the rock wall with ease, and looked through to find the other half of the cave deserted. He slid to the floor, kicking up dust as he went, and stood at the entrance to the cavern beyond. In front of him was a scene of chaos. The rivers of lava that had punched through the walls and windows had widened, and they fizzed and hissed as they wound sinuously around fallen lumps of stone, leaving islands of untouched floor in their wake. There was no sign of the dragon or the djinn. His heightened hearing detected a slither of movement in the city beyond, but whether it was lava or dragon, he couldn't tell.

Negotiating the path out to the city was going to be more difficult than it had been days earlier; his jumps needed to be longer and higher. It meant testing his new-found strength. Oh well, better to test it here first than wait until he met the dragon.

Finding the closest place to leap to, he took a deep breath and a running jump. His legs flexed beneath him and he covered the space with ease, shocked at how far he travelled, almost overshooting the island and landing in the lava on the other side. He stopped just in time, perfectly balanced. Wow. That was intense.

Sweat was already beading on his face and down his neck. He could clearly see his path through to the arched entrance and the city beyond, so he pushed on, leaping from island to island and stone to stone, until he landed safely on the other side. He looked back, wondering how he would ever return to the portal if he killed Giolladhe, because his super strength would have gone. He shook the thought out of his head. Too much to do before then.

The shadowy half-collapsed passageways stretched away on either side, and he listened, detecting a slither away to the right. Beneath the smell of dust and sulphur he detected something earthy, a strong musky odour.

Dragon.

He followed the sound and smell along passages he hadn't seen before. The tunnels here were bigger – this must be why the dragon was in this part of the city.

Every now and again he stopped and listened and adjusted his path, crossing collapsed rooms barely lit by smouldering trickles of lava. It was a labyrinth.

And then Tom heard the slow hiss and slither of dragon, but much closer this time. A movement to his left made him spin around and he saw a mammoth wall of flame hurtling towards him. He rolled out of the way into the nearest room, and flattened himself against a wall. A huge roar echoed down the passage, chilling his blood.

Enormous footfalls thudded down the passage, and Tom looked frantically for his best way out. His most effective form of attack would be to circle around behind it, but that was impossible from here. The only way was forward. He ran to a gap in the collapsed wall and passed through to the next room. Another jet of flame followed him, and another roar. He flattened himself along the floor, breathing heavily. He hadn't even seen it yet.

The dragon laughed and then spoke, its voice deep and gravelly. "I know you're there, boy. I sense Galatine. It has been many years since I have seen it."

Tom jumped to his feet and ran into the next room, looking for a way to circle back. He shouted, "Are you Giolladhe? Hiding here beneath the desert like a worm?"

The thump and rumble of dragon's feet stopped. "How do you know my name?"

"Because it's my business to know it," Tom yelled, trying to gauge where the dragon was. He stood at the entrance to the main passage and saw another room opposite. "Any reason you're trying to kill me? Wouldn't you like to chat first? Catch up on old news, find out why I'm carrying Galatine?"

The dragon's voice echoed around him. "If you're carrying Galatine, you're here to kill me. How did you find it?" he growled. "I sent it far from here."

Tom took advantage of the break in fire, and ran across the passage into the room beyond, cursing as another jet of flame followed him. He had to keep the dragon talking while he tried to find a way to attack.

"Your friend Raghnall had it in his weapons collection," he yelled back, running into another room.

The dragon roared, "He is no friend of mine."

"Then you'll be glad to know that we killed him. And then we met your brother!" Tom yelled back, curious to see how that would provoke Giolladhe."

The dragon fell silent, and all Tom could hear was the thumping of his own heart. "Is that a surprise? That he still lives? We've saved him from your curse."

At this Giolladhe laughed, deep and guttural. "So then *you* are cursed, boy. Now I know why you are here and not Filtiarn. You should run, for I am stronger than you."

The rumble of feet headed towards Tom and he darted through another room, finally spotting a door that would allow him to circle back. He scrambled through fallen masonry and caught a glimpse of the dragon through a gap in the wall. It was the colour of sulphur, with deep red flashes of colour along its scales and wing tips. As yet he couldn't see its head. Without hesitation he ran forward, dived through the gap and stabbed Galatine deep into its side.

The dragon howled and roared and whipped around, throwing Tom against the wall, masonry and sand falling as the dragon struggled to manoeuvre in such a small space. Tom scrambled free and ran back along the passage, diving into the first available doorway.

He waited for the sound of falling stone and sand to stop, hoping the entire city wouldn't fall on his head before he killed Giolladhe and got out. Spying a gap at the top of the wall, he scrambled up to look through to the passage beyond, planning to leap onto the dragon's back, but it had disappeared.

Tom saw a flicker of dragon tail heading into a room further along. He leapt down and ran towards it, following Giolladhe into a much larger space with a domed ceiling and beams running under it. Now he could see him fully, his nerve almost failed. Giolladhe had turned to face him, and he was huge, his head bristling with sharp spiky scales, his eyes red and burning. He flexed his wings, smacking them off the walls. Lowering his head, he opened his mouth, giving a glimpse of razor-sharp teeth before spitting a wall of flame.

Tom dived out of the way, and taking advantage of the ruptured walls, scrambled upwards, grabbing a beam above his head and pulling himself onto it. He raced along until he was above the dragon and out of his line of fire. He was just about to leap onto the dragon's spiny back when a swirl of dust and sand rose in front of him and the djinn appeared, settling on one of the beams.

"You need to stop, boy," the djinn said, looking regretful.

Beneath him, Giolladhe roared, flexing his wings as he tried to turn and look upwards.

"Why?" Tom demanded, frustrated he would miss his chance.

"Because I can't let you kill him."

"Well that's just tough, because I *have* to kill him. He's cursed my sword, and now me." Tom launched himself onto the dragon's back, bringing Galatine down with enormous force, puncturing the dragon's wing and piercing his thick scaly skin with a satisfying crunch. As it flexed and howled, Tom fell off, slithering to the ground, where the edge of a wing caught him, throwing him across the floor. He rolled to his feet and found the djinn in front of him. He picked Tom up and flung him across the room and into the wall, where he landed with a crash.

Adrenalin surged through Tom, dulling the pain. He staggered to his feet, furious. "What are you doing?"

"If you want to kill the dragon, you have to kill me first."

Tom pointed Galatine at the djinn. "Why in the Realms do you want to keep that thing alive?"

"Because it was us – the djinn – who turned him into this creature, as a punishment for many transgressions. It is my job to keep him alive so that he suffers here forever. I will not let you kill him and relieve him of that torture."

Tom couldn't believe it. "I hate to break it to you, but he seems pretty fine with being a dragon. He's not exactly letting me end his years of torture."

Giolladhe sent a blast of flame at the djinn, causing him to dissolve into sand and whirl across the floor. Tom ran headlong at the dragon and again plunged Galatine deep into his side, before ducking out of reach of his giant wings. Giolladhe's roar thundered around the room.

The djinn reappeared, lifting Tom up around the throat with his hideous long clawed hands, until he was at eye level and Tom's feet were dangling in the air. "If you don't stop, I will have to kill you."

"Then you'll have to kill me," Tom managed to say, struggling to speak. And before he knew what he was doing, Tom thrust his sword at the djinn, feeling the slight resistance of flesh, before the djinn turned into sand and dropped Tom to the floor.

Tom ran for the wall and bounded up, his feet easily finding footholds, and then leapt onto the beams overhead. He couldn't believe he was having to fight a djinn and a dragon. Fortunately it seemed the more he fought, the stronger he became, the wild power of the boar within him raging with strength.

The djinn reappeared, clutching his side, dark green blood leaking onto his clawed hands. "You struck me!" He was more puzzled than outraged.

"You won't stop me," Tom said, surprised by how calm he was feeling. He had never felt so determined. It was if he stood in the eye of a storm. "I don't want to hurt you, but I will if you don't walk away."

For a second the djinn hesitated. "You are not what you appear. You are too quick. Too strong."

"You better believe it."

Beneath them Giolladhe turned and twisted, furious at being attacked. Then he looked up, and was about to send a burst of flame at Tom when Tom dived over his head and landed on his back. Shocked at his own agility, he again plunged his sword through the scales and between the spines that ran along the dragon's back, feeling the crunch of bone. He pushed deeper as the dragon howled in pain, and Tom felt something snap as the dragon's neck flopped downwards.

If dragons had a spinal cord, Tom was pretty sure he'd just severed it. Galatine was buried up to its hilt in the dragon's back, and he wrenched it free then slid down the side of the dragon onto the floor. He glanced up at the djinn, but strangely the djinn didn't try to stop him; he just watched, green blood dripping down his side.

Tom circled to Giolladhe's head. The dragon was struggling to keep his eyes open. "What have you done to me?" he grunted, his guttural voice becoming more difficult to understand.

"What I had to do," Tom said, feeling regret at the situation he found himself in. "Filtiarn was your brother, Giolladhe. He trusted you. How could you do that to him?"

"Because he would have ruined everything."

Tom wanted to ask so many more questions, to try and understand, but he didn't think he ever would. And Giolladhe, even now, didn't seem to have an ounce of regret. Tom looked in wonder at the huge bulk of his body, the slow heave of his chest, the wings collapsed at his side, and felt an overwhelming sadness. He readied Galatine, raising it above his head.

"I'm about to release both of us, Giolladhe. You may not deserve it, but I know I do."

He brought his sword down and sliced through sinew and bone, taking off Giolladhe's head in one clean cut.

37 The Tale is Complete

Tom staggered back and sank to the floor, leaning against the wall. He was exhausted. He felt the beast within him struggle and thrash around, and then a supernatural mist oozed out of every pore.

As it left him, he felt incredibly weak; his muscles ached and his vision dimmed, making him aware of how powerful his night vision had been. Now all he could see was the big black bulk of the dragon, lit only by the palest fiery glow of lava.

But he had done it. He had lifted the curse. He laughed into the darkness, like a madman.

Now he just had to get out.

The djinn reappeared in front of him, still clutching his side. "You were possessed?" he asked, his eyes lit by the pale flames which burnt within him.

"Yes," Tom said, staggering to his feet. His legs trembled with weakness. "Ow. That really aches." He looked warily at the djinn. "Are you going to kill me now?"

"No, why would I do that?"

"Well I did stab you and ruin your life's mission," Tom said, trying to suppress the shake in his arm as he held Galatine.

"How many beings do you think have ever injured me?"

"I don't know. The dragon must have a few times."

"No-one except you." The djinn was looking at him curiously. "I'm impressed – even if you were possessed. I have never seen my own blood spilt before in battle. I do not like it."

"Lucky you," Tom said. "I've seen mine plenty of times – including now." He looked down at his arms and legs, which were covered in scratches and cuts.

The djinn laughed, although it sounded more like a growl. "We will both live."

"Will we? Because I'm not sure I'm going to get back to the portal," Tom said. If he could walk back down the pathways of the underground city, it would be a miracle.

"Come, my friend. I will help."

Before Tom could protest, the djinn picked him up and bounded down the corridors with loping grace, despite his injury. He leapt across fallen walls, chunks of stone and lava with ease, depositing Tom outside the portal door once more.

Tom felt dazed, and stood swaying, looking around the room at the remnants of equipment and tools, wondering what dark and strange magic Giolladhe would once have woven down here. He looked at the djinn. "Thank you. Where will you go now this is over?"

"Azkrill, the capital of our fair realm, far to the east, in the blazing deserts of Sansarkan. I will speak of Tom, the dragon slayer; slayer of Giolladhe, the Forger of Light, savour of Filtiarn, beast possessed, djinn-wounding warrior, bearer of Galatine."

Tom had to admit that sounded quite impressive. Maybe he should adopt it as his title. "And your name?"

"Valaal, Keeper of the Forger of Light."

Tom smiled, grateful for this crazy experience. "Good to meet you, Valaal." He gestured towards the workshop. "I guess this will be the last time I see this?"

"Yes. I will seal the portal once you have gone," Valaal said. "The whole city will collapse soon anyway, 'tis best no-one comes here again."

Tom felt strangely reluctant to go. "Maybe we will meet again one day."

"Maybe we will," Valaal said, a slow smile spreading across his face.

"Before I go, will you tell me a little bit more about Giolladhe and why he was turned into a dragon? I really want to know. Everything he did is so mysterious, and so long ago."

Valaal nodded. "All right. But my heart hurts to think of it."

And for a little while, Tom ignored the threat of death by lava, and listened to the djinn.

For a few seconds Tom thought he was stuck in the portal, the room beyond was so dark, and then he remembered he'd come here with no light to guide him. To his left a faint grey strip leaked into the room, revealing the edge of the doorway. Staggering to his feet, he stumbled through the central room and down the corridor to where the front door hung open, early morning sunshine blazing through.

He shielded his eyes, temporarily blinded by the light. He was halfway down the path when he heard a shout. "He's here!"

Woodsmoke ran towards him, closely followed by Beansprout. They both looked worried, and if Tom was honest, a bit distracted.

Woodsmoke crushed him in hug. "Where have you been?"

"And what have you been doing?" Beansprout said, looking shocked. "You're filthy! And covered in blood. Are you hurt?" She reached out and hugged him, regardless. "Great Herne, you stink. Again. And what's that weird green stuff on you?"

"Beansprout," Tom protested, "will you stop asking questions!"

Bloodmoon and Arthur rounded a corner, Bloodmoon looking quite cavalier and not the least bit worried, whereas Arthur was frowning. Bloodmoon grinned as he saw Tom, and then looked a little put out. "I smell sulphur. Someone's been hunting dragons. Could've let me know, Tom."

Arthur ran forward, pulling Tom into a hug, and then looked at him carefully. "Dragons? Don't be ridiculous, Bloodmoon. Are you all right, Tom? We've been searching for hours. This is the *last* place we thought we'd find you. Merlin and Nimue are in the passageways beneath the house."

"Where did you think I'd go?" Tom asked, incredulous.

"I honestly thought you'd gone to sulk, you know how you do sometimes," Beansprout said, sounding slightly sheepish at her accusation.

Tom was about to complain when, with a whirr of wings, Brenna landed next to them on the path. "Tom! I've been searching the forest. I'm so relieved …" She trailed off as she took in his appearance. "What have you been doing?"

Arthur ploughed on regardless. "We've been trying to figure out a plan to get rid of this curse." His voice was grumpy, now his relief at finding Tom had worn off. "You can't just go wandering off."

Tom was tired and starting to get annoyed. Did everyone really think he was so stupid? "I have been fighting a dragon, and getting rid of this curse. What do you think I've been doing?"

"Getting rid of the curse?" Arthur said, looking startled. "What do you mean?"

"I mean I've killed Giolladhe. I thought I would take matters into my own hands."

"You killed a dragon?" Beansprout said, admiration in her eyes. "Tom! You're amazing."

"Yes," he said smugly, "I am. And now I need a bath and a sleep."

Arthur looked put out. "You didn't tell *me* I was amazing when I killed a dragon."

"Oh, Arthur," Beansprout said. "You're always amazing, you know that."

Tom pushed through them all, trying to suppress a grin, but they followed him doggedly back to the house, asking question after question, until he reached the door of his room. "All of you, please, leave me in peace! I'll tell you later." And he shut his door with a big smile.

Hours later, after a bath and having slept most of the day, Tom headed down to the balcony and found the table glittering with candlelight, silverware and cut glass. The entire household was either gathered around the table, or reclining on chairs looking out over Dragon's Hollow.

Nimue rose to greet him. She was as dazzling as the silverware. Her dark hair cascaded over her shoulders, and she wore a deep green silk dress that matched her eyes. "Glad you're here, Tom. I gather I need to congratulate you." She stood on tiptoes and kissed his cheek. "I'm not sure whether you're crazy or brilliant."

Tom couldn't help blushing. "Brilliant, of course." He thought he'd try and cover his embarrassment through bluffing, and besides, he could see Woodsmoke smirking. Ignoring him, he said, "I'm sorry if I worried everyone. I just knew what I needed to do and got on with it. And I didn't want to risk anyone else getting hurt."

"Very noble of you," Merlin said, coming over to shake his hand. "If a little foolhardy."

Arthur frowned at Merlin, then pulled a chair out for Tom and pushed a drink into his hands. "Come, sit down, Tom. You're the guest of honour. We've cooked roast suckling pig especially for you."

"My favourite beer! And my favourite food! Wow, I am being spoiled," he said, laughing.

Brenna slid into the seat next to him. Her dark eyes looked huge in the candlelight, and the fine feathers around her hairline reflected the light, giving her a dark glow. She gave him a playful punch on his arm. "How did you know the dragon was Giolladhe?"

"Because it spoke to me, and it knew what Galatine was. Who else would know that?" He shrugged. "It bothered me when I was leaving the Realm of Fire the first time, but I was in such a rush to get back, I didn't really think about it. And then, last night, I just knew."

"So you found my brother," Filtiarn said. He looked solemn and sad, and not as relieved as Tom thought he would.

Tom met his eyes across the table, noting how old and frail he looked. After his initial jubilation at the curse being broken, he now looked like an old man again. "I did, and I'm sorry I had to kill him."

"You had to do it, Tom, or you would have suffered my fate, and I wouldn't wish that on anyone. I have lost my youth, my life, my love and my children, all for the possibility of my making peace with dragons." Filtiarn looked puzzled. "And you say he was a dragon, which seems fitting. How did that happen?"

"Valaal, the djinn, told me their magician had transformed him years ago when they found the depth of his betrayal of them. For years Giolladhe had a second workshop in the Realm of Fire. It was beneath the citadel on the edge of the city of Erfann – it's where the portal led – and he used the fire of the mountains to fuel his more complicated spells. But his experiments caused problems. The mountains of fire erupted, the dragons attacked, and eventually Erfann was destroyed – this was sometime after the dragons wars. Years later, after the sylphs found out Giolladhe had double-crossed them with his so-called gift of protection, he had to flee the Hollow, pretty much as we guessed. Raghnall had refused to stand by him and essentially blamed him for everything. The djinns offered him refuge in the Azkrill, their capital city. However, Giolladhe got up to his old tricks, betrayed people, double-crossed them, and eventually ended up endangering Azkrill, so they took him to Erfann where their magician transformed him, and Valaal was appointed his keeper. I felt really sorry for the djinn, and I liked Valaal. And that's as much as I know – if I've remembered it properly."

Filtiarn was silent for moment, and then took a long drink. "So much betrayal, so much greed. I feel like I never knew him."

"You never suspected?" Arthur asked.

"We were very different," Filtiarn admitted, "but I never suspected him of such deception. It makes me question everything. Every conversation, every interaction. But I wonder where all his wealth went? He lived in a cave. It was plain, unembellished."

"That is an excellent question," Bloodmoon said. "I must make enquiries."

Filtiarn looked at Tom with an almost pleading expression. "Did he say anything about me?"

"Not really," Tom said, "other than he did it to stop you ruining everything. I'm sorry."

Filtiarn pushed his plate away, falling silent, and Tom thought he should change the subject. He turned to Beansprout. "It was the djinn's blood on me earlier – the green stuff."

"You killed a djinn?" Beansprout said, looking both horrified and impressed.

"No! I injured it. It was trying to protect Giolladhe to prolong the punishment. Anyway, he forgave me, and now we're friends – sort of."

"You injured a djinn?" Bloodmoon asked, stopping eating in surprise.

"Yes. Accidentally."

"Not many can do that, Tom."

Tom swallowed a mouthful of delicious pork. "That's what he said, but it was only because that supernatural beast was in me. It gave me superpowers. It was very cool," he said, thoughtfully, wishing he could have kept the superpowers. "That's another reason I went there straightaway. I was strong and I knew it, and I didn't know how long it would last."

Elan interrupted. "It should have been me. Who was cursed, I mean." He had been quiet up until now, watching Tom and the others. He seemed very worried.

Tom looked at him, confused. "You mean you should have had the sword?"

"No, I mean as Filtiarn's relative. You shouldn't have had to suffer that."

"Elan, it wasn't your fault. I activated the sword, not you. It was just the way it was." Tom really loved Galatine, despite everything that had happened, and he knew Filtiarn didn't want it – but what if Elan did? What if he thought it was his birthright? "Do you want Galatine? If you do, it's yours." He pulled it free from its scabbard and placed it on the table. He had shined and polished it that afternoon, cleaning away every trace of blood and flesh.

Arthur frowned and said, "Tom!" at exactly the same time as Filtiarn said, "Elan!"

Tom stopped them both with a calm look. "It's OK."

They watched as Elan picked up the sword and ran his hands along it, the swirling opals quickening at his touch. And then he looked at Tom and smiled. "No, it yours. You've earned it. But thanks for asking."

Tom grinned. "Thanks for not having it. I *really* like that sword." And he put it back in its scabbard.

Woodsmoke gave Tom the ghost of a smile, and then turned to Filtiarn, Rahal and Elan. "So what now?"

"Now we go home," Rahal said, glancing at Filtiarn. "Our family will want to see Filtiarn. I suppose we'll have a celebration."

"And I suppose I will die very soon after that," Filtiarn said, staring into his drink.

"What?" Tom said, almost choking.

Everyone stopped eating and looked at Filtiarn.

"I am dying. I know I am. Ever since the curse has broken I feel my vast age pouring back into me. The beast has taken its toll. I want to make it home, spend my last days there overlooking the ocean, remembering better days. And then you can bury me in the family tomb, next to my love." He directed this last statement to Rahal and Elan.

"But I wanted you to have many happy years yet," Rahal said, her eyes starting to fill with tears.

He patted her hands. "My dear, you have nothing to feel sorry for." He turned to the others and raised his glass. "But tonight we celebrate, because the curse is over."

There was a resounding clinking of glass and calls of congratulations, and then Nimue turned to Arthur. "And what about you? I suppose you'll be returning to New Camelot?"

"Of course, with Merlin, Tom and Woodsmoke."

They nodded in agreement.

"What about you, Bloodmoon?"

"I'll join Filtiarn in their ride across the moors," he said, looking at Rahal rather than Filtiarn. Tom grinned and Rahal blushed. "And then, who knows? I'll go where the adventure takes me."

"As long as it's not into trouble," Woodsmoke said. "I don't want to have to break you out of prison."

"It's good to know that you would, should I ever need it," Bloodmoon said in all seriousness, leaving Woodsmoke gaping at him.

"I will journey to New Camelot with you, and then return to Aeriken," Brenna said with a sigh. "There is talk of a coronation."

"Really?" Beansprout said, excited. "You've finally agreed?"

Brenna shrugged. "Sort of. As long as you all come for the ceremony."

A chorus of agreement ran around the table, and everyone looked excited except Arthur, who seemed a little worried. "You shouldn't do it unless you're absolutely sure. It's a lot of work, you know."

"I'm already doing the work, I may as well just go ahead. It will make the Aeriken happy." She glanced around the table and wagged an admonishing finger. "But don't you dare leave me out of anything!"

"Or me!" Beansprout added. "I'm staying here, of course. I have to continue my training."

Tom looked around the table, at his friends laughing and talking, and felt excited for his future. He grabbed his drink. "I'd like to propose a toast!" He grinned at them as they raised their glasses. "To friendship!"

Author's Note

Thank you for reading *The Cursed Sword*, originally called *Galatine's Curse*, the third book in my series Rise of the King. I hope you enjoyed reading more of Tom's adventures with King Arthur.

I wanted to explore more of the Other and was keen to revisit characters from the first book, as well as develop some new ones. Writing about the history of Galatine – my invented history – was lots of fun.

All authors love reviews. They're important because they help drive sales and promotions, so please leave a review on either Amazon or Goodreads – or another retailer of your choice! Your review is much appreciated.

If you'd like to read more about Tom, you can get a free short story called *Jack's Encounter*, describing how Jack met Fahey – a longer version of the prologue in *Rise of the King* – by subscribing to my newsletter. You'll also receive a short story prequel about how Excalibur was made, called *Excalibur Rises*.

By staying on my mailing list you'll receive free excerpts of my new books, as well as short stories and news of giveaways. I'll also be sharing information about other books in this genre you might enjoy.

To get your FREE short story please visit my website - http://www.tjgreen.nz

About the Author

I write books about magic, mystery, myths and legends, and they're action packed!

My YA series, Rise of the King, is about a teen called Tom and his discovery that he is a descendant of King Arthur. It's a fun-filled clean read with a new twist on the Arthurian tales.

My second series is adult urban fantasy and is called White Haven Witches. There's magic, action, and a little bit of romance.

My third series is called White Haven Hunters, and is a spin-off about some popular characters from White Haven.

I've got loads of ideas for future books in all my series, including spin-offs, novellas and short-stories, so if you'd like to be kept up to date, subscribe to my newsletter. You'll get free short stories, free character sheets, and other fun stuff. Interested? Subscribe at my website, www.tjgreen.nz.

I was born in England, in the Black Country, but moved to New Zealand 10 years ago. England's great, but I'm over the traffic! I now live near Wellington with my partner Jase and my cats Sacha and Leia. When I'm not busy writing I read lots, indulge in gardening and shopping, and I love yoga.

Confession time! I'm a Star Trek geek - old and new - and love urban fantasy and detective shows. Secret passion - Columbo! Favourite Star Trek film is the Wrath of Khan, the original! Other top films - Predator, the original, and Aliens.

In a previous life I've been a singer in a band, and used to do some acting with a theatre company. On occasions me and a few friends make short films, which begs the question, where are the book trailers? I'm thinking on it ...

For more on me, check out a couple of my blog posts.

Why magic and mystery?

I've always loved the weird, the wonderful and the inexplicable. Favourite stories are those of magic and mystery, set on the edges of the known, particularly tales of folklore, faerie and legend - all the narratives that try to explain our reality.

The King Arthur stories are fascinating because they sit between reality and myth. They encompass real life concerns, but also cross boundaries with the world of faerie - or the Other as I call it. There are green knights, witches, wizards, and dragons, and that's what I find particularly fascinating. They're stories that have intrigued people for generations, and like many others I'm adding my own interpretation.

And I love witches and magic, hence my second series set in beautiful Cornwall. There are witches, missing grimoires, supernatural threats, and ghosts, and as the series progresses more weird stuff happens.

Have a poke around in my blog posts and you'll find all sorts of posts about my series and my characters, and quite a few book reviews.

If you'd like to follow me on social media, you'll find me here -

Website: http://www.tjgreen.nz
Facebook: https://www.facebook.com/tjgreenauthor/

Twitter: https://twitter.com/tjay_green
Pinterest:
https://nz.pinterest.com/mount0live/my-books-and-writing/
Goodreads:
https://www.goodreads.com/author/show/15099365.T_J_Green

Printed in Great Britain
by Amazon